The Outsider

ALSO BY C.R. HOWELL

STANDALONES
The Woman In My Home
The Outsider

the
outsider

C. R. HOWELL

JOFFE
BOOKS

Joffe Books, London
www.joffebooks.com

First published in Great Britain in 2025

Cover art by Jarmila Takač

ISBN: 978-1-83526-977-0

For Siôn

CHAPTER ONE

Megan

They slept with the curtains open. In the faint early light Megan could see the aluminium roof of the lambing shed. The land was shadowed but a glow infused the heavy blue of the sky. The mountains were black. Ewes in the top field munched on the dewy grass, the rest of their flock spread over the hundred acres beyond. Noah's bedside lamp was on and Megan watched him moving around the bedroom, opening his drawer to find socks, buttoning his shirt.

"Did you hear those noises in the night?" she said.

He looked up at her. "No?"

"I'm sure it was nothing. Foxes."

But a fox had got into the chicken coop a few months ago, taking out all their hens. He came to the bed and bent down, kissing her head.

"Do you want tea when I come back?"

"I won't be here," she said.

He frowned. "Where are you going?"

"The class."

He stepped back, looking betrayed in the half-light.

1

"What?" she said, though she knew perfectly well.

"I forgot."

"How could you forget? I've told you a hundred times."

"I wasn't sure if you'd go."

"Why wouldn't I go?"

He didn't answer.

"Come on," she said. "I'd rather get it out of the way now."

He sighed. "I just don't know why it's a priority. If you want things to do—"

She sat up, holding the duvet against her chest. "I do not want things to do."

"Well, there's a lot."

"I'm aware," she said. "You remind me every day."

"So then?"

"So then what?"

"Even if you don't want to help on the farm—"

"I do loads to help on the farm!"

"I just mean, even if you don't want to do any more than you do now — there's the cottages."

She closed her eyes, lay back against her pillow. "Those cottages — I'm sick of talking about them."

He sat on the bed beside her, taking her hand. "Look — I've told Dad we'll have them ready by Christmas."

She opened her eyes. "Christmas? Are you mad? That's in three months!"

"If we focus, we can do it."

"You mean if I focus. It's not going to be you, is it?"

"I can help."

She sighed. "Since when do people go on holiday at Christmas?"

"Apparently, they do. Especially to cosy cottages in north Wales. It's money down the drain if we miss out. After that there's no market until Easter, really."

"When did I become in charge of the cottages?"

He gave her a steady look, clearly thinking how to manage her. "We did agree," he said.

"Did we? I don't remember that."

"You're good at this kind of thing, Meg."

"Oh, please," she said. "Anyone could do it."

He shook his head. "You make things look a certain way. Dad agrees. He specifically wanted you in charge."

"God forbid we should displease his highness."

Noah pulled a face, like she had said something distasteful. She knew how ungrateful she sounded. She couldn't help it. Ray owned this house and land, asking no rent from them. Now he was giving them the cottages, too. But all she felt was resentment. Because there was a charge, it just wasn't money. Managing the cottages was the kind of thing she would agree to in the abstract. But there were things she hadn't anticipated, like how people had reacted when word got out that they were turning them into holiday homes. It had been worse than she had expected.

Noah watched her. "All I'm saying is he thinks you'll do it better than the rest of us."

By "the rest of us", he meant himself, his sister Imogen and her husband, Aled. Ray Robinson's subordinates, the four of them. She knew he was right. She vaguely remembered agreeing to this. And it was true that no one else could do it, not in the way Noah meant but practically. Imogen was too unwell. Aled had a full-time job. Noah worked the farm virtually every waking hour. And though she resented the implication that she wasn't entitled to go to a Welsh class on a Saturday morning, she could see Noah's point about that, too. The farm was so dominant in his life that he had no time or opportunity for much else. Though Megan wondered, sometimes, if he just refused to create any.

"I'll get started on the cottages this week." This was as much of a concession as she could manage; she wasn't cancelling her class.

He nodded. "You'll be back after?"

Having reached a semi-truce, she was reluctant to tell him the next thing. "I'm visiting Imogen."

His expression darkened. "Since when?"

"I arranged it last week."

He sighed.

"You could come?" she said.

He shook his head. "I don't think so."

* * *

She couldn't get back to sleep. In the intimate quiet she heard Noah below the window, whistling the dog, starting up the quad. She got out of bed and did a few quick jobs, emptying the dishwasher, scrubbing wet crust from the casserole pan she'd left soaking overnight. She got dressed, deciding she would make an effort with her appearance for her class. Sifting through her drawers, she put on her pale blue tube top that would accentuate her tanned shoulders, then looked in the wardrobe for her lightweight black cardigan. She found her navy jeans in the drawers, too, pulling them on, threading the brass button at her waist. Though she was still relatively slim, she had gained weight over recent years. This was her last pair of jeans that still — just about — fit her. In the mirror she brushed her thick hair, straight lines of dark blonde streaked with highlights from the summer sun. She put on her flat sandals, picked up her handbag and went downstairs.

She didn't say goodbye to Noah, who was still out in the fields. She got in her Land Rover, checking her appearance in the mirror. She looked nice, she thought. She didn't know why it mattered, except that there was excitement in doing something new and she was glad for an opportunity to be noticed. She and Noah lived an invisible life. She found her sunglasses on the passenger seat and put them on. It was a warm day in early September, birds trilling in the high trees along the winding track that delivered her eventually to the road. As she drove along the lanes, her mind went back to Noah. Underlying her anticipation about the class was the unpleasant aftertaste of their conversation. She was angry, she realised, a sharp spike

4

lodged in her middle. She had known that Noah would forget she was going; he would forget by choice, putting it out of his mind because he didn't approve. She also knew that, when she reminded him, he would act put out, making her feel, once again, that she shouldn't go. She was tired of their disagreements. Tired of the endless practicalities. Farm, cottages, leaking roof, tractor repairs, tumble drier, animal feed. Their life was constructed from these things. They had become one of those couples she pitied, fixated on practical trivialities, sidestepping everything meaningful. But what was meaningful now? The only thing that mattered had been denied.

Perhaps this was why she was angry. It was hard to admit it, but she was angry all the time. It seemed to simmer beneath her skin, waiting for provocation. She was ashamed, knowing it was toxic and vulgar, that it manifested unreasonably, like refusing to deal with the cottages. But she had a sense of things being constantly imposed on her, that she had no say over her own life, and she didn't know what to do about it.

Her knuckles whitened as she gripped the steering wheel. She let go, placing her fingertips against the bottom, letting the blood rush back. She lowered the window. The class was in Glanllwyd, not their local village but a ten-minute drive. She knew the café, one of the sustainable community hubs that had popped up in the area over recent years. As she approached the village, wide fields sailed by. Mountains rose through white mist. She turned a sharp bend, angles shifting so she faced the rising sun and was momentarily blinded. She flipped down the visor. A car hurtled towards her. As it fled deafeningly past her open window, she was flooded with rage. She leaned into the rushing air, narrowly missing the low stone wall on her left as she shouted at the car vanishing in the distance.

* * *

The café was not as she remembered, the shopfront red with mounted gold lettering. From across the street the interior

5

looked dark and unpeopled. She parked on the road, lowering her head to read the street sign through the window. It permitted only an hour. Irritated, she pulled out and drove to the high street, finding a space in the car park. The machine didn't take cards, only change, which she didn't have. She refused to ring the number and work through a menu. Choosing the lesser of two evils, she downloaded the app. Her signal was poor. For the thirteen years she had lived here, she'd been meaning to change her mobile provider; she had been specifically told, more than once, which company would give her better coverage. But she put off such tasks, making her life more difficult than it needed to be.

By the time she had input her information and paid, she was late. She hurried across the street and down the side road, pushing open the café's heavy door, the bell overhead tinkling. When she booked the course over the phone, she was told to look for a ramp at the back of the café. She saw it now, a dark slope with a silver railing. She hurried between tables of coffee drinkers, a rowdy family with young children, plates smeared with baked beans. The ramp led to a small landing with three closed doors. One was a disabled toilet. Another was marked for staff. She grasped the stainless-steel handle on the last door, pushing it open. She was met with chatter that quietened quickly to silence as she entered the large, sunny room. A small gathering of adults was sitting round a rectangular table, their faces turned towards her. Windows stretched along the wall behind them, overlooking a concrete courtyard. The walls were red and framed prints hung in the retro Art Deco style Megan disliked. There was a record player on a table, vintage sewing machines collected on the floor, a steel urn gleaming in the sunlight. Beyond the learners stood the teacher, young and slim, light-haired, hands in the pockets of his shorts. A flip chart stood to his right, the date scrawled on a blank sheet. In his hand, still poised in mid-air, he held a lidless marker pen.

Megan became immobile where she stood. The teacher moved towards her, dragging a chair from the corner and placing it at the table for her.

"Megan," he said, not really a question.

She nodded. As he resumed his position by the flip chart, she felt sure she knew this man. She didn't know from when or where, and she couldn't be sure she had actually met him as opposed to having seen him around. Strangely, she felt she knew him from a long time ago, from childhood, perhaps. But that would mean she knew him from the south, which seemed very unlikely. It was all unsettling, the décor of the room, the quietness of the group, the way she knew the teacher but didn't know how. She sat down, anyway, beside a black-haired, spectacled woman who didn't even turn her head, though a bearded man opposite smiled broadly across the table. She was flooded with panic, unprepared, self-conscious in her tube top. This did not feel exciting at all. It felt like school, with all its tension and distrust.

She should leave, she thought, go back to the safety of her car. Maybe she could learn by herself, after all? Download one of the apps? But she knew she wouldn't. Thirteen years she had lived here and picked up nothing but basic phrases, uselessly singular and disjointed, and sounds she didn't know what to do with. It made her ashamed. In shops and cafés, she wanted to speak the language. She was Welsh herself and felt that conversing in the native tongue might finally give her the sense of belonging she yearned for. But she lacked the courage, and the fundamentals, and she chickened out at the last minute, falling back on English, watching the look of recognition pass over the eyes of the person in front of her as they realised she was not one of them.

The teacher stood before the class now, stepping over Megan's interruption to resume the lesson.

"*Gethin dw i*," he said. "*Athro Cymraeg dw i. Dw i'n byw yng Nghaernarfon.*" He looked around at their silent faces. "Who can tell me what I just said?"

Megan had understood but kept her mouth closed, as did everyone except the bearded man who had smiled at her, and who burst out now with a startlingly loud voice and American accent. "Well, Gethin, you said your name is Gethin, you're a Welsh teacher and you live in Caernarfon."

Gethin, thought Megan. Knowing his name, she was more certain she knew him. She watched him closely. His mannerisms were familiar, the way he moved. His hair was soft and sandy blond, his eyes dark blue. He was thin at the waist but broad-shouldered. His shorts were beige, his T-shirt navy blue. On his feet he wore Timberland boots with white socks. His accent was local and familiar. The harder she tried to place him, the more out of reach he became.

After praising the American for his correct translation, Gethin prompted the man to take a turn introducing himself. While his ears turned pink, the man could correctly use the three phrases, telling the class his name was Jim, he lived in Llanrug, and he was a researcher at Bangor University. He didn't pronounce Llanrug correctly but it was a sincere try, not sloppy or careless, and she felt bad for Jim, knowing her own pronunciation would never be quite right, either.

They went round the table, Gethin nodding as they stumbled their way through. Megan paid little attention to the information her classmates provided, which hardly seemed the point, though it occurred to her later that knowing their names might help. By the end, she remembered that the American was Jim and the youngest learner was a university student called Rhys. She went last, feeling her cheeks grow warm as the group's gaze fell on her. She looked around helplessly at her classmates. Her eyes settled on Gethin, who was leaning forward, palms resting on the rim of the table. His expression lacked the gentle encouragement he had shown the others. She recited the phrases carefully. When she finished, Gethin considered her. "*Da iawn*," he said — well done — but with no conviction.

* * *

Three hours passed, a neat vacuum of time inside a four-walled room, and Megan felt vastly more comfortable with her classmates by the end. She had learned all their names and gained a basic sense of their personalities. Jim was easily her favourite, his enthusiasm genuine and infectious. He didn't — as she might have expected from a man his age in an adult-learning class — condescend or dominate. He was curious and considerate, listening intently. They worked together once, Gethin rotating the pairs so they could get to know one another. Jim told her he had a cousin, as well as several friends and colleagues back in the States, who were called Megan, pondering why the Welsh name was so popular there. Aside from Jim, there was Denise, the unflinching woman Megan had originally sat beside. Denise was Korean and spoke in blunt, broken English. There was Rhys, the student, who explained to Megan that he had been raised in the north of England by his English father and Welsh-speaking mother, but his mother hadn't spoken Welsh with him. The other two were Roger and Sally, a married, retired couple who had moved here from Hampshire last year.

She liked the group. She was less sure about Gethin, who wasn't trying to hide his dislike. He hadn't once encouraged her, though she had completed the exercises as well as everyone else. Denise had even commented on it, in her unfiltered way, saying to her, as Gethin walked away, "He don't like you." Megan was mortified that the others had noticed. She wondered if it was because she was late, if Gethin was the kind of person offended by such things. But surely it would be extreme to hold a grudge like this about something like that? She began to worry that she had done something to make him hate her, and forgotten that, too.

* * *

As the class prepared to leave, sliding textbooks and pencil cases inside bags, Jim stayed behind to talk to Gethin. Megan waited, too. What she was going to say, she didn't know. But she knew that if she didn't confront the issue now, she wouldn't come back, and it had taken long enough to get here. Jim talked to Gethin about Duolingo, asking whether it was worth using the popular app even though it taught the southern dialect of Welsh. Gethin said he wouldn't recommend it. The definiteness of his response surprised Megan. Jim looked taken aback, too, and a little disappointed, saying, "They really should add a northern option."

Gethin went on to explain that the Welsh course was campaigned for and created by volunteers, and that Duolingo wasn't intending to develop it any further at all, let alone adding another dialect. Finally, Jim left, thanking Gethin profusely and politely nodding to Megan before he disappeared through the doorway. With Jim gone, Gethin began to tidy up as though Megan wasn't there, tucking chairs under tables, collecting abandoned worksheets. Refusing to stand there and be ignored, Megan gathered up dirty mugs from their tea break and took them to the sink. She turned on the tap, awkwardly rinsing the mugs in a basin too small for washing up.

"You don't need to do that," Gethin said, looking over at her. She ignored him, squirting hand soap on the white porcelain, rubbing her thumbs over splashes of tea. There didn't seem to be a cloth anywhere but she used the hand towel to dry the mugs and stacked them beside the urn, as they had been before. She turned to Gethin, who was tearing up big sheets of flip chart paper and sliding them among the flattened cardboard in a blue recycling box.

"Have I done something to upset you?" she said.

He kicked the recycling bin back under the table and went to the flip chart, carrying it under his arm to the back of the room. One of the markers slid off, falling on the carpet with a silent thud. He leaned the flip chart against the wall and went to retrieve the pen.

"I'm sorry if I was rude," he said, sighing as he stood up, wiping his palms on his shorts.

"I just want to know why," said Megan.

He looked away towards the window, pushing his fingers under the neckline of his T-shirt to scratch his shoulder. He was uncomfortable, just the two of them in the room, but he showed some underlying hint of satisfaction, too, like he had wanted to get her attention and now he had it.

"Have we met before?" she said.

He smiled. "Many times."

"Oh," she said. Her cheeks grew warm. "Where?"

The second she asked, the answer came to her with shocking clarity. It was the farm; he had worked there. This was years ago. Seven? Eight? He had been a teenager, at the time, perhaps fifteen or sixteen. He had helped with the lambing. Then he was gone. Noah had told her, at the time, that he had never intended to keep him on long-term. Megan hadn't believed him, wondering if something had happened.

"I'm so sorry," she said.

"No need to apologise."

"No, it was rude of me not to remember you. You were a big help on the farm."

His expression darkened. She was patronising him, she realised, making things worse.

"I just mean — I'm sorry, that's all."

"Don't worry about it. It was a long time ago. So why are you finally learning Cymraeg?"

She laughed. "Finally?"

"I didn't mean it like that."

"It's fine," she said. "It's just . . . time." Inexplicably, she began talking about the cottages. "Noah wants me to run them. He's so busy with the farm. I was thinking it would be helpful if I could speak Welsh."

She had no idea why she was saying this; it wasn't even her reason for learning. It wasn't as though holidaymakers were usually Welsh speakers, which Gethin was quick to point out.

"Oh, I know," she said. "You're right. I don't know what I'm saying."

"So you're going ahead with the cottages?"

She looked at him. Reflexively, she said, "Yeah, why wouldn't we be?" As though this wasn't perfectly clear.

"I thought you might have changed your minds, after everything."

"It's not really my decision," she said. "I mean, it's Noah's father. I'm just going to be taking bookings and cleaning up after the guests and things."

She knew how this sounded, the hollowness of her defence. But after everything that had happened over the summer — protestors at the top of the track, graffiti on the lambing shed — she felt herself becoming hot and prickly, a hedgehog putting up its quills. She didn't know Gethin — she hadn't seen him for years. He was bringing this up out of nowhere. Although, thinking about it, she was the one who had brought it up, completely unnecessarily. And why wouldn't he voice his objections? He lived here, like everyone else. He was probably teaching Welsh precisely because he worried about the threat to his language from people like the Robinsons.

He was looking at her now. "Is that how you're justifying it?"

She stared at him. "What?"

He sighed. "Never mind."

They faced each other silently. He looked almost deflated, as though he had broached something personal and she hadn't reacted how he'd hoped. He didn't move; neither did she. The exchange had slipped beyond the bounds of what was normal between a teacher and student, and neither of them quite knew how to handle it.

"Is that what this has all been about?" she said. "The cottages?"

He opened out his hands, as though to say, *what did you expect?* Then he walked to the back of the room and lifted a black rucksack from the ground, bringing it to the table. As he unzipped it, she noticed his hands were trembling a little.

She folded her arms. "I think the people who run this course might like to know about this vendetta you have against me." She meant to sound assertive but it came out pompous and childish.

"Vendetta?" he said. He picked up a handful of pens and stuffed them inside the rucksack, zipping it closed, swinging it on to his shoulder.

"That's how it seems," she said. "I've come here to learn and you're treating me like I'm a terrible person. Why are you looking at me like that?"

He smiled mockingly. "I'm just waiting for you to say, 'It's not fair.'"

She shook her head. "You're not a nice person."

"If you say so."

He watched her. She went to the chair he had placed at the table for her when she first walked in, pulling her handbag roughly from the back. Clumsily, she put on her jacket. Her own hands were shaking, too.

Much later, she would look back on this exchange — and all their conversations afterwards — and wonder if things might have been different if she had just listened — really listened — to what he had to say. But for now she said, "It was nice to meet you. I think I'll find another class."

CHAPTER TWO

Noah

He was keen to get down to the bottom field and check on the lambs, particularly since Megan said she'd heard noises overnight. They were bigger now, five months. Some had already been sold. But he had plenty left, most of them getting close to their target weight. There had been livestock thefts in the area recently, the rural crime team posting stories on Facebook about sheep loaded into the backs of trailers. According to farmers he knew, the criminals didn't take more than ten or fifteen at a time, but for a small farmer like Noah, that was a lot, especially at this time of year.

The quad bumped noisily along the parched track. Mai — his border collie — raced alongside, looking up now and then to check for any new instruction or change of plan. He loved this time of day, the slow-rising light dispersing the dark blue of the night. The sun would break soon and the wild hills would be there again, rushing towards the thick bluebell wood and the black shining lake. Technically, these hundred acres weren't his; his father owned the land. But it belonged to Noah in every other sense and one day it would be theirs — his and Megan's — on paper, too.

14

But lately he wondered if it would be enough for Megan, now that they were not going to have children. There had been a time, after they met and when she first moved here, when she loved the farm almost as much as he did. But that was in the early days of their marriage, when they planned to raise a family. Thirteen years later, with three failed rounds of IVF behind them, Megan had turned against the farm, as though it were directly to blame for their infertility. He didn't want to be angry with her about that. But he couldn't help feeling resentful.

He was even more annoyed by her refusal to engage with the cottages. There had been countless discussions and she knew, as much as he did, that there was no way round it. His father was offering them a way out of this unending struggle to make enough money from the farm. They had no choice but to accept. But just like turning against the farm, Megan's resistance to taking on the cottages was a protest against child-lessness, a way of expressing her anger with him for failing to give her children. She would never admit it, of course, but this was what it came down to.

So they wasted their time arguing about things that were inevitable. Like this morning, if you could call it an argument. As ever, it was tight-lipped and half-realised. They tended to be careful and restrained when talking about difficult things, rarely releasing the full store of their anger. A handful of times, Megan had lost her temper. Once she threw the remote control at his head. Whereas he never raised his voice. He held on to himself, tightly.

* * *

When he and Megan met — in a pub in Cardiff, the city she was living in at the time — she was restlessly unhappy. She worked for an advertising company in the bay, building campaigns for products she didn't care about. She was glad to abandon her conventional life and come here. At first, she'd delighted in the vast outdoors, gathering wildflowers from the grounds, arranging them in glass tumblers on the kitchen table. She operated the tractor like she was born to it. She got the place organised, sorting through years of junk piled in the shed, collecting stray feed buckets and broken Tupperware, installing an urn in the lambing shed so he didn't have to walk back to the house every time he wanted a cup of tea. As their fertility struggle dragged on, she began to say she wasn't cut out for farm work. But the truth was she was like every good farmer he knew — thorough, tough, unafraid of work.

The irony was, as well as alleviating financial pressure, running the holiday cottages could be just what Megan needed. Noah knew she'd be good at it. She had that attention to decorative detail that eluded him. She was much better with people. More than anything, she would have something that was her own. But the fuss made by the locals over the course of the summer — when she'd been forced to drive her Land Rover through a small mob of protestors at the top of their track — had made an impression on her. She couldn't, at first, comprehend the strength of feeling. When she understood it better, she didn't know what to do about the fact they were on the wrong side of such a sensitive issue, at least according to the people who were angry. He explained to her that tourism brought millions to this area every year, and thousands of jobs. The people campaigning were not rational. She didn't really listen. She was emotional, too, disturbed by the idea that they could be the targets of such bitterness and reproach. And she had been frightened, too, especially when, at the height of it, someone broke on to the farm and sprayed graffiti on the lambing shed.

* * *

He was nearly at the bottom field now. Mai was panting wildly after her unbroken run down the track, tongue lolling from her mouth. But her tail was high with anticipation at seeing the lambs. Though Noah was a close second, the sheep were Mai's steady purpose in life; she lived in quiet, obedient expectation of any opportunity to be near them. Noah, on the other hand, was anxious. As they neared the gate, he had to remind himself again that the lambs were fine. Noises at night meant nothing. This was a remote farm, its perfect silence heightening the cry of every bird, the scamper of rodents, foxes overturning the recycling then fleeing the bark of the dog. There was an owl whose ephemeral hooting sounded like a baby crying. At one point it had become unbearable to Megan, and Noah had seriously considered taking his shotgun out there and tracking down the taunting bird.

After the hens were killed, he started leaving Mai outside at night to keep watch. But she barked at the smallest movement and they grew tired of being woken by her frantic woofing only for Noah to go out and find there was nothing there.

* * *

Megan's visit to Imogen was on his mind, too. Really, this should have upset him most of all, given it was directly against what they'd agreed. His sister — Imogen — was being held at the psychiatric unit of the local hospital, having been diagnosed in her early twenties, first with bipolar disorder, then borderline personality disorder, then schizoaffective: bipolar type. Now she was officially schizophrenic. Noah didn't know whether the label mattered, though having a clinical diagnosis had helped explain her rambling monologues, black depressions, sudden delusions — and given her access to life-changing, antipsychotic medication. When they were teenagers, Noah thought she was just over-imaginative. Imogen later explained this was probably her prodromal phase, the illness incubating invisibly inside her.

There was a short time, after she met her husband, Aled, when Noah had been hopeful that Imogen might live a normal life. Aled was about as dependable as people came and his steady support had temporarily helped contain Imogen's turbulence, enabled her to maintain the basic conditions for staying well: medication, exercise, therapy. Then they had Hari. Imogen had wanted a child for as long as Noah could remember and he knew, once she'd decided she was well enough to become a mother, that no one was going to stop her. Noah would never say Hari had been a mistake. He loved that child, and Imogen herself was adamant that, however much strain Hari had put on her, he had also saved her life many times, giving her a reason to live when she was clawing at the edges of depression. Nonetheless, four years since having him, Imogen had never really got back to where she was before. Somehow, she was more resistant to staying on her medication now she had a young child in her care, which made absolutely no sense to Noah. "Why would it make sense to you?" Megan had asked him once. "You're not Imogen."

The last time she came off her tablets was three months earlier, when she went missing from a barbecue at Aled's parents' house and the police found her, hours later, on the edge of a lake on Anglesey, saying there were monsters in the water. She'd been at the unit ever since, the longest she'd ever been detained there. Noah's sympathy was depleted virtually to nonexistence, particularly given, in his view, it was entirely her choice to be there. All she had to do, if she wanted to go home to her four-year-old child — whom she hadn't seen at all since she was sectioned, because Aled refused to take him to visit her at the unit — was take her medication. That was all the doctors wanted. She didn't have to try a new drug or go on a higher dose. All she had to do was resume what she was taking before.

She refused. Week by week, the doctors met with her, reviewing her case, trying new angles of persuasion. Her answer was always the same: not this time. Eventually, Noah and Aled made a decision. If they stopped going to see her, she might more acutely feel the peril of her situation and reconsider her position.

Megan had not liked the idea but had said she would go along with it; Imogen was Noah's sister, she would do whatever he thought was best. Yet here she was, weeks later, visiting Imogen as though this conversation had never taken place. She hadn't discussed it with him first; she hadn't told him she was going at all until this morning. Which was why this was the thing he should have been most annoyed about. But the truth was, he hadn't expected Megan to go along with it for long. Though she had wanted — and, he was sure, intended — to, she just wasn't capable of acting with this degree of pragmatism when it came to his sister.

* * *

As he got off the quad at the bottom gate, Noah felt a wrongness through his body. A lamb beyond the hedge was emitting a manic, high-pitched bleat. The pink baler twine that had held the gate shut lay strewn on the ground. The gate was ajar. He felt a rush of sickness. Looking down the track, he felt a presence close by, as though someone might be watching. His heart began to beat violently. Clutching the cold bar of the gate, he pushed it open, lifting the bolt to stop it juddering over the ground.

Mai stayed at his side, creeping watchfully, her back low. The first thing he noticed was the lambs, clutched in the far corner of the field. Mai raced towards them, uncharacteristically breaking free from his charge, and began to bark. Noah whistled, calling her back. She ran to him, sitting promptly at his feet, looking up, wide-eyed. *What are you going to do about this?* she seemed to say. But he didn't know what this was, yet. He took a step in the direction of the gathered lambs, treading on something. Staring into the grass, it took him a moment to grasp what he was looking at. The skin of a lamb lay strewn at his feet. Looking to the right of it, he saw a severed head, flies mounting the open wound. Mai moved towards it, craning her neck, her tail sceptically low. She sniffed the disembodied face and jumped suddenly back, barking furiously.

Panic swelled in Noah. He took another step, his eyes searching the grass. He found another skin, a second head. A clutter of hooves. Tangled, fly-infested guts. Remnants of a small massacre, scattered in the grass. Blood pounded in his ears. He moved with terror, not as though something appalling had already passed but as though the danger was present. He looked back at the gate, his quad parked silently on the track. He turned his gaze to the fence at the bottom where the hills sloped quietly towards the woods. There was no one here but him.

* * *

The shock was total. It thundered in his ears and seemed to expand the world around him like he had taken a hallucinogenic drug. The police officers, when they arrived, appeared fake to him. The clouds through the window rushed falsely, alarmingly fast. The trees were plastic and pretend, the sky surreally blue. The officers were talking but he had little sense of what they were saying. There was a mug of tea in his cupped hands; one of them had given it to him. Vaguely he remembered calling Chris, a local officer who worked on the rural crime team.

He sipped his tea, scalding his tongue. Wincing, he stared down at the mug in distrust. It was very full. Should he put it down? He shouldn't be holding all this hot liquid, surely? He imagined turning over the mug and pouring it on his legs. He was not himself, oddly removed from the world. He felt he was floating, alone. It frightened him.

Then he thought — Megan. She would make this go away. He looked at the officers. Chris was quiet, watching Noah with a concerned frown. Noah couldn't remember the name of the woman with him, if she had told him her name. They were in full uniform, as incongruous in the quiet house as the words coming out of their mouths.

"I need to see my wife," he said. The words floated around his head like they had come from elsewhere. The female officer stopped talking, staring at Noah.

"Have you rung her?" said Chris.

Noah frowned. "I don't think so."

He thought about it. He was almost sure he hadn't. But he didn't trust his mind. He put his mug down on the floor. He wondered if he might vomit. Had he vomited already?

"Will she be back soon?"

Will she? thought Noah. Where was she, anyway? He couldn't bring the knowledge to mind, though he must have known; she must have told him where she was going. What was happening to him? He was finding it hard to send signals from his brain to his body, to move a finger or shift his feet. He stared stupidly at his hands, which seemed not to belong to him.

He looked at the clock.

"Welsh class," he said. "She's at a Welsh class."

He was so surprised by this, he started to laugh. The officers stared; they didn't think it funny.

* * *

Her phone was off. He left a voicemail, which he had not done for years. The officers left, saying they would take his statement when he was feeling better. But it seemed impossible to him that he would ever feel like himself again. He went outside. His body was light, his limbs full of air. He felt he might be lifted to the clouds. He walked slowly down the track, careful on his feet, as though he were drunk. Mai spotted him and rushed to his side, whining. He reached down and felt her soft, reassuring back.

He didn't trust himself to drive the quad. He was going to walk down to the field and try to feel like himself again. The birds in the trees sounded manic and disturbed. But the walk was helping him. When he reached the bottom, there was a woman in the field. She wore plastic over her shoes and white coveralls on top of her clothes. She was taking photographs. While he stood at the gate, watching, he remembered

21

something Chris had said — that the butchering was probably carried out by a gang they were investigating, coming in from out of county to steal livestock.

He took his mobile from his pocket and rang him.

"Why would they butcher my lambs in the field? Why not just take them, like they did with the others?"

Chris listened patiently. Then he said, "I can't answer that yet. But it could be anything, mate. Maybe they couldn't get hold of a vehicle."

"Do you realise how long it would have taken them to do this? It was risky, don't you think? And for what? The meat from twenty-six lambs? If these thefts are part of some big out-of-county operation, why jeopardise it for that?"

Chris seemed to take his point of view on board, saying he would bear it in mind. Noah felt he was coming back into himself, beginning to feel a restless rage. He wanted to know why this had happened. Putting his phone away, he looked out at the field. The remaining lambs were still gathered in the corner, keeping their distance from the woman and her shuttering camera. One of them, he realised with a start, was still letting out that high repetitive bleat. Feeling terrible that he hadn't checked on the lamb earlier, he crossed the field and walked among them, Mai at his feet. The lambs scattered, moving in all directions. With the rest dispersed, the bleating lamb was exposed, a white bundle in the grass. Noah knew the lamb, the second in a difficult birth who had struggled to gain weight. It remained, still, a runt. Noah went to the lamb, collapsed in the grass as though injured. Mechanically, it opened and closed its hard mouth like a wind-up toy stuck on repeat. It didn't flinch, even when Mai nudged it with her snout. Noah bent down, pulling the lamb to its feet. It blinked in surprise and shook its head, ears waggling, bucking away. The bleating stopped.

Noah sat down on the grass. He took out his phone, staring at the blank screen. He touched his wedding ring, turning the gold band between his fingers. His feelings towards Megan were shifting, unpredictably, between needing her helplessly and feeling furious that she wasn't here. Mai lay beside him, resting her head on his lap.

Noah looked over at the runt, munching on a tuft of grass. He thought back to last spring, when it was born. Noah had checked the camera feed on his phone in the middle of the night and seen the ewe in distress. Knowing she'd been scanned with triplets, he woke Megan. They'd gone to the shed together. Noah had caught the ewes and reached inside, feeling not one but two pairs of front legs and a nose. Quickly, he'd worked out which legs belonged with the nose and pushed the others back, giving him enough room to pull the first lamb clear and place it on the straw in front of the ewe. He'd reached back in and felt for the legs of the second, easing it out. The third was dead. Megan had tried to revive it, clearing mucus from its nostrils, swinging it back and forth. But it was gone. This had been the week after their final round of IVF. Megan had held the tiny dead lamb, a bloodied lump. She'd looked devastated, a despair that had little to do with the lamb. He'd put his arm around her in the cold night, no noise in the shed but the surviving twins, suckling furiously from their worn-out mother.

CHAPTER THREE

Megan

As she left the café, she was pulsating with rage. Who did that man think he was? Surely he was not allowed to treat students like that? She wanted to report him. But it had all been so subtle, the bulk of it down to his sneering attitude. He hadn't said anything explicitly offensive, had he? Hurrying to her car, she tried to remember. Her mind was reeling. The question about whether they were going ahead with the cottages had been implicitly judgemental, though Gethin could say he'd just asked an innocent question, that she had taken it the wrong way. Then there was the comment about justifying it to herself; she remembered that vividly. But they'd been alone. He would deny it. And they would take his side, while pretending to take her seriously. He was one of *them*. And who was she, except exactly what Gethin saw — an outsider, married into an English family turning local houses to holiday homes.

Noah had been right, she realised, slamming the car door closed, jamming the key in the ignition, hands trembling with outrage — she should never have gone to that class.

* * *

And now she was late. By the time she reached the unit, she would have only twenty minutes with Imogen. Visiting hours ended at one o'clock, though whether this was enforced depended on which staff were on shift. As she drove through the sun-dappled lanes and down the rushing bypass, she felt briefly reassured by the landscape. The mountains always seemed to belong to everyone; or rather, to belong to no one. But this consolation was quickly soured by the unpleasant reality pressing down on her: people like Gethin thought she didn't belong here. Since she first came to live here she had never been able to escape her sense of being unwanted. She was an intruder. Even Noah, who had come here as a child, had more claim to the place than she did, in spite of him being the English one.

Before the summer, her sense of unbelonging had been a faint background hum. The backlash against the cottages had pulled it into the foreground. Now she was tormented almost constantly by feelings of illegitimacy. How had these people — most of whom she didn't know — made her feel so wrong in herself? Why couldn't she be indifferent to it, like Noah was? And was what they were doing really so terrible? What Noah said was true — tourism drove the local economy. New holiday homes would bring more visitors, who would spend their cash in the cafés and attractions that employed the local workforce. Megan would hire tradesmen to refit kitchens, sort out plumbing and electrics, tidy the gardens.

At the same time, she understood their basic point: they were denying these homes to local families and instilling ghost houses, empty half the year, occupied the rest of the time by fleeting holiday makers, oblivious to the village, chattering in their loud, obnoxious English.

* * *

She found a space in the vast hospital car park and walked through the sunlit grounds towards the unit. With trepidation she speculated about Imogen's mood, how lucid or muddled she might be. The last time Megan visited, she thought Imogen was a lot more stable and coherent than the day she'd gone in; she had almost felt she could talk to her about her medication, though decided, in the end, to wait until next time. Withdrawn from her tablets, it was always better to talk to Imogen face to face. Technology only heightened the distrust that so often characterised her psychosis. In fact, having just had her phone returned, Imogen had been texting Megan the night before. It was like receiving messages from a drunk friend, a meandering, random, sometimes disturbing stream-of-consciousness.

Megan didn't believe that being inside the unit did Imogen any tangible good. They didn't even provide therapy. But Megan also knew that Imogen couldn't be allowed to go about her life without her medication. She wasn't safe without it. God forbid, neither was Hari. The problem was that Imogen somehow routinely convinced herself she no longer needed the tablets. *Look how well I'm doing!* she would say. Maybe now was finally the time to lead a normal life, free from drugs? The psychosis came back almost immediately, worming into their lives like an imposter. Out of nowhere — or so it seemed to them — Imogen revealed its grip on her mind — could anyone else hear the grass whispering? Had they all been replaced by robots? Was someone trying to kill her? Had she killed someone? The more delusional she became, the harder it was to convince her to go back on the tablets. Trying only proved her paranoia — you wanted to hurt her, you were one of them, you're all the same.

It was sad, and immensely frustrating. Megan entirely believed Imogen that her medication came with unpleasant side effects. She had seen how the tablets dulled her senses and made her sick, especially when they were reintroduced. But it was also one of the only things that made her better. When she was taking it regularly, she lived a basically ordinary life. She probably couldn't have held down a job — her time-keeping was not great, her communication style unconventional. On her tablets or not, she was still a kook. But she painted, occasionally selling her work at local shops and craft markets. She was a doting mother, collecting Hari from Cylch, taking him to the swings and beach, reading to him at bedtime. It had never been clear to Megan why she decided to stop taking her tablets, except that the better things were, the more she longed to be rid of them. She didn't discuss it with any of them first. Sometimes she told her therapist, who broke confidentiality to tell Aled if he felt he had to. But by that point, Aled usually knew. He was versed in the signs, powerless as her speech became nonsensical and rambling and her clothes began to smell of stale sweat. She neglected Hari, too, sending him to Cylch in dirty clothes, forgetting his packed lunch.

It became dangerously easy, at these times, to alienate her. Noah and Aled made things worse, Megan felt. They were too hard on her. Noah belittled her, told her off, making her stressed, which worsened the psychosis. Aled wasn't much better. Since Hari had been born, his criteria had shifted. Imogen wasn't his number one priority. That was fair. They had a child. But Megan had seen the effect on Imogen of knowing that Aled put Hari first, hesitating hardly at all before ringing the police and having her locked away at the unit. Between them, Aled and Noah had come up with this policy not to visit her. Was it working? No. Its only outcome was that Imogen had spent the last month alone. What was the point, then? Were they trying to punish her? Noah would say they hadn't maintained it for long enough. But Megan couldn't bear it any longer. She hadn't intended to hide from Noah the fact that she was coming; it was just that every time she'd considered telling him she was afraid he'd talk her out of it.

* * *

Walking from the car to the unit, she realised she had forgotten Imogen's bag, which was still in her boot. She swore to herself, looking at her watch. It was a quarter to one. Hesitating, she decided to go back. If she wasn't allowed to see Imogen, she could at least drop off the bag. She sprinted back through the grounds, running along the narrow road to avoid a man on crutches and a young boy in a wheelchair. Her Land Rover was in the overspill car park, furthest from the hospital. By the time she got there she was panting, rummaging breathlessly among her jumble of bags for life and charity donations. She found the bag — one of Imogen's bohemian-patterned hand-stitched totes — and grabbed the strap, hurrying back towards the unit, thinking over what she had put inside.

When Imogen had messaged a week ago, asking Megan to bring some of her things to the unit, Megan agreed immediately — a practical, useful task. Then she realised she would have to go to Aled and Imogen's home and ask to root around in Imogen's things, making it known to Aled that she was breaking the agreement. As she waited at the front door, she had felt brazen and ashamed. She didn't want Aled to think she was challenging his method of dealing with Imogen — she wasn't. Megan was firmly aware that her relationship with Imogen was different; there was less at stake for her than there was for Aled and Hari.

When Aled opened the door, he had looked depressed. He hadn't shaved for days. His belly sagged over the waistband of his joggers, peeking beneath his T-shirt. She could hear Hari playing somewhere in the house. She was filled with guilt and considered making up some other reason for her visit. But what would she tell Imogen? When she explained to Aled why she was there, he sighed and stood to one side, gesturing for her to go up to the bedroom.

"I haven't had a chance to tidy up there."

"Oh, don't worry about that."

In fact, the entire house was a mess. As she crossed the hall, she glanced through the open door to the living room and saw dirty plates on abandoned trays, toys all over the floor. Sprawling piles of unwashed clothes blocked her way to the stairs. There was a suspicious smell of urine, making her wonder if Hari had begun wetting the bed again. She made a mental note to talk to Noah, aware they should have been helping Aled more. It was the end of the school holiday, Cylch still closed, but Aled working full-time. Even with his mother helping, he was clearly struggling. Megan knew she should have offered more childcare. She was Hari's auntie and she had a lot more free time than Noah. But with their last round of IVF only six months behind them, she didn't feel ready to spend that kind of focused time with him yet.

She had walked up the shadowed staircase and into the main bedroom, where the curtains were closed, blocking out the daylight like an intruder on their private tragedy. Dust rose in the stifled air. Tea-stained mugs and scrunched-up tissues littered Aled's bedside table. She took her phone from her pocket, checking Imogen's list. Trying not to touch anything that belonged to Aled, she opened and closed drawers. It didn't take her long to find the unspecific items of clothing: clean socks and underwear, pyjamas, a warm sweatshirt. The rest lacked an obvious place and Imogen had given no instructions. She looked in Imogen's bedside drawer for reading glasses, finding a pair that didn't match the description. Aled appeared in the doorway, ascending the stairs so quietly he startled her.

"What are you looking for?"

"Reading glasses?"

He pointed to Imogen's oak drawers perched on claw-like feet. "Have a look in the box."

Megan walked over and stared at the black slate chest sitting on top. Lifting the heavy lid, she found a sienna case, prying it open to see Imogen's reading glasses nestled within.

"Thanks," she said. "I just need her sketchbook and pencils now."

"I think the sketchbook is downstairs. Hari might have been drawing in it, to be honest. I'll have a look."

Every word he uttered seemed to require great effort. Megan felt awful, roping him into this. She found the tote bag in Imogen's wardrobe, putting the clothes and reading glasses inside. She started collecting up dirty mugs then changed her mind. As she checked the list again, sighing to see that Imogen had asked for headphones, Hari came bounding upstairs with his inexhaustible store of energy.

"Auntie Megan!"

He ran to her but stopped short of hugging her, as though his enthusiasm had evaporated in her immediate vicinity. His hair had grown, his dark curls — just like Noah's and Imogen's, and their mother's — buoyant and full. His eyes were angelic, his lashes long and thick, his irises shining hazel.

"Is my mam here?" he said, ecstatic with the possibility.

She crouched down to face him. "She's not. I'm sorry."

Crestfallen, he turned to point at the doorway. As though talking to someone in his imagination, he switched to Welsh. Turning back to her, he remembered who was in front of him, and switched again. "My dad is looking for her sketchbook now," he said. He pronounced the English words with effort, as though they were foreign to him. He spoke more comfortably in Welsh, which wasn't surprising. Though his mother was English, and she and Noah spoke English to him, everyone else he knew — his father, grandparents, friends, neighbours — were Welsh-speaking. He spent little time with Ray compared with his extended paternal family, who lived nearby in the village. It was also the case that Imogen had taught herself a great deal of Welsh, speaking it with Hari whenever she could. She sang him Welsh songs, read him Welsh-language books, named things around them bilingually. She felt strongly about the preservation of the language, a conviction Megan had always admired and wanted to emulate while feeling an ambivalence on the subject that she didn't understand.

"I know," she said, in answer to his comment about the sketchbook. "I'm taking some things to the hospital for her."

He stared at her. "Can I come with you?"

She sighed, taking his soft hands in hers. "I don't think children are allowed. But she'll be home soon."

She didn't know if this was the right thing to say. She was not very good at talking to children, even Hari. She also had no idea what Aled had told Hari about his mother's absence. It must have been relatively new territory, as Hari was so much more aware of the world now than the last time she was at the unit. It was also the longest she had been there; the longest Hari had been without his mother. Three months must be an eternity for a four-year-old. Sometimes, overcome with frustration, Megan wanted to shake Imogen and shout, *Just take the drugs! What's wrong with you? Don't you care about your child?* Then she'd take a breath and remember that she knew nothing about what it was like to live with a psychotic illness, to be forced to take powerful, mind-altering medication, to reach such depths of despair that you cut your own legs with nail scissors.

In the hallway, Aled handed over Imogen's hardbound sketchbook and tin of charcoal pencils, plus a big bar of vegan chocolate. Looking at the chocolate, which she hadn't asked for, tears welled in Megan's eyes. She lowered her head, putting the items in the bag. She decided to forget the headphones; Imogen could have hers. Hari appeared at his father's side, tugging his hand, looking up pleadingly at him. He was crying, tears spilling down his cheeks, saying something to his father that Megan couldn't translate. Aled looked at her.

"He wants to go to the hospital with you," he said coolly.

Megan put her hand over her mouth. "Oh, I'm so sorry," she said.

Aled shrugged, opening the front door, keen for her to leave so they could get back to the quiet morning into which she had carelessly intruded. She stepped on to the lane, Hari's wailing pursuing her all the way to her car.

* * *

The unit was a single-storey building in clean red brick. There was a yard at the back with high wire fencing but nothing

31

else about the place suggested incarceration. The windows were big and unbarred. The grass lawn at the front burst with flowers. Mentally ill patients had once been treated on a psychiatric ward in the main hospital. Imogen claimed the unit was built because patients on the other wards complained about the relentless shouting and screaming, which Megan had thought Imogen exaggerated until she heard it for herself.

She hadn't had a chance to turn on her phone since leaving her class. Approaching the entrance, she opened the screen to find three missed calls and a voicemail from Noah. The voicemail alarmed her. In fact, Noah calling her at all made her anxious. Normally, he would text. She didn't have time to ring him back, nor listen to the voicemail. She couldn't get embroiled in a crisis on the farm, not if she was going to have any chance of seeing Imogen. Whatever it was, Noah could deal with it. He tended to panic, thinking he couldn't cope without Megan. But he always did. She would ring him when she came out, which might be in a few minutes, if they didn't let her visit.

She put her phone away and went to the desk, sighing when she saw the nurse behind it, a sharp-boned Scottish woman whom Megan had dealt with before and knew to be a rule-obsessed tyrant.

"Hi," said Megan, smiling. "I'm here to see Imogen Griffiths."

The woman glanced at the clock behind her. "Visiting hours are over in ten minutes."

"Not quite ten," said Megan. "But yes, I'm late. But I would really like to see her. She's expecting me. I don't mind if it's only a quick visit?"

The woman looked at her.

"It's important that visitors are here on time," she said. "It can make the patients anxious if they're kept waiting."

"I understand. I'll make sure I'm not late next time."

The woman glanced at the two bags Megan was carrying. "Are either of those for Imogen?"

Megan nodded.

"I'll need to check them," said the woman.

"It's just this one," said Megan, handing over the tote bag. The woman glanced suspiciously at her handbag but said nothing. Though she'd known they would check the bag, she was irritated. She waited. The woman put the bag down on the floor beside her chair and looked at Megan, smiling. "I'll bring it to her once I've checked it."

Megan sighed. "Fine," she said.

She had wanted to give Imogen the bag herself but never mind. The woman pressed a button. The doors to her left opened slowly, mechanically. Megan walked through them and down the sunlit corridor, a stretch of glass overlooking the courtyard. Patients were gathered in the sunshine, smoking, talking, some of them staring slack-jawed at the ground or walking in circles. She found Imogen in the day room, sitting alone in a high-backed blue leather armchair, staring at the wide-screen television. Her jaw was sunken, tortoise-like, beneath the neckline of her aqua hoodie. Her eyes, dark like Noah's, conveyed the characteristic look of distraction that belied her intelligence and fierce will.

"Imogen?"

Megan moved closer, placing her hand gently on Imogen's arm.

Imogen looked up, anger flashing in her face.

"Oh, it's you," she said, looking back at the television. "I thought it was them. They're coming soon. All of them at once."

Megan knelt beside the armchair and took Imogen's hand. It was cold.

"Who is coming?"

Imogen didn't reply. The television showed a swimming race, the camera moving over the crystal-blue water of an Olympic-size pool. Sunlight spilled through the windows, pooling on the carpet in front of Imogen's chair.

"Why are your hands cold?" said Megan.

Imogen turned her head and looked at her blankly. Her hair — dark, thick curls like her mother's, though cut defiantly short at her chin — was damp. Megan thought it was from showering rather than not having washed it. She fought the urge to reach out and touch it.

"Shall I get you a blanket? I brought the bag, by the way. They're just checking it."

Imogen looked at her, frowning. "Bag," she said, as though not quite sure of the word's meaning.

"The one you asked me to bring? It has your sketchbook inside. There's chocolate, too. Aled wanted you to have it."

Imogen nodded slowly. "Swimming is bad. Very dangerous."

"You love swimming."

Imogen looked at her. "Are you going to kill me?"

"Of course not."

"Who are you?"

"Megan. I'm Megan."

"How can I be sure?"

"Because — look at me. I'm Megan. I'm sorry I haven't been for so long."

"They were taking time to replace you. They had to take away the other Megan and make a new one. Now you're not Megan. I know all about it."

"Oh, Imogen," said Megan, sighing. She told herself not to cry.

"They sent you to kill me."

Megan watched Imogen for a moment. "I have an idea," she said. She reached into her pocket and pulled out her phone. "Let's look at some pictures — okay?"

Out of the corner of her eye, Megan noticed one of the nurses looking over, watching them. She scrolled through her camera reel, swiping past hundreds of photographs until she found a picture of the two of them. It was a selfie, taken at the start of the summer, before Imogen came off her tablets. The four of them went to a lake in the mountains and had a picnic. Imogen swam in the cool still water. It was a beautiful day, the sun high, the lake shrouded by hills. Megan remembered thinking that maybe she would be okay; she would live a life of beauty and leisure, unlike her friends who complained about the constant stress of having children. In the picture, Imogen's hair was wet and she wore a dry robe, hanging open over her damp swimsuit. They were both freckled in the sun, skin bronzed and glowing.

"This was a few months ago," said Megan.

Imogen looked at the picture. "They gave you this. They told you to show me."

"No one gave it to me. This is my phone. This is us."

Imogen pushed the phone away and drew her knees to her chin. She began rocking gently back and forth on the leather-padded seat, the hems of her joggers lifting to show faded cuts on her ankles. Megan looked at the nurse, still watching them. She knew she would be asked to leave if they thought she was upsetting Imogen. Megan put away her phone and stood up, dragging a plastic chair over from one of the tables.

"Imogen?" she said. "Everything is okay. You just have to take your medication. Okay?" Her voice was unhelpfully desperate. She was upset. She knew she should go.

"No medication, thank you," Imogen said. She closed her eyes, muttering rhythmically to herself. "No, thank you. No medication. No, thank you. No, no, no."

* * *

Megan drove home the back way, along the lonely lanes, unable to face the bypass. Tears streamed down her face. The day stretched behind her, long and exhausting between her encounter with Gethin and brief visit with Imogen. It wasn't even two o'clock. She wanted to go home and tell Noah everything: the things Gethin had said — Noah would be livid about that — and her experience with Imogen. He would be sympathetic about that, too, even if he was angry with her for going in the first place. She would have to try hard not to blame him for Imogen's state. But she did. This was his fault. Aled's, too. They had isolated her and now she was even worse than when she went in. Why hadn't the doctors told them? And what was the point of her being there at all if it was making her more unwell? They just wanted to lock her up. The whole thing made her so angry, she could scream.

The sky was cloudless and blue, the mountains strong and clear. She felt suddenly alone and she thought, as she often did, how everything came back to the fact she didn't have children. Maybe it had once been that kids were peripheral; certainly, she had felt that way as a child — unseen, shut away, told to be quiet and keep to herself. But now, at least here, the Cylch and school were the centre of the community, mothers the governing tribe. Through farming, Megan knew mothers who, while helping their husbands run a thousand acres of land, baked for fundraisers, sewed costumes for the Christmas play, volunteered at the sports day and Easter egg hunt. They invited her to the bingo nights and fairs they helped organise. She never went. She wouldn't go alone, and Noah could seldom be persuaded to do anything that wasn't farming-related, in which case he only went to find out what other farmers were doing, and at what cost.

She was finally home, where she would see Noah, tell him everything, maybe feel better. But as she drove down the long track, something did not feel right. She slowed down, a sense of danger all around her. A bunny leaped from a bush and hopped across the track, disappearing into a burrow. Their beech tree, fallen in last winter's storm, lay collapsed, trunk stretching into the field, roots tangled and exposed. Though it had lain like this for months, the uprooted tree appeared, like everything else, stark and wrong. She didn't know why she felt this way until she reached the house, pulling round the work shed to find an unfamiliar car on the drive and a woman, removing her forensic-looking coveralls, packing away her camera.

CHAPTER FOUR

Noah

The day after the slaughter of the lambs, Noah woke as though hungover, in spite of not having touched a drop the night before. His mouth was stale and bitter-tasting. His head felt taut, a sharp pain pressing within. He could smell sweat and remembered, vaguely, turning over in the night and feeling a wetness on his back. It was light outside now. He hadn't slept this late in years and didn't feel he'd benefitted. Megan had turned off the alarm, saying he needed to recover. Trying to get up, he felt like a dead weight. He slumped back under the covers, closing his eyes.

There were things to do. Time had not stopped. There were all the ordinary demands and now, after what had happened, new ones. When Megan got back the day before, she had rung Chris and asked things Noah had failed to consider, like how they would be updated about the investigation, whether they were eligible for compensation. Then she sat Noah down and calmly talked him through practical tasks, like phoning the insurance company. She asked if he thought they would be covered for a situation like this. He said he didn't know; it was rare for sheep to be butchered in the field. She asked if their payments were up to date. He said he thought so. She asked if they were meeting the conditions for the insurance to be valid. He said he wasn't sure. She talked about the mess in the bottom field, how the smell would only get worse. So would the flies. They should have started the clean-up already, but no harm done, as long as they got straight on with it tomorrow. By which she meant Sunday — today. They would need to bring the remains to the yard, ready for the fallen stock man to collect on Monday. Initially, Megan had assumed the police would help with this, asking Chris about it when she rang him back. When he explained that they couldn't help, she found this hard to accept. But it wasn't the job of the police to clean up dead livestock — even in the state he was in, Noah could have told her that.

But Megan had understood, the minute she saw Noah, that she needed to take control. He had tried to listen, knowing, somewhere in his mind, that the things she was saying were important. But there had been a blackness enveloping him, a lingering disconnect between himself and reality. His thoughts were heavy and dampened, as though dunked in water. He remembered thinking that something of himself had been taken with the meat of his lambs and as she talked, handling things, carefully planning, she had seemed almost a stranger. He had found it overwhelming and difficult to follow her thoughts, as though she was talking him through a complicated maths problem. He couldn't imagine doing any of these things, even basic tasks like finding paperwork. He couldn't have explained it, certainly not to Megan. He felt ashamed. But she seemed to understand, taking note of his slow reactions, remaining unusually gentle and patient.

Now all these tasks were upon him. Downstairs he could hear Megan, moving around in the kitchen. Her footsteps drew closer. There was a clattering on the stairs, then she appeared in the bedroom, carrying a tray. She wore her white towelling dressing gown and mule slippers. As she placed the tray on his lap, he stared at the thick buttered toast and hot tea.

"You didn't have anything to eat last night, did you?"

He thought about it and realised she was right. He sipped the tea, hoping it might alleviate his headache. It was sweet. That was not how he took his tea, but he found it comforting. He looked at Megan, too tired to make the observation that she had put in sugar without asking, remembering that one of the police officers had done the same thing the day before. She sat down, moving his legs over so she could perch on the bed.

"Noah," she said.

He looked at her. "What?"

She pointed at the toast. "Eat."

He picked up half a slice, taking a bite from the corner, chewing feebly. She watched him. He found it oddly difficult to chew, even harder to swallow. His throat felt closed-up, somehow. He put the toast back on the plate.

"You have to eat."

"It hurts my throat," he said, feeling ridiculous.

"How about porridge?"

"You don't need to make a fuss. I'm fine."

"Don't act like it's nothing."

He looked at her. "It was just a few lambs."

"No. It wasn't."

* * *

One of the many things he had not been able to face the day before was telling his father. He didn't much like the idea today.

"Do you want me to do it?" said Megan.

He was in a towel now, looking for his phone. He glimpsed himself in the mirror above his pine chest of drawers, his face pale against his damp hair and the stubble on his chin. He needed to shave. One thing at a time. Megan had offered to run him a bath. He'd been tempted by the idea of wallowing in hot water. But there was only so much babying he could take.

Unable to find his phone, he was feeling more anxious by the minute.

"I'd better do it myself," he said. "I just need to find the bloody thing."

"Do you want to use mine?"

Every time she spoke he felt unreasonably provoked. "I need to find it, anyway."

"Maybe you left it in the field?"

"Why would I do that? It's not like I'd have put it down on the grass."

She looked at him, clearly trying not to say that he might have done anything, the state he was in. He resented this, though it was probably true. The thought of speaking with his father was making him agitated. It wasn't easy to ring the man at the best of times. He got dressed and went outside, finding his phone on the seat of the quad. It must have fallen from his pocket, though he'd had it when he went back to the field and he had not used the quad then. Thankfully, it hadn't rained. But the battery was flat. He took the phone to his bedroom and plugged in the wire, sitting hunched at the edge of the bed, waiting for the screen. His father would be at home, reading the paper. His housekeeper didn't work on Sundays, which meant Ray would be alone, enjoying the fact he could eat what he wanted.

He didn't answer his mobile. Noah rang the landline. After a couple of rings, his father came to the phone.

"Ray Robinson," he said.

"It's me," said Noah.

"What's wrong?"

"How do you know something's wrong?"

"Noah."

"It's nothing. It's just — someone got in our field."

He was quiet for a moment. "How many?" he said.

"Twenty-six."

"Have the police been round?"

"Yesterday."

"When did this happen?"

"Early yesterday morning. I was asleep." He said this apologetically, as though he should have been awake at four in the morning.

"You're only telling me now?"

"Yesterday was — I don't know."

"I'll be there in a couple of hours."

Noah's heart jumped. "There's no need for that. We're handling it. It's fine."

"I'll be there by twelve," he said, then hung up.

* * *

Noah's mother had been an adventurous, headstrong woman with dark curls and many passions. Music, nature, books, food, her children. From a young age she'd wanted to work a sheep farm in north Wales. She had a Welsh grandmother in Porthmadog whom she'd stayed with during childhood summers, instilling in her a romantic love for the landscape and people. She'd watched the locals, speaking their secret language, and longed to be one of them. This was the only thing she had ever wanted, as long as Noah could remember.

The contrast between his mother and father was so striking, their relationship so apparently devoid of affection or respect, it was hard for Noah to believe — especially as the years went on and he understood the world better — that their decision to make a life together was anything other than a necessity. His mother had been fifteen years younger than Ray, twenty when Noah was born, which had made him wonder over the years. He had his suspicions but he didn't know anything for sure. He would never have asked his mother, out of respect, nor his father, out of fear.

Either way, they never married — another strangeness, particularly for the time. But his mother's attachment to a wealthy man raised the possibility — repeatedly, relentlessly — that he might buy for her this farm that persisted in her dreams. For years his father refused. In fact, he derided his mother for it, calling it her castle in the sky, a foolish dream. Noah knew she would never let it go. The older he and Imogen grew — the less they depleted her energy and time — the more fixated she became. Tensions grew. Noah felt certain, as his mother became increasingly unhappy in their cobbled Midlands village, that she would do almost anything.

One day, something changed. To him, it was imperceptible, a magic trick performed by grown-ups after bedtime so that when you woke the world was different and no one told you why. He and his sister were bundled into the back of the car and transported from the pale fields of England to the primeval green of northwest Wales. There was an auction at a town hall. Everyone spoke Welsh except for them, including the auctioneer, though the bidding was done in English. Noah watched, in horror and fascination, as his father outbid everyone there, including the neighbouring farmer whom everyone had assumed would get it, for an eighteenth-century farmhouse and a hundred acres of land.

Purchasing it was one thing. The farm then demanded constant injections of cash, from the investments in livestock and machinery to the endless repairs to outbuildings, fences and the two-hundred-year-old main house with its rotting window frames, leaking roof and mammoth nest hidden in the dark of the lower attic, waiting until summer to reveal itself with the sickening hum of a hundred baby wasps. The money they made from selling lambs was pitiful compared with the money his father had to put in.

Meanwhile, Ray had not come with them. He stayed in Warwickshire, an abandoned bachelor keeping track from across the border with restless typewritten letters. When Noah's mother died — fifteen years ago — his father wanted to sell. He had always hated the farm. Noah persuaded Ray to let him maintain it alone, without his mother, promising he would finally make it profitable. His father agreed. But he said things needed to change fast. If they didn't, he would not hesitate to sell.

* * *

Ray pulled up just before noon. Noah watched through the dining room window as his blacked-out Range Rover crunched into the drive. After calling Ray, Noah had gone outside to tidy the yard, trying to make the vicinity of the house a little more presentable, feeling the pressure he always did when his father came. If he'd had more time, he would have mucked out the stable, cleared the stream, cut the front lawn; anything to avoid giving the impression he could not keep up. Megan often reminded Noah that his father didn't care about such things, preferring to stay in the house and talk about money. He specifically wanted to know how Noah was covering his costs, given he hadn't asked for a penny since his mother died. Noah hadn't told Ray about the loans, knowing he would use it as evidence that the farm was still making a loss — which would be true. But things had been improving, even before his mother died, but particularly since Noah took over. Year by year, he had made the operation more efficient. The farm wasn't completely self-sufficient, yet. But it would be. In the meantime, he just needed a little help with maintenance. He had wondered, in the recent past, if Megan should find work, never wanting to bring it up. There was no need anymore. The cottages were going to make the crucial difference, providing the extra income they needed to not only cover the farm's costs but maybe even allow them to live a little, too.

As the Range Rover came to a stop, Noah put on his boots and went out to meet his father, who was standing with his hands behind his back, squinting at the top field.

"How the hell did they manage twenty-six?" he said.

"I wondered the same," said Noah.

His father chuckled to himself. "It was ballsy — you've got to give them that."

"I think there must have been a few of them," said Noah. "There's been a gang around for a while, stealing livestock."

"Stealing?"

His father looked at him.

"Yeah," said Noah. "I don't know."

His father eyed him then turned back to the field. They stared quietly at the sheep. The ewes seemed different to Noah,

43

since the slaughter. Surely it was impossible they would have been aware of it from up here. He didn't know how far the noise might have carried but he was haunted by the idea they had been butchered barbarically. He'd heard it said plenty of times that illegal slaughter was often botched and inhumane. At the same time, he'd had some notion, when he found the remains the day before, that the job had been fairly clean.

"Megan's got the kettle on," said Noah.

His father followed him into the house. The air inside felt suddenly heavy with apprehension. Noah noticed chips in the paintwork, the cracked glass of the hall window. In the normal course of things he pushed these defects out of his mind, focusing single-mindedly on running the farm. His father's presence in the house brought it all crashing forward. In the kitchen Megan had set a tray with thick slices of the bara brith she'd rushed out to buy when Noah told her his father was coming. She smiled when they walked in. His father nodded at her across the room. Megan never hugged Ray. At most, she put a hand politely on his arm. Given his father was too proud and cranky to initiate physical contact, they kept their distance. It was strange, in a way. But why should she hug his father? Noah didn't hug him, either.

Ray pulled out a chair at the table. Megan brought over the tray of tea and cake, placing it at the centre, sitting down opposite Ray. She looked at Noah, who loitered near the door, feeling oddly unable to sit down.

"Tell me what happened," said his father.

Noah looked at Megan, who stayed respectfully quiet. Noah told his father everything he could remember. He didn't notice that he was moving around the kitchen island as he talked, not until his father snapped at him.

"Will you sit down, Noah? You're making me nervous."

Noah hesitated then did as he was told.

"Are the insurance payments up to date?"

"Yes," said Noah, after a moment's pause.

"What?" said his father.

"The padlock on the gate was broken."

Megan looked at him. "Really?"

"Yeah," said Noah. "Not that it would have made the slightest difference. They would have broken it, or just lifted the gate off the hinges."

"How do you know?" said his father.

"A padlock isn't going to stop a gang, is it? They must deal with locked gates all the time."

"Why hadn't you replaced the padlock?"

"I've been meaning to."

"Did you tell the police?"

"I don't think so," he said. "No."

"If the police don't know, there's no reason for the insurance to know. The criminals broke it. End of story."

Noah hesitated.

"Got it?" said his father.

His gaze seemed to penetrate Noah's skin. Noah closed his eyes. Yesterday's sensation of being untethered was coming over him again. He did not like this feeling. He had an urge to go outside and feel rooted on the land. He looked down and saw that someone — Megan, presumably — had placed a slice of bara brith and mug of tea before him. His father munched slowly on his own piece of cake.

"There need to be changes," he said, his mouth full.

"This wasn't my fault," said Noah, sounding childish. He knew he mustn't whine; his father despised it. Noah looked at the table. This powerlessness when his father was around — he was so tired of it. Why did he always feel like a child around him?

From across the table came Megan's voice, firm but also pleading. "This wasn't Noah's fault. What difference would it have made if the gate was padlocked? Like Noah said, they'd have broken it. They slaughtered a load of lambs in the middle of the night. They must have had all kinds of tools with them. You can't think a padlock would have stopped them?"

Megan seemed genuinely hurt by the implication that Noah was to blame. His father hadn't said it explicitly, but it was how he thought. Noah didn't feel indignant. It was too predictable. He just felt a deep dread coiling up inside him.

"Details matter," his father was saying. "You have to be on top of things."

"We are!" said Megan.

"You're disorganised. Noah is disorganised. He always has been."

"That's not fair," she said. "That's really unfair, Ray."

Noah brought his fingers to his temple.

"What's the matter with you?" his father said, looking at him accusingly.

"Nothing," he said, pulling his hand away. "I've just got a headache. Look, just — please — don't sell the farm."

"I'm not talking about selling it."

"What, then?" said Noah.

"Just some changes. You'll be running the cottages, now, okay?"

"Yeah," said Noah. "So?"

"That'll be enough on your plate."

"What do you mean?" said Noah.

"I mean you can't do both."

Noah looked at Megan, then back at his father. "Of course we can."

"You've made no progress getting the cottages ready."

"That's my fault," said Megan quickly. "I'm going to start on them this week."

"I'm not blaming anyone," said his father, holding up his hand. "I'm just talking about some redistribution. To make things run more smoothly."

"Redistribution to who?" said Noah. Looking at his father, it dawned on him. "You're not serious?"

"It will be better this way," said his father.

"What way?" said Megan, looking between them. "What are you talking about?"

"Imogen," Noah muttered, looking at Megan.

Megan stared at Noah, then looked across the table at his father. "What?"

"Not just Imogen," said his father. "Aled, too. Well — mainly Aled, I imagine."

"Aled doesn't know a thing about farming," said Noah. "And he has a job."

"He grew up on a farm," said his father. "And he understands business. He's been running one for years. And he'll have Imogen."

"Imogen doesn't know anything about farming, either," said Megan.

His father shook his head. "She knows more than you realise. She grew up here, too, didn't she?"

"She didn't work the farm," said Noah.

"What about Aled's job?" said Megan.

"He's going to take a step back," said his father.

"I see," said Noah. "So you've discussed this with them?"

His father didn't answer.

"This is our home," said Megan. "Where do you expect us to live?"

"I'll help you find somewhere else. A place in the village — you can be close to the cottages."

"This is insane," said Megan. "Are you trying to punish us? Because of the lambs? Because we're suffering already — believe me."

He looked at her sharply across the table, then at Noah. "Now get a grip. You're not a pair of children, are you? I've made my decision; you'll have to make your peace with it."

CHAPTER FIVE

Megan

A week had passed since her first Welsh class. She hadn't spoken to Noah about Gethin. Having planned to tell him everything, she'd got home last Saturday to find that twenty-six of their market-ready lambs had been butchered by criminals and Noah wasn't the same as before. It wasn't just that first day, when he was shock-stricken and barely able to speak. All week he'd been a slow-moving husk of his former self, slipping out in the early hours, returning like a ghost at night, staring at her blankly when she talked to him. She worried he was having a mental breakdown. Or maybe he was simply coming to terms with the emotions churned up by this violation of his livelihood and land.

Personally, she wanted to kill the men who had done this and had fantasised all week about hurting them. She was outraged by their shamelessness, all the while knowing her outrage was pointless and naive. These were criminals. This was what they did. She'd also been trying to reason with herself that it was only twenty-six lambs. They would be compensated by the insurance, even if they didn't get market value.

In the end they would lose only a small percentage of their income.

But that wasn't the point.

The work that had gone into bringing those lambs to size — people didn't know the half of it. Raising lambs was a year-long labour, starting in September when they weighed their ewes, checked their teeth and teats, bought replacements, sold off culls. They tupped them in November and scanned them in January, selling barrens, splitting the rest into groups according to how many lambs they were carrying. Expecting ewes had to be fed adequately but it was dangerous to over-feed, which could lead to difficult births. Left to their own devices, ewes often ate less in the last weeks of pregnancy, when growing offspring pushed against their paunches. Noah had to correct for lowered appetite, increasing nutrient den-sity to make sure the foetus was nourished, udders developed, colostrum was produced; all the while remaining vigilant against overfeeding.

Meanwhile, through the winter, they — mainly Noah — built new pens and repaired old ones, cleaned and disinfected the shed, restocked antibiotics and iodine, tubes and syringes, bottles and teats, heat lamps, thermometers, electrolytes, for-mula, lubricant, wormer, glucose, gloves. As April approached, they gathered the ewes into paddocks and watched them like hawks. Lambing was how Megan's friends described the early months with a newborn baby — exhilarating, exhausting and fuelled by adrenalin, caffeine and sugar. She often felt she was on drugs, snacking furiously, drinking sweetened coffee, not caring, when she collapsed on the couch in the early hours of the morning, that her clothes were stained with mucus and blood.

There were always complications. But they had no time to stop or think, treating navels, docking tails, vaccinating. Each ewe and her lamb (sometimes two, very occasionally three) were monitored for twenty-four hours and then, if the weather was kind, turned out to the field. Outdoors was where they thrived. Noah kept a beady eye on the weather. It was a mild climate here so they didn't worry much about the cold — but rain and wind could be deadly and they had plenty of that. Every year there were orphans. They tried to adopt them to ewes who'd lost their own lamb, covering the orphan in the dead skin. Or they gave them to ewes with single lambs and plenty of milk. If none of this worked, Megan bottle-fed the motherless newborns, holding them against her on the hay as they sucked formula through a silicone teat. They weaned the lambs in summer, herding them into the bottom field. Megan hated this part, lambs mewling at the fences, wanting to get back to their mothers.

The financial cost, never mind the time, physical work and mental toll, was an investment injected over the course of a year with the promise of reward at the end. Aside from the lambs being their biggest source of income, there was pride in sending them to market, fat and healthy, knowing they'd fetch a price that honoured their hard work and the reputation of their farm. And there was reassurance in knowing their lambs would be slaughtered without fear, stress or even knowledge of what was happening. It was hard to contemplate twenty-six of them cut to pieces with no thought for humane killing, contaminated meat or any of the standards they farmed by. And all of it inflicted by faceless men in the night who may never be found. She didn't know how she would get over it. She was frightened to think Noah never would.

* * *

The strangest thing about the last week was how often she'd thought about Gethin. Far from forgetting about her Welsh class, as she'd intended to when she stormed out of the café, her thoughts went back to him repeatedly, as though she was having some perverse reaction to the disturbing events at home. It was a distraction, perhaps, her way of coping. Whatever the reason, she didn't know what to do about her class. Not going back seemed less attractive in retrospect; what did it say about her if she let someone treat her like that and slunk quietly away? After what they'd been through with the lambs, she was less inclined now to disappear. Wasn't that exactly what Gethin wanted? Wouldn't it mean he had won? And wouldn't it prove him right, that she should be ashamed about the cottages and hide herself away? But at the same time, how could she stay in a class with a teacher who hated her?

When she walked through the classroom door — she was early this time — Gethin looked surprised. Within almost the same second, he appeared to exhale in relief. She wasn't sure how to react and looked away, taking her seat. Apart from the student, Rhys, everyone from the week before was there — Jim the American, Denise the Korean, and the English couple, Roger and Sally. As soon as the class started, Megan noticed a difference in Gethin. He was less sure of himself and distinctly nicer to her, offering the same gentle guidance and encouragement he showed the others. Meanwhile, Roger, having been fairly quiet in the first lesson, had evidently become frustrated by his inability to pronounce certain Welsh sounds, concluding it was the fault of the language.

"I just don't see how anyone can make that sound," he said. "It's not possible."

"Pronunciation is one of the hardest nuts to crack," Gethin reassured him. "You'll get there. It's early days."

"It's not just hard," said Roger. "It's impossible. You can ask Sally — I've been trying to say this all week!"

His whingeing caused an air of discomfort to settle over the group. Megan was embarrassed by his petulance. It began to seem as though he wanted to provoke a reaction; perhaps he was looking for a reason to give up. Gethin was endlessly patient, armed with a string of platitudes about perseverance. Towards the end of the lesson, he inadvertently used a mutation, explaining quickly, apologetically, that the class needn't worry about those yet.

51

Roger laughed vigorously. "Oh, but we do worry, Gethin!"

Having been so concerned about facing Gethin, Megan wondered if it was Roger who would drive her away from this class. She also wondered what teachers were meant to do about difficult students in adult-learning classes. It wasn't like they could tell them off or send them out.

"You speak Welsh very well," Gethin said to her at the end. The others were chatting as they packed away their things. Gethin had come over quietly, talking to Megan under the radar as Roger's booming voice filled the room.

"Thanks," she said, though she didn't feel she could take the compliment at face value. "I am Welsh, I suppose."

"You suppose?"

"I'm from the south."

"Is that not part of Wales anymore?"

She laughed. "People round here don't always think so."

He nodded. "I can't argue with that."

"I do understand it. More than I did when I first moved here. It's just hard because—" She sighed.

"Because you are Welsh."

"Yeah. Well, that's how I felt before. But now I wonder if maybe it's true."

"What's true?"

"That I'm not as Welsh as people who speak the language. It's just made me think, you know — what does being Welsh mean, if you don't really have anything to do with the culture? I didn't used to feel that way. But maybe I did, deep down. I remember when I got to comprehensive school and suddenly we did Welsh every week. I hadn't learned a word of it before. We had a really bad attitude, like, laughing at the words and making fun of the teacher. It was awful how we behaved, when I think about it now. But I wonder if we felt ashamed. Like we'd been able to ignore the fact we couldn't speak the language until it was thrown in our faces at the age when everything feels humiliating."

She felt her cheeks grow warm, realising she was rambling on about something quite personal. She didn't talk about these things, even with Noah. He wouldn't have understood. Noah was not only English but he didn't really think of Megan as Welsh. It was as though she passed for English with him, because her accent was subtle and she didn't express it in any way he would recognise. But these thoughts seemed to surge out of her, and they felt strangely private and close to the bone.

"Sorry," she said. "I don't know what I'm talking about."

He looked at her. "I do."

He didn't apologise for the week before and she was glad. She didn't want an awkward conversation. She could see he was regretful, and the fact he had changed his behaviour meant more to her than an apology. After everyone had gone, she found herself lingering again, helping Gethin tidy up for a second time. It was more pleasant this time, quietly tucking in chairs and rinsing mugs without the hostility of the week before. But now there was a different tension, which she didn't understand.

The waste-paper bin beneath the tea station was full. She decided to empty it, lifting out the bag.

"Do you know where the bin bags are?" she said.

Gethin was watching her from the other side of the room.

"Try that thing," he said, pointing to a lopsided wooden cupboard behind her. She went over and opened it, searching the cluttered shelves. There was a carrier bag at the bottom, stuffed with more carrier bags. She extracted one and opened it out inside the bin, folding the edge over the rim. She went to the sink and washed her hands. It was strangely domestic, the way they tidied quietly, as though they were accustomed to doing this all the time.

"I need a coffee," said Gethin.

She looked at him. He was by the door, his rucksack on his shoulders. He wore cargo shorts again, this time with a white T-shirt and Adidas trainers. She took his comment about coffee as an invitation, picking up her bag and following him out of the classroom. She assumed they would have coffee here, but he headed across the floor of the café to the door. A man at the counter, presiding over a spread of cakes and muffins in glass domes, called something to him in fast Welsh. Gethin replied, raising his hand in a gesture of goodbye.

They walked together among the grey pebbledash houses. It was sunny, hardly a cloud in the sky, but a cool breeze blew around them. There were leaves in the gutter, collected against the kerb. It was unclear where they had come from since there were no trees in sight. There was very little green anywhere, just a planter here and there, breaking up the grey with bright flowers and hand-painted sides. Graffiti covered the brick walls and the ends of terraced rows, bringing colour to monotony like the planters. Graffiti round here was hardly ever the crude vandalism Megan had grown up with in the urban south; it was vivid, intricate paintings of scenes from local history, punctuated with Welsh-language poetry and nationalist slogans.

She sensed Gethin knew where they were going. She knew no one in Glanllwyd but she felt afraid of bumping into someone. She had an unsettling sense that she was doing something wrong. Maybe she was doing something wrong. She had told Noah she'd be home after class. When she considered texting him to say she was having coffee with her teacher, she found herself suspiciously reluctant. For one thing, she knew it would irritate him, extending her time here beyond the three hours her class already consumed. But more than that, he would wonder why, and she didn't have an answer.

The longer they walked alongside one another in the cool sunshine, the more she felt aware of herself, her body. Her heart was beating fast. There was a light tingling in her skin. When they drew close, her hand brushed against his.

"It's just here," he said.

She looked at the pebbledash house with its mahogany door. The glass panel was fan-shaped and faintly stencilled, though she couldn't make out the words. Squeezed between a kebab shop and a library, Megan wasn't convinced this was a café at all. There was no chalkboard, no shopfront, no sign. But through the small, tinted window to the right of the door, there did appear to be tables, and people sitting at them. Gethin held the door open. Megan had the odd sensation he was taking her somewhere private, like she might find his parents waiting inside. She walked into a shadowy room, dark at the back, speckles of sunlight on the brown carpet at the entrance. There was a counter along the left wall, a young aproned girl behind it. The cakes in the display fridge were extravagantly topped with berries and whipped cream.

Gethin took off his jacket and placed it on the back of a couch, which was brown, like the carpet. "What can I get you?"

"An Americano, please," she said. "Or whatever they have is fine."

"I'm sure they can manage an Americano."

She sat on the couch, next to where Gethin had draped his jacket, feeling the heat of the sun through the window on her back. She was self-conscious, unsure what to do with herself. Gethin seemed to know the girl behind the counter, who couldn't have been older than sixteen. Gethin himself wasn't older than twenty-three or twenty-four, though he carried himself like an older man. When she met men in their twenties these days, they were like teenagers to her — awkward, insecure, often still suffering from acne. Young women were the opposite, she thought. They had accepted their insignificance in the world long before, saving everyone the aggravation of dealing with their egos and making them seem infinitely more worldly and mature.

When Gethin came back, he carried two white mugs and a small jug, clinking it all down on the glass-topped table. There was a chair opposite but he moved round the table and sat next to Megan. As he poured milk into their coffee, she wondered what she would say to him. The argument from the previous week floated between them. She wanted to know why he had hated her so much, which she didn't believe could only have been about the cottages. She wanted to tell him about the slaughter of the sheep, and what Ray had decided to do with the farm. The feeling she'd had when she first saw him — that she knew him from an earlier time in her life — had grown stronger with seeing him again. As he sat beside her and she smelled his aftershave, mingled with the underlying fragrance of his skin, she realised it was more than having once known him; it was a feeling of having once been close with him. Perhaps this was why she had thought about him so much, because some memory of an emotional bond had been stirred. She wondered if she was, in fact, attracted to him.

Was this how it felt to be attracted to someone? She couldn't remember. She had not fallen in love since she met Noah. She had been twenty-seven, then. Before that she'd had a string of self-obsessed boyfriends, unwilling to give her what she wanted. Noah was the opposite. He had wanted to commit to her and wasn't afraid to say so. That had been attractive in itself. Many things had made her fall in love with Noah. His passion for the farm. His disinterest in going out drinking, playing sports or doing anything she considered infantile in a grown man. His grief for his recently dead mother. His sensitivity.

Gethin was watching her. He had his back to the window, too, sunlight dappling the back of his T-shirt.

"Did we talk at all?" she asked him.

"When?"

"When you worked for us."

"Hardly ever. But—"

"What?"

He was quiet, sipping his drink. He put his mug down, clanging the porcelain against the glass. "I was aware of you."

"What does that mean?"

He looked at her. "How unhappy you were."

She turned her face away.

"Sorry," he said.

"It's fine," she said. "So you felt sorry for me?"

"I wouldn't say that. I could just feel the sadness. It was, like, everywhere on that farm."

"Maybe it was Noah's."

"Maybe." He sipped his coffee again.

"Some of our lambs were killed," she said.

"I heard."

"From who?"

He shrugged. "Word gets around."

This was true, round here. But she disliked the idea of people talking, humiliated to think anyone might feel sorry for them. Maybe, worse, people thought they deserved it.

"Is that why you're being nice to me now?"

He shook his head. "No."

"Why then?"

He sighed, sitting back and propping his elbows on the back of the couch. "It wasn't fair, how I treated you."

"I agree."

He laughed. "Do the police have any leads?"

She shrugged. "They're investigating some gang who've been stealing livestock. Noah doesn't think it's related, though."

He watched her. "Who does Noah think it was?"

"He doesn't know. But he says it doesn't make sense that the sheep were stolen in these other cases, whereas with this . . . You know."

"I can see his point."

"Also . . ."

"What?"

"Well, I don't know. With all the backlash about the cottages — maybe it was more targeted." She looked at Gethin, feeling that this had been the wrong thing to say. Gethin clearly identified with the people who had protested against the cottages. Maybe he wouldn't take kindly to her suggesting that one of them might have butchered their lambs.

His expression was still, though, hard to read.

"And what do you think?" he said.

"I don't know. It would be a strange way to express your anger about the cottages, wouldn't it? But we did have someone come into our field last month and spray the lambing shed."

"I didn't know about that. So does Noah think it was someone from the village?"

"He doesn't actively suspect anyone. He just thinks that's a more likely explanation than this gang. But it's hard to know what Noah thinks about anything. He hasn't been very communicative lately." She felt a pang of guilt. Talking about Noah felt like a betrayal.

"It can't be easy, I guess." said Gethin, "Getting past something like that."

CHAPTER SIX

Noah

Every noise in the night disturbed him, though many of them seemed to rise from broken dreams. He slept in fits, awakening sweat-slick and frantic to find it dark, an eerie stillness hanging outside the house. Had it always been this quiet? Sleepless and agitated, he thought of getting up, going out to check for intruders. He could start up the quad and drive down to the bottom field. He talked himself out of it, slipping back into sleep by four or five.

He was out on the farm by seven and his mind was relentless, thinking about the slaughter constantly. If this had been the gang in question, his meat was sold by now. The black market was supposedly thriving, the cost-of-living crisis pushing meat prices so high that when someone came offering lamb on the cheap there were plenty of buyers. It was all bizarre to Noah, surreal, and removed from his realm of existence. But whatever the police said, he found it hard to believe that these were the culprits. The crime seemed far more personal. Maybe that was just how it felt when you were the victim of a crime, easier to believe it was targeted and meaningful than random and insignificant. He had other issues with the police's assumptions, though. For one thing, no one had explained why these people had butchered his lambs in the field. Chris's line that maybe they didn't have access to the right vehicle did not ring true. This was not some last-minute decision based on a broken-down lorry. It was planned. They would have needed refrigerators, the right kind of knives. They had known how to butcher. It hadn't been a perfect job but when they were cleaning up the mess, one of the things Noah thought was: they knew what they were doing.

Police officers didn't understand what was entailed in butchering twenty-six lambs. There was no reason they should. But when he looked back on his interactions with them, it was as though they'd already decided who was responsible. They weren't going to consider anything else. He tried to express his concerns to the detective, a woman called Mandy who went over his statement with him at the station. She was a nice enough woman, trained to listen. Victims had certain rights, these days. At the same time, he'd had a distinct feeling that listening was all she was going to do.

* * *

It was Saturday — a week since the slaughter — and he was behind on everything. He didn't know where the week had gone, except that he had spent far too much time on bureaucracy, like his back and forth with the insurance company. His father had been trying to contact him. Noah was ignoring his calls and texts, unsure how to respond to his recent threat to transfer ownership of the farm to his sister. First, Noah needed to understand what exactly his father was doing. Was this a genuine plan? During the meeting, there had been an air of intention that made Noah fear it was. But you couldn't trust the man. This could be a strategy aimed at scaring Noah into agreeing to some other scheme. The discussion had arisen as though it was a reaction to the slaughter of the lambs. It would be characteristic of his father to sense fear and vulnerability, use it to his advantage. Or he might have been planning this for months, years.

Noah didn't know; that was why he needed to think.

He also had a long list of things to do — a fence to mend, wood to chop from the fallen tree, paperwork to complete before sending the last batch of lambs to market. The ewes were not ready for tupping, which was six weeks from now. And he had a new ram to collect. He got himself dressed and went out to the yard. Megan had gone to her Welsh class; that was how late it was. The sky was clear, the mountains stark in the distance, free of mist. He let Mai out of the shed. She looked at him, as though to say, *Slept late again?* then went off to do her business.

He had bought a new topper for the truck that needed assembling. The sun rose higher as he worked, shadows shortening on the ground. Mai lay close by, panting gently, watching as he spread panels, divided nuts and bolts. Inevitably it was more complicated than the manufacturer promised. He read each direction aloud, Mai cocking her head as she listened. Birdsong from the thick canopy was shrill and loud. His mind wandered. He thought of the lambs in the bottom field, how exposed they seemed to him. But it was no more the case now than it had been a week ago. In fact, it was less likely than ever that anything would happen to the remaining lambs. They were probably safer than they'd ever been. But they didn't feel safe to him. Nothing felt safe. It was a kind of grief he felt, the heightened state that came when somebody had died. There was a pulsing in the air, as though death was very close. He had felt like this after his mother died, aware that he was meant to feel sad when all he felt was afraid. He felt that now.

He pulled out his phone and checked the social media pages of the rural crime team for the hundredth time that week. They had posted frequently, redoubling their efforts to encourage farmers to protect their livestock and machinery.

Mostly they doled out pointless advice that farmers either followed already or chose not to, usually because they couldn't afford it or didn't have the time. Make regular checks of your field. Keep fences in good repair. Use capping hinges on field gates. Lock cattle grids out of position. Join your nearest watch scheme. Consider CCTV. Report suspicious activity.

A week or two before the attack, Noah had seen a car on the track at the lower edge of the bottom field. He spotted it again a day later. The second time he saw it, unmoving beyond the hedge, he wanted to go and confront whoever was inside. He didn't have a right to ask — it was a public track, though no one used it except him. But there was something about this car. He considered taking a photo and reporting it to the police. In the end, he had done nothing. This was one of the many reasons he blamed himself.

* * *

By the time he was finished building the topper, the back of his truck was bedecked with a wide, gleaming crate. There was plenty of room for a ram; in fact, he could transport two or three sheep in there, if he ever needed to, without having to attach the trailer. Mai sat back on her haunches, looking sceptically at the new structure.

"It's not for you," he told her.

She stood up and wagged her tail, trotting round to the passenger door. Noah opened it. She jumped on the seat, light as an eel, positioning herself as she always did, at a tilted angle so she could face both the windscreen and the driver. It was ten now, later than he'd wanted to set off. He was anxious. This was not a good time to be bringing in a new ram. The ewes were starting to smell, the existing rams getting restless. This was when they became territorial. But one of his rams had died in the summer and he needed another for tupping.

He drove slowly, worried about the topper, which rattled on the back. He would have to drive more slowly on the way home, with the ram inside. He thought about the slaughter again. Something that had bothered him was the way the criminals left the scene. The mess was one thing but on Sunday, when he and Megan were cleaning up, they found rubble sacks in the hedges, stuffed with severed heads. This explained why he hadn't been able to find all the heads in the field. But why leave some remains in the field and stuff a portion of heads into sacks? And why shove the sacks in the hedges, when the crime was going to be discovered, anyway? Either way, those mutilated heads, the eyes of his lambs staring from the dark bottom as flies crawled and droned, were somehow more upsetting than the remains in the field.

* * *

The farmer selling the ram was Kevin — Kevin Nefyn, as he was known, Nefyn being the location of his vast farm. Noah had been there many times over the years, including with his mother, long ago. You had to drive through a pay-and-display car park at the entrance from which Kevin raked in cash from tourists who parked there to access the beaches; then past his towering wind turbines and vast stretches of solar panels. Eventually you found Kevin, somewhere near his state-of-the-art lambing shed. The man was practically drowning in government grants and private profit from his impeccably timed business decisions.

"*Sut wyt ti*, Noah?," said Kevin as Noah got out of the truck. Kevin squinted into the sunlight, sleeves pulled to the elbows of his dirty arms, the sea glittering behind him in the distance.

"Fine, thanks. How are you?"

"*O da iawn, diolch*. Can't complain. *Sut mae'r defaid?*"

"Well, I suppose you heard what happened?"

"I did. Absolutely disgusting, I couldn't believe it. I saw your dad just after, he came down for a *panad*."

"Oh yeah?"

He knew his father and Kevin were friends, but he hadn't known his father came here last weekend.

"He was asking about the turbines," he said, pointing towards the structures in the distance.

Noah nodded. He knew he should have got into renewable energy years ago. He was aware his father felt this way, too.

Kevin watched him. "So you're getting out, I hear?"

"Getting out?"

"Handing over the farm to your sister, your father was telling me?"

Noah shook his head. "Not a chance."

"Oh! Right," said Kevin. "My mistake. Your dad must have been pulling my leg."

Noah nodded. "Expect he was."

* * *

Driving home, the ram grunted, topper rattling, and Noah trembled with uncontained rage. He had worked hard to hold it inside while he and Kevin manoeuvred the ram. Even now, alone in the truck, he didn't know what to do with it. He slammed the dashboard with his fist, shouted into the air. Mai stared at him and let out a quick bark.

"Shut your mouth," he shouted. "Just shut it."

She watched him, fearful and alert. He could hear Megan's voice in his head: *you're angrier than you'll ever admit.* He took the ram back to the farm, leaving it in the shed. Then he got back in the truck, letting Mai jump in again. It was half twelve now. Megan still wasn't back. She might have gone to the cottages, though he doubted it. She'd claimed she would start on them during the week just gone but she hadn't done a thing, as far as he knew. What did he care now? There was no way he was giving up the farm, so why give his father the satisfaction of making progress on the cottages?

As he bumped back down the track, he took his phone from his pocket, finding the number for the unit.

"I need to see my sister."

The woman at the other end went quiet, sensing his tone. "Who's your sister?"

"Imogen," he said. "Griffiths." He still wasn't used to her married name, though it had been five years now.

"When were you thinking of coming?"

"I'm on my way."

"Have you made an appointment?"

"I'm making one now."

"It's better to use our online system, if you can?"

"Well, I haven't. But I wanted to let you know I'm on my way."

There was a short silence. "Just give me a minute, please."

Another woman came on the line. "We're doing visits by appointment, now. It's a new system. It helps the patients have a sense of routine."

"I know about the new system," said Noah. "That's why I'm ringing — to let you know I'm on my way."

"It's better if you make an appointment in advance. That way Imogen knows to expect you."

"Are you saying I can't see my sister?"

The woman paused. "Let me just check with Imogen if she's happy to see you."

"Go ahead," he said. "I'll be there in fifteen minutes."

* * *

As he drove to the hospital, Mai lay flat on the passenger seat, ears low, watching him. The topper rattled violently now he was driving fast. He must have installed it wrong, he thought. He couldn't do anything right. He stared ahead, teeth clenched, thinking things he had no wish to think about. This had been happening a lot over the last week. A memory came to him now, vivid and unwanted, of a certain time during primary school. He must have been ten, maybe eleven; it wasn't long before they left the Midlands and moved to the farm. His best friend was a freckled, scrawny boy called Stuart. They were close, the two of them. Often, they went to each other's houses after school. Stuart's family was ordinary within the parameters of the middle-class village in which they lived.

Stuart's mother worked at the offices of the local council. His father was a teacher. When they were deciding whose house to go to, Noah preferred his own. This annoyed Stuart. They argued about it, Stuart accusing Noah of thinking his house was better. Noah couldn't tell Stuart the real reason, which was that, although Stuart's parents and sisters were perfectly nice, Noah had a bad feeling when he was there. He couldn't explain any more than that.

One day, Stuart was not in school. There were whispers in the classroom. The teacher told the children off for gossiping. When Stuart came back, he told Noah — privately, ashamed — that his father had been arrested and Stuart was not allowed to see him. When the police interviewed Noah, he sat next to his mother on a soft couch in a room full of teddies. His mother's face was stricken, her body stiff as wood as she held Noah's hands, fearing the worst. Two officers in plain clothes sat across from him, asking gentle questions about terrible things. Noah told them the truth — nothing had happened, not the things they were insinuating. Noah didn't tell them about the feeling he had in Robert's house. And he didn't tell them about the time he'd gone upstairs to use the bathroom and bumped into Stuart's father, making his way down the landing back to the little room in which he sat listening to his CDs. Though he talked freely to the man when he was with Stuart, Noah had gone very still, unable to look him in the eye. He hadn't wanted to move past him to get to the bathroom.

"I'm just going to the toilet," Noah had said.

Stuart's father was clutching a CD. He'd held it up, showing Noah the front. It was classical music, like his mother played, and which Noah didn't like. Lightly, Stuart's father said, "Do you want to come in and listen to it?" The expression on his face was full of vulnerability. He waited no more than a few seconds before he laughed softly, embarrassed, and said, "Never mind." Then he'd gone into his music room and closed the door. The music came on, loudly, and Noah knew he had upset him. Stuart had run out from the kitchen, calling to Noah, and Noah went back down, forgetting to use the bathroom.

* * *

Imogen was in the day room, sitting by the windows. The sun had vanished behind cloud and the light in the room was dull.

"What's wrong?" she said when she saw him. She sat upright in the chair, clutching the armrests. "What is it? Something has happened."

He took a chair and positioned it next to her.

"Nothing's happened," he said, sitting down. "I just wanted to see you."

She looked at him. "Please tell me what's true."

Dirty hair. Dark shadows under her eyes. Strange speech patterns. He had never asked Megan how her visit with Imogen had gone the previous Saturday. Too much had been going on. He had assumed that Megan would have said something if Imogen had been markedly worse.

"How are you, Imogen?"

She glanced away from him towards the windows. "I'm very sad," she said. She looked back at him. "Can we go home?"

"Your home?"

"Our home."

"We don't live together, Imogen."

"We did before," she said. "You were my best friend. I wish we were children. Running around on the farm, chasing the bunnies."

Noah was struck with the familiar sensation of being edited into experiences that weren't his. Imogen embellished childhood memories, and not just when she was unwell. In reality, she had roamed the farm alone, immersed in her imagination, while Noah helped his mother.

"The lambs," she said. "It was nothing to do with me."

"I know," he said. "How did you hear?"

"Daddy called me."

"I thought they took your phone?"

"I have it now," she said, taking the device from her pocket and holding it up. The screen flashed then darkened. She glanced at a nearby nurse. "They'll take it again, though."

"So Dad has been calling you?"

Beyond the doorway there was a raising of voices, the thudding and squeaking of shoes. It died down quickly. Noah looked at his sister. Now he was here, he wasn't sure she was lucid enough to ask her what she knew about the farm. He wasn't sure he could trust her at the best of times. It might have been her illness, making her vulnerable to manipulation, but he had always suspected her of encouraging their father's favouritism. Megan said that Noah was too hard on Imogen, that she actually had no malicious or competitive feelings towards him, that she loved him dearly, almost above anyone. She feared his rejection, that was it.

He looked at Imogen again, trying to see her the way his wife did rather than his own image, filtered through resentment. She did look frightened, he thought. But that didn't mean she didn't want to hurt him.

"When did it happen?" he said.

"When did what happen?" she said, eyes wide.

"The decision about the farm."

She stared at him, appearing genuinely perplexed. "What decision?"

He leaned towards her. "Imogen, do you remember — maybe a while ago, I don't know — having a discussion with Dad — probably Aled, too — about taking over the farm?"

She stared at him, horror in her eyes. She drew her knees to her chest. "Who is taking over the farm, Noah? Is it those people in the village? They want to kill us."

Noah sighed. "I don't mean that. I'm talking about you and Aled taking over the farm. That's what Dad has decided."

She looked at him, relaxing. "Why would he give us the farm?"

"My thoughts exactly."

"Are you sure about it?"

"Yes."

"Have you asked Aled?"

"No."

She began to nod slowly, looking towards the window. "They've discussed this. Yes. I think so."

"How do you know?"

She was busy in thought, brow furrowed, lost in the machinations of her disturbed mind. She leaned towards him, putting her hand on his. "They're in it together," she whispered. "Yes. I'm sure of it. It all makes sense now."

"I've never known Aled express any interest in the farm," said Noah.

"But he and Daddy have been close lately. Aled went to see him."

"When?"

She shrugged. "A few weeks ago, I think."

"How do you know?"

"I rang Daddy. One night, before they took my phone. Aled was there. At the house. I was so confused. I thought it was — you know—" She tapped the side of her head. "But he was there. I talked to him."

"Why would Aled want the farm? He knows nothing about it. He has his business. He can't do both."

Imogen shook her head. "The business is in terrible trouble, Noah. Aled has been trying to hide it, even from me. He lies to me, you know. I can't trust him, Noah. He's been asking people for money. The bank told him, no. Maybe he was asking Daddy for money — or maybe it was about the farm? Who knows what they're up to."

Noah shifted uncomfortably, worried that he had planted a new conspiracy in Imogen's mind. He looked down at her fingertips, pressing urgently into the backs of his hands. The way she touched him had always repelled him. She'd struggled with boundaries for as long as he could remember. On her first day of junior school, as her year group filed into the hall, she had spotted Noah, lined up at the back. She broke away from her peers, running over, flinging her arms round his waist. His friends laughed. Her friends laughed. Everyone laughed except the teachers. Noah pushed her away, telling her to get back in line and do as she was told. He told her off again when they got home. He'd been doing some version of the same thing ever since.

"Imogen," he said. "Have you said anything to Dad about wanting the farm? Because if you did, he might have taken that to heart; you know how he wants you to have what you want. I've heard you say it would be nice for Hari to grow up on the farm, like you did. I won't be angry with you. I just need to know."

"I only meant if we all lived there! I thought Daddy could build another house and we could all be together, wouldn't it be nice? I would never, ever want to take the farm away from you, Noah."

He watched her for a minute. Gently, he pulled his hands away. If she'd been involved, she would have let it slip, one way or another. And it made sense to him that his father and Aled had shut her out. She wasn't exactly reliable in keeping a secret. Besides, she had little to contribute to such discussions. It made him feel a little better to know she was in the dark, too.

As he stood up, she was looking at him, a bemused expression on her face. "There was something I needed to say to you. But I can't think what it was now!"

"Can't have been that important."

She looked sad. "But it was."

He zipped up his jacket, keen to get away. However hardened he had become towards his sister's situation, he was flooded with guilt every time he left her here. That was the worst part about coming.

"I know what it was!" she said.

He waited. She looked at him with studied concentration.

"I don't want the farm," she said. "I have never wanted it in that way."

"Good to know," he said, not pointing out that she had just told him this. He bent down and gave her a hug. She clung to him. To extricate himself, he took hold of her wrists, peeled her hands away from his back.

"Why were you ringing Dad, anyway?"

"What?"

"When Aled was there — why were you ringing Dad? You never ring him. He's always complaining that you don't."

She tugged her sleeves down over her hands.

"I made a mistake," she said.

"What do you mean? What mistake?"

"I thought Mummy would be there."

* * *

Pulling out of the hospital car park, he felt immensely tired. Seeing his sister was fatiguing. But he also felt an overwhelming helplessness. It had been simmering inside him for years, he felt, this sense he could not control his own life. When he took over the farm, he thought it would go away; he would be in charge. But every time he felt things were moving in the right direction, life pushed against him. He couldn't go home. He felt there was something he must do, though he didn't know what it was. He drove down the bypass. Mai beside him, panting lightly. Between collecting the ram and visiting Imogen, she'd been in the car for hours. But she far preferred that to being stuck in the house or locked in the shed.

It was early afternoon. The sun was high in the sky. Turning off at the next roundabout, he realised where he needed to go. He moved along the narrow lanes, sunlight breaking through the gaps in the high trees. Eventually he turned into the estate, a maze of executive homes huddled together in bright sunlight. A clean tarmacked road wound between them. His window was open and he could hear children in their gardens. They weren't on the streets like they used to be. They were hidden from view. But you could hear them. The houses were in pairs, side by side with neat driveways and sparkling full-length glass alongside the front doors. He could never live somewhere like this. He had wondered, before, if he would feel the same way if his father hadn't bought the farm. Had that single decision made him who he was? Would he otherwise have been normal? Like Iwan Williams, whose driveway he pulled on to, parking his dirty truck behind his friend's immaculate BMW.

He looked at Mai, panting urgently now as he turned off the engine.

"I won't be long," he said.

She stopped panting for a second, pricking her ears. Then she opened her mouth again, tongue hanging out. He reached into the back, finding her pop-up bowl and an old bottle of water. It wasn't fresh but it was better than nothing. He walked round to her side, putting the bowl on the ground, letting her out to have a drink. She lapped the water greedily. He ushered her back in to the truck, leaving the window open.

"Don't bark at children," he told her. She settled down on the seat again, watching him walk to Iwan's door. His truck was conspicuously filthy, his boots not much better. He didn't like bringing all his muck here. At the same time, he was offended on some level by the immaculate estate, how prudish and unnatural it was, every car in sight shining. The little pretend road was clean, barely a leaf in the gutter. Noah assumed the people who lived here, if not solicitors like Iwan, were professionals of some kind or another: pharmacists, opticians, accountants, teachers.

Noah stood in front of the dark painted door. Through the glass, he could see the open staircase, cream carpet rising, shoes jumbled at the bottom.

"Noah!" said Katy, pulling open the door. She did her best to appear pleased but looked alarmed to see him. "*Ti'n ocê, cariad?*"

"Yeah. Fine. Sorry to just turn up like this. I was hoping to speak with Iwan?"

"*Wrth gwrs!*" she cried. "*Dwi'n meddwl fod o'n llofft. Tyd mewn — anwybydda'r holl lanast 'ma.*"

He nodded. She was telling him Iwan was upstairs, that he should come in, excuse the mess. Noah understood more or less all the Welsh he heard. Through his teens, seeing that he could increasingly understand the language, his mother pestered him to speak it back to people. She was an avid learner herself, watching S4C in the evenings, listening to Radio Cymru in the kitchen. But really it was the social implications that worried her, that people might dislike him for refusing.

Katy left the door open for Noah while she went to the stairs, shouting up for Iwan. After a moment she sighed and climbed the stairs, her large backside pushing out behind her. They had been in high school together, him and Katy and Iwan. Katy and Iwan weren't a couple until later, but the three of them were friends, always together.

Noah took off his boots and left them outside the door. Minutes later, Iwan appeared, padding downstairs in his socks. He wore shorts and a T-shirt, his arms and face golden against his light bleached hair. Undoubtedly, they had recently returned from a long summer holiday abroad.

"It is you!" he said, taking Noah's hand and pulling him into a hug. His skin smelled faintly of lotion, which might have been sunscreen but could just as easily have been moisturiser, knowing Iwan. His face was smooth and clean-shaven, soft hair wafting fruity shampoo. Katy stood behind him, lingering impatiently. When Iwan turned back to her, she told him he should take Noah into the living room, and that she'd keep the kids outside so they didn't bother them. Then she disappeared into the kitchen.

Through the window above the sink, Noah glimpsed the children in the garden. They had three kids, all under the age of seven. This was one of the reasons Iwan and Noah rarely saw each other anymore, as well as the fact Noah was basically terrible at staying in touch with anyone.

73

Iwan let Noah into the living room, where it was cool and quiet, the wide front window overlooking the estate. Noah's truck on the drive looked even filthier from this angle. Noah perched awkwardly on the edge of the pristine light-grey couch, feeling that his clothes, too, were probably dirty in this context. He looked up at Iwan, who was closing the door surreptitiously. Sitting on the matching armchair opposite, Iwan leaned forward, looking at Noah.

"Mate, I've been meaning to text you all week. Work's been a ball-ache. I heard what happened to your lambs — those bastards. I couldn't believe it."

Noah nodded. "Thanks. I mean, that's not why I'm here. But thanks."

Iwan nodded. His joviality had dissipated and he looked sombre now. When Noah said nothing more, Iwan went on. "I actually know someone you could talk to. Not that you can't talk to me. You can. I just mean, I know a really good therapist. She helped me a lot, a year or two ago."

"Oh — no," said Noah. "It's not that."

"There's nothing wrong with it, mate. I had to speak to her myself."

Noah shook his head. Then he looked at Iwan. "Did you? Oh. Are you okay?" He didn't really want Iwan to tell him anything about it. He knew that was selfish, but he just couldn't cope with it right now.

"I'm fine," said Iwan. "Much better. I'm just saying there's no shame in it."

"I know. But it's not that. I just need—" Noah pressed his hands together, looking at the clean cream carpet. "It's my dad."

Iwan laughed. "What's the bastard done now?"

For some reason, Noah couldn't even bring himself to smile. Iwan went quiet.

"It's not what he's done," said Noah. "It's what he's planning. I don't know if there's anything I can do." He shook his head again, feeling the whole thing rising in his throat like a sickness, swallowing it down. "I expect there's nothing. But I need to know — I need you to tell me — what my options are."

Noah looked up at his closest friend, who was watching him closely. Iwan sat back in his armchair. "Start at the beginning," he said.

CHAPTER SEVEN

Megan

Coming home from her coffee with Gethin, Megan wondered what she'd tell Noah. She couldn't say she'd been to the shops, she had nothing to show for it. Almost everyone she knew locally, Noah knew too. She settled on saying she'd had coffee with her Welsh class, which was closest to the truth, plus he was unlikely to ever meet them. Meanwhile she wondered — why not just tell him the truth? She'd had coffee with her Welsh teacher — what was wrong with it? But she had a vague sense that if she told him about the coffee she was compelled to share the full truth, including her confusing feelings about Gethin — and what would he make of that? And wouldn't it be thoughtless to make a fuss about such a thing, a week after the slaughter of the lambs? In the end, what she did or didn't plan to tell Noah was irrelevant. He wasn't there when she got back. And while she'd been the one out with another man, she found herself unreasonably upset that Noah was out and she didn't know where he was.

When his truck pulled in, she went out to meet him on the drive, standing at the front door.

"Where have you been?" she asked, folding her arms. Noah got out of the truck. Mai jumped out after him, running over to Megan, circling her legs.

"I was at the hospital," he said.

"What? Are you okay?"

"No, I mean — I went to see Imogen."

She stared at him. "Really?"

"I needed to talk to her."

He walked towards the house, giving her a kiss on the cheek as he passed. In the porch he bent down and unlaced his boots, pulling them off and placing them on the rack. Megan waited then followed him into the kitchen.

"So?" she said. "What happened?"

He sighed, wandering over to the fridge. "She claims not to know anything about Dad and the farm."

Megan watched him.

"I believe her," he said, glancing over his shoulder at her.

She nodded. "Good. I do, too. Not that I've talked to her about it. I just mean — if you believe her, then I do."

He gave her a quizzical look. She was behaving oddly, she realised. It was the guilt. Noah opened the fridge, staring plaintively at the bare shelves. She'd promised she would go to the supermarket today, which was what she should have done instead of having coffee with Gethin.

"Are you hungry?" she said. "I'll make you a sandwich. There's some cheese in there somewhere."

He nodded, wandering over to the window beyond the kitchen table. He had a distracted air, though Noah was always a little like that. He was like Imogen, in that way, and how Megan imagined their mother had been. They were cerebral creatures, lost in their thoughts. Conversation seemed to move too fast for Noah. He hated parties and dinners — anywhere that small talk was expected. She found a half-eaten block of cheddar in the fridge and placed it on the chopping board. She cut away the hardened edges then carefully sliced three wedges. She took two pieces of bread from the packet by the toaster, buttering one, laying the cheese on it. She cut the sandwich in half and put it on a plate.

Noah stood at the window, staring out at the fields of the neighbouring farm. A long time ago he'd wanted to buy that land, a distant dream now. As much as she hated Ray for what he was doing, she wondered if it might be in their interest to give in. Better for Noah than the endless slog of trying to make the farm work. But then wouldn't they just be transferring their financial burden to the cottages? She had done some calculations and she wasn't sure the income would be enough on its own. It was as though Ray had realised that letting them have both would finally allow them to relax and decided to nip that in the bud.

Anyway, none of that was the point. Noah had never had the slightest interest in catering to tourists. In fact, he'd resisted it as long as she'd known him, even when other farmers were reluctantly putting up glamping pods and tipis. Noah saw visitors as a necessary evil but not anything he wanted to get involved with. He got just as annoyed by their behaviour — getting drunk and being sick on the side of the road, leaving litter around their campsites that blew on to nearby farms — as people whose families had lived here for generations. It had been one thing when Megan was going to run the cottages; to have the farm taken away, the holiday homes their sole way of life — it seemed almost a deliberate humiliation.

"Noah?" she said.

He turned from the window, staring at the plate she was holding as though there had never been a discussion about a cheese sandwich.

"Sit down," she said. "Eat."

He did as he was told, pulling out a chair. She placed the plate in front of him. He clearly wasn't going to ask anything about her day; he wasn't in that frame of mind and he didn't know she hadn't come straight home. But something compelled her to say, "I had coffee with my Welsh teacher after class."

He wasn't listening. He was deep in thought, chewing on bread while clutching the sandwich in his fingers. He seemed newly disturbed, perhaps from visiting his sister.

"What did you say?" He looked up at her.

"I said I had coffee with my Welsh teacher."

He nodded slowly. "Good," he said. "That's good."

He took another bite of the sandwich. He didn't ask her why, and he didn't explain why it was good. Instead he looked at her and said, "Did you get hold of Elwyn?"

She sighed. Elwyn was the builder. Megan was meant to ring him this week about work on the cottages.

"I did try," she said. This was half true. She had got hold of Elwyn's number then failed to ring him. There was a reason for this. After their meeting with Ray, she and Noah hadn't discussed what they were going to do; they hadn't even talked about how Noah felt about it. Noah had said he didn't want to discuss it and hadn't brought it up since. Surely they needed to have this conversation before Megan went ahead contacting Elwyn, and everything else regarding the cottages?

"Maybe try him again today?" said Noah. "You have to be persistent with tradesmen. You know what they're like."

She looked at Noah for a second, wondering if she should state the obvious.

"I'll ring him later," she said. "So I've been meaning to tell you all week that this teacher — my Welsh teacher — used to work here."

Noah looked at her. "Used to work where?"

"At the farm."

He frowned. "What's his name?"

"Gethin. Gethin Williams."

"Oh," he said. "Him."

"What do you mean 'him'?"

"Nothing really. How old is he now?"

"Not sure," she said. "Twenty-four?"

"Sounds about right."

"Why did he leave again?" she said, trying to sound casual as she took Noah's empty plate.

"I didn't trust him."

Megan stared at him. "What do you mean?"

79

Noah sat back in his chair, lifting his arms over his head and yawning. "Well, I couldn't prove anything. But I started to get a bad feeling about him."

"Why?"

"I can't remember, exactly. Nothing I could prove, anyway."

"So you sacked him?"

He nodded, staring behind her. "Wasn't his dad a butcher?"

"No idea," said Megan.

Noah was nodding. "Mark the butcher," he said. "I remember. He used to come here to pick him up. He has a shop in Brynhalen."

"The one on the maes?"

"I think so."

Megan found it hard to get her head round the idea of Gethin having a father at all, let alone him owning the butcher's in Brynhalen.

"I never understood why he wasn't working there, instead of here."

"Because he was interested in farming?" said Megan. "I think I'd rather work here than in a butcher's."

"Hmm," said Noah.

"What?"

"Nothing."

"What is it?" she said. "If you know something, you should tell me. Because I've been wondering—"

"What?"

"Nothing, just — In the first class, he was off with me."

"Off how?"

"Oh, it was stupid, really. I just got the sense he didn't like me. But if you sacked him then it's not surprising, is it? He made a comment about the cottages. But I knew there was more to it."

Noah stood up, taking his plate back from her hands.

"Noah?" she said.

"What?"

"What is it?"

"I was just thinking."

"Thinking what?"

He looked at her. "It's probably nothing. But when I went into the station on Tuesday, I told the detective a few things that have occurred to me; things I think they should be considering when looking for the men."

"Okay," she said. "What kind of things?"

"Just how I don't think it was related to the other thefts."

"Yeah, you already told me that. So what?"

"Well, I felt like it was personal."

She nodded. "I know what you mean. I felt the same way about it."

"And I think—" He trailed off, glancing at her.

"What? Just tell me!"

"I think they did a pretty clean job. I think they had someone with them who knew how to butcher."

She looked at him, wondering why he had found this so difficult to say. Then it dawned on her. "Oh, Noah. Don't be ridiculous."

"I'm not saying it was him," he said. "There are dozens of butchers round here, obviously. But you see what I mean. He wasn't happy when I sacked him. And now we've bought the cottages, which you just said he made a comment about. I'm just thinking, that's all."

She shook her head. "No. The thing about it being personal — I get that. But you sacked Gethin when he was sixteen, right? You can't think he's been holding a grudge ever since?"

He walked away from her, dumping the plate in the sink. "Like I said, I'm not saying it was him."

* * *

The cottages stood opposite the primary school, right in the middle of the village. Their position was partly what made their conversion to holiday homes so offensive. If Ray had bought three houses on a remote back lane, the reaction wouldn't have been the same. But in this tightly woven village, where certain families had lived for generations and the language was spoken in every house, installing holiday cottages in front of the school was sacrilegious. The school, in grey stone with huts at the foot of the yard and daffodils skirting the railings, was itself sacred, one of the three anchors of the community. The second was the church, partially covered by a stone wall, though you could see its single stained-glass window, the deep red and blue glistening on sunny days. The third was the pub, a grand eighteenth-century listed building with a cobbled stone façade. If Megan had to choose, she would say the school was the most ferociously protected. Ten years ago, when starting a family seemed innocently on the horizon, she and Noah went to a meeting at the community centre about the council's proposal to close it. The meeting was translated through headphones, she and Noah able to listen to the whole thing. Megan had watched, captivated, a little unsettled. In her life she had never known anyone care so much about anything as these people cared about this school. A woman took the microphone and collapsed into tears before she could say a word. Grown men were crying, explaining why this closure imperilled everything important — their language, the future of the village, their way of life.

Megan understood, by now, that the transformation of the cottages to holiday homes encompassed the same existential threat. People saw it as another stage in the incremental loss of their way of life. Megan knew they had a point. At the same time, she noted that these houses had been empty for a while. The landlord, whose wife was unwell, had stopped renting them, no longer able to cope with the stress of tenants. Nor could he bring himself to put them on the market and show them to a succession of house-shoppers who might pull out at the last minute. When Ray Robinson came along, asking to take all of them off his hands at once, he had probably hardly cared what happened to them.

Megan parked in front of Tŷ Gwyn, the middle cottage, and walked up the lane, raising the hood of her jacket. She needed to go to the cwt, the shop inside a shed in the pub garden, and get some milk. It was Tuesday now; she still hadn't been shopping. Over the road there were children in the school yard, shrill shouts echoing across the lane. As she turned through the pub gate, she avoided looking in the direction of the people at the tables and headed straight for the hut. Since the protests, she avoided the village altogether. It was worse now, knowing she was here to visit the cottages, though no one else knew that.

It was sunny but mild, a light breeze blowing over the grass. The back door was wedged open with a rock and she saw the pub was empty inside. It was quiet on weekdays. She and Noah never ate or drank here. They'd been once, years ago, and felt out of place. It wasn't the fault of the locals — no one had said or done anything — but just a feeling they'd come away with. Since the backlash against the cottages, Megan assumed they would never come again.

She pulled open the door to the cwt, stepping into the cool shadows. She was surprised to find a man inside, thin and tall with a white beard. She smiled, avoiding his eye. The space between the shelves and counter was small and she moved against the wall, waiting as the man laid out his items. The cwt was run on an honesty system — you wrote down in the book what you'd taken and followed instructions about how to use the card machine. On the floor by her feet was an open cardboard box, bursting with leafy vegetables, a note scribbled in Welsh that she understood to say people could help themselves. She stared at the ground, waiting for the man. Collecting up his items, he looked back and nodded at her before pushing open the door and disappearing into the sunshine. She took a cold glass bottle of milk from the fridge and placed it on the counter. She scribbled the item and quantity in the book, making sure to write in Welsh. She double checked the price. She was terrified of making a mistake and people thinking that, on top of everything else, she and Noah were short-changing the cwt.

Stepping into the garden, she came face to face with a table of men, laughing raucously, half-drunk pints of lager on the table. As her gaze moved over them, she realised one of them was Gethin. He looked up, catching her eye. He didn't seem surprised to see her. Maybe he had seen her going into the cwt. It wasn't surprising that she would be here, either way. This was her closest village. Whereas he lived in town, a ten-minute drive from here, and with plenty of pubs closer than this.

She looked away from him, clutching the milk to her chest and hurrying to the gate. She had a strong feeling of not wanting to talk to him here. Whatever was between them didn't belong here. As she hurried down the lane, she heard him behind her.

"Megan! Wait a minute!"

She stopped, turning to him. "What are you doing here?" she said.

He looked at her, surprised, and put his hands in his pockets. "What are you doing here?" he said.

"I live here," she said.

"No, you don't," he said. "You live a mile over there." He nodded at the fields beyond the school.

She looked at him. "You know what I mean. This is my village, not yours."

"Your village?"

She sighed. "Never mind. I have things to do. You probably know the kind of things I mean, so I really don't need you making me feel bad about it."

"I wasn't going to mention it. You're the one making a scene. Why are you being weird?"

She didn't have an answer. "I don't know," she said.

"We haven't done anything wrong, you know."

"Haven't we?"

"We had coffee," he said. "It's not a crime."

But if the attraction between them had been only incubating then, it felt irrefutable now, facing each other on the quiet lane. She needed to get away and never see him again.

"I have to go," she said.

"Can I see you again? Before class on Saturday, I mean."

She looked at him. "No. And I don't think I should come to class again, either."

"Why not?"

"Gethin," she said. "Don't."

* * *

She opened the passenger door to her car and placed the milk on the seat, looking in her handbag for the keys to Tŷ Gwyn. She felt inexplicably sad, as though she had experienced a terrible loss. How could this person possibly have this effect on her? It made no sense. It must be the accumulation of everything else, she thought. Tensions in her marriage, failed fertility, Imogen, Ray, the farm, the cottages. Months and years of unresolved, unspoken stress and disappointment, all bundled together and converging in the figure of Gethin. Desire was never created by the object alone, it was just as much an expression of one's own history and circumstances. But she still wanted more of this. At the same time, she despised herself for it. She had been with Noah for thirteen years of her life. She loved him primally. He was her family, her best friend, her unwavering ally in a cruel world. This — Gethin — could not happen.

She opened the gate. Tŷ Gwyn was built in stone, like the houses on either side, but it was distinct from the other two with its smooth, white-painted render. After a long summer of neglect, the front gardens were wildly overgrown, in slightly shameful contrast with the tamed bushes and orchestrated bursts of flower further up the lane. As she walked up the path, she looked through the keys for the single Yale, carefully labelled "T.G." She pushed the key into the lock. Her hands were still trembling from her encounter with Gethin, her tummy disturbed by flutters. "Get a grip," she said to herself. She felt ridiculous, but also somehow exhilarated.

Inside the cottage it was cool and dark. Tŷ Gwyn required the least work of the three. Her plan was to get only this house ready for Christmas, directing the resources at her disposal to one instead of three. There was a chance she could actually achieve that. Whereas the other two, with their poor plumbing and dilapidated kitchens, would consume all her time and energy, at the expense of finishing Tŷ Gwyn. Ray didn't like to be told that anything was impossible but he would have to deal with it.

When she had eventually spoken to Elwyn, he told her to take pictures and send them to him. She walked through the empty rooms now, her thin jacket zipped to her chin. It was somehow colder in here than outside, the shaded rooms giving off the sad sense of abandonment emitted by uninhabited houses. Small things needed fixing — lights and cracked tiles. It needed a deep clean. But the fundamentals were good. Standing in the kitchen, she selected the photos and sent them to Elwyn. She looked back towards the hall, noticing a door in the corner of the kitchen. She had forgotten there was a cellar here, converted to a flat for the previous tenant's disabled mother. She hadn't considered what to do with it. Would anyone want to sleep down there on their holiday, a basement flat with disability fixtures? She couldn't rent it out separately, not without removing access from the main house. In which case the only entrance would be through the garden, which you couldn't get to without going through the house.

Megan walked over to the door. Opening it, she flicked a switch and looked down at the carpeted staircase. She wandered down, finding it surprisingly pleasant when she reached the bottom. A small window at the back overlooked the garden, which sloped gently upwards. A tidy modern kitchenette stood in the corner. A door opened to an en suite. There was an overall impression of light and space, the walls white, the carpet cream, mirrors on the walls. Aside from some dust and dead moths, it was more like a holiday rental down here than the rest of the cottage.

* * *

She went to her Welsh class the following Saturday, having told herself emphatically that she would not. An unbearable tension seemed to crackle in the air as Gethin moved around the classroom, brushing the back of her chair. She tried to concentrate. She had sat next to Jim when she arrived and they were doing all the pair work together. Roger and Sally always sat together, an unbreakable unit. This was fine with everyone else, as no one wanted to listen to Roger's constant moaning. Rhys, who had come back for the third lesson, was working with Denise, who was surprisingly maternal towards him in spite of her blunt manner.

"It's nice to see you again," Jim had said when he saw Megan. She almost laughed before realising he was being sincere. They were doing an exercise together now, working through a list of place names, saying they were from each town or village. Megan was finding it difficult, though it shouldn't have been. Meanwhile, Jim was calmly engaged, muttering things like, "I did not know that took a mutation; how interesting." Gethin worked his way around the table. When he got to Megan and Jim, he stood directly behind Megan so she couldn't see him. He had done this deliberately, she felt, giving him all the power as he watched her, poised to criticise and correct, while she couldn't see him at all. As she attempted the next phrase, she felt the heat from his body behind her, and her grasp on the activity fell apart completely. Her mind went blank. She stuttered, started again, got it wrong, then gave up altogether, putting her hand over her mouth. Her face was burning. Jim looked at her in confusion. Gethin leaned over her from behind, his hand brushing hers as he reached for her workbook, and read the line for her in his melodic, perfect diction.

When he walked away, Jim whispered to her, "Do you know him?"

"No," she said. "I actually don't."

* * *

After class she waited behind, yet again. Gethin tidied. She didn't help. She felt hot and agitated. Her heart pounded as she watched him moving around the room. She had a sensation of being outside herself. They didn't talk but simply left the café together and walked to the car park, moving past her Land Rover and stopping at his small black Vauxhall Corsa. He opened the door for her. She climbed inside, stretching the seatbelt across her body, staring ahead at the dull sky. Gethin moved round the car and got silently in the driver's seat. When he was sitting in the car, they were quiet for a moment. She had an urge to say something, to stop what was happening. But she didn't.

He started the engine. They left the village behind. Megan looked through her window at the fields. She had an overwhelming heat in her body. She had assumed Gethin would take her to his home but after a while in the lanes, he turned down a shaded track. Tall trees shadowed the dry mud. The car bumped along. He pulled over in a clearing. It was deadly quiet, nothing but wood in front of them, the leaves orange and green. A muted chorus of birds seemed to shield them, along with the dense canopy.

Gethin turned off the engine. For a while, he stared through the windscreen. She felt he wanted to say something. She hoped he didn't. She didn't want this to be discussed or named. She turned to him. He looked at her, reaching out to grip a handful of her hair, tugging lightly. She closed her eyes, letting him push his head forward and brush his lips against hers. They kissed deeply, finding a rhythm despite their urgency. His fingers kneaded the back of her neck. His mouth was foreign to her and she thought of Noah, so familiar but whom she had not kissed like this for a long time. They had not been intimate at all for months, as though deciding to abandon their struggle to have children had signalled the end of their sex life. Gethin was new terrain. In another way, his body was in some way known to her, like everything else about him. The kissing wasn't enough, it wouldn't get to the heart of whatever this was. She lifted herself from her seat, climbing over the gear stick, finding herself on top of him, her head touching the roof of his confined car. When she pressed against him, twisting her neck, she was unable to separate the fast beating of his heart from her own.

CHAPTER EIGHT

Noah

Finding Megan on the drive, he wanted to tell her everything. But he refrained, sharing only his visit to Imogen. He didn't like lying to her, even leaving things out. There was enough making him feel out-of-control without undermining his marriage. Despite their problems, his relationship with Megan was grounded in trust. But he wasn't ready to talk to her about taking his father to court. For one thing, she would have an opinion about it, one way or another. He imagined her preference would be not to do it, that she would say it was too much stress and expense, they'd been through enough, they should move on from the farm and make do with the cottages. She would be right in many ways and he would find it hard to argue.

Promissory estoppel was the term Iwan had used to describe Noah's legal right to challenge his father. He had been surprised to learn that a promise from his mother might be enough, in spite of the fact that, when she died, the land had passed to his father, who had been listed as the joint owner. The solicitors would need to prove three things, according to

Iwan; first, that a promise had been made to Noah about the future of the farm; second, that Noah had made important decisions based on that promise; finally, that he had made these decisions to his own detriment, should the promise not be fulfilled. It was not difficult to prove the second and third. He'd sought no qualifications beyond school, instead working the farm his entire adult life. The first condition was trickier. While it was true that his mother had promised him the farm, she was not here anymore and it wasn't written down, as far as he knew. She hadn't left a will.

"So how can we prove it?" Noah had asked Iwan.

"It won't be easy. But we'll call witnesses. Your sister. Megan. Anyone who can give evidence that it's likely your mother said this, or that it was understood between you. You'll say your bit, of course. Ultimately it will come down to who the judge believes — you or your father."

Noah had been thinking about going to see Imogen again, asking her how she felt about giving evidence in his favour. While there was no way his sister believed anything except that his mother intended for Noah to have the farm, saying so in court would mean going up against not only their father but her husband. And what if she did agree to do it? Was she a reliable witness? It was on record that she suffered from a psychotic illness. According to Iwan, she was key, the only person to have lived with Noah and his mother after they moved here. Whereas Megan had never known his mother. Her testimony would simply be that Noah had consistently maintained, throughout their marriage, that he would one day inherit the farm, and that Megan, as Noah's wife, had made her own decisions based on that promise, too.

* * *

On Wednesday afternoon, while Megan was out, he went upstairs and stood on the landing, pulling down the long ladder to the attic. He climbed the skinny rungs, slender bars

91

of wood digging into his feet, and pushed open the hatch. It was raining, the drumming of water on the roof steady and persistent, and as he raised himself into the stuffy heat, the noise grew louder and more urgent. It was pitch dark up there. He groped for the switch on the bare wall, flicking it on, the blackness abruptly steeped in a hazy light from the single bulb hanging from the rafters.

Among the boxes of CDs and DVDs, abandoned computers and childhood keepsakes, his mother's things were sealed in long plastic boxes. He and Imogen had sorted through her belongings after she died. Many things they had given away, her dresses and shoes and old-fashioned handbags. Imogen had taken her jewellery and studded hair grips. Everything else they packed away up here. Imogen took some boxes home, which Noah hadn't minded at the time, though it was troubling to him now that he may have to go there and ask to look through them.

He brought the boxes down awkwardly, one at a time, sweating and dust-covered by the time he sat on the floor of the landing, his mother's things spread around him. He didn't know what he was looking for, but Iwan said anything that remotely indicated his mother's intentions would be valuable. He knew he needed to be thorough, but he was overwhelmed before he'd even begun. There was so much here. Most of the letters and paperwork he'd never looked at. After she died, he'd been keen to get it all packed away. But he knew his mother had kept diaries. He would never have read them except in these circumstances. Even now, he was deeply uncomfortable about the violation.

From what he could see, most of the diaries were kept during the early years of his and Imogen's lives, as Joan wrote down her experiences of new motherhood. He became momentarily absorbed in these, which she had never shown him, and which scrupulously detailed night-waking, hospital visits, colic, breastfeeding . . . He made a mental note to show Megan, and Imogen, before telling himself to move on — they predated the purchase of the farm and were therefore of no use. He was sure she'd kept notebooks in the early years after they moved to the farm, writing down what she was learning and keeping track of the flock. Eventually he found them, hardbacked black Moleskine with lined pages, filled with his mother's neat, black-inked script. He read them carefully. She wrote — with endless detail and fascination — about sheep. There was little mention of him; when his name did appear, she was generally commenting on how well he was adapting to the tough physical work. At one point she noted how torn she felt about taking advantage of his labour — was it okay to use him for real work on the farm at the age of twelve, even if he enjoyed it? This made him smile.

He was becoming tired, though he had four more boxes to investigate. He opened the next one with a sigh, looking down at the scattered mess, wishing he and Imogen had organised it better. At the bottom he found letters stuffed inside a brown padded envelope. He recognised immediately what they were: letters sent from his father to his mother after they moved. He remembered her opening them, raising her eyebrows in muted contempt, putting them to one side. As a child he had not wanted to read them; he didn't want to now. He and Imogen had carefully avoided them when they sifted through these things thirteen years ago.

Warily, he took them from the envelope, reading them one by one. His father's style was as jarring and brash on paper as he was in person. Noah recoiled at his tone, even when the content was unremarkable. A lot of the time he was simply asking that their mother send Noah and Imogen back to the Midlands for the school holidays. In others, he was answering a request for cash, usually with a note of gloating. Requests to see his children turned quickly to threats and eventually tirades of abuse. There was a letter written in April 1994 — they'd been at the farm just over a year by then — in which his father had clearly realised Joan had no intention of ever sending the children home. He threatened legal action, which

Noah didn't believe he'd ever taken. This seemed strange to him now — why had it never gone to court, if his father was upset about it? It had never occurred to Noah, either, to wonder why they'd never gone back to Warwickshire. The relief from being away from his father had been so great he wouldn't have dared ask.

Halfway through the letter, a line stuck out to Noah. He read it several times. *I've said it before and I'll say it again: these are malicious lies and you are a fool to believe them.* Nowhere in the letter did his father name the lies he was referring to. It could have been anything; Noah didn't want to know. Whatever had passed between his parents before they came to the farm — and he was sure it was something, even if only a tipping point in the emotional havoc his father had inflicted over years — Noah had never had the stomach to know anything about it.

* * *

He had something else on his mind. Megan was right that Gethin was unlikely to have held a grudge for eight years. But that wasn't entirely what he'd meant. After the campaign against the cottages eased off, Noah felt there were bound to be participants who were unwilling to give up so easily. If someone had arranged the slaughter of the lambs as retaliation, or a warning, Gethin would be an ideal participant. He knew the layout of the farm. He presumably knew how to butcher. Clearly he had strong views about the cottages. It would have been an added incentive that Noah sacked him all those years ago.

There was something else, too. He hadn't wanted to tell Megan this, not yet. But the whole time Gethin worked at the farm, Noah had felt there was something off about him. It was only a feeling at first, a sense of something awry, hard to pinpoint. One afternoon, they had a disagreement. Lambing had come to an end, all the newborns and ewes turned out to the field. Gethin had come to find Noah, flustered, saying there was a ewe with a broken leg. The boy was disturbed, more so than he should have been over a lame sheep. Noah went to the field with him, examining the ewe. He flushed the wound and bandaged the leg. When he stood up and began walking towards the gate, Gethin ran after him.

"Are you just going to leave her there?"

Noah stopped, looking at the boy. "I'll bring her to the shed."

Gethin nodded with a kind of knowingness that Noah knew was common in teenagers but he still found it irritating.

When they'd transported the ewe and laid her in a pen, Gethin said, "Won't she need pain relief?"

"She'll be fine."

"But she's moaning?"

"Don't worry about it."

"My uncle's a vet," said the boy. "I could ask him to come down, give her something? He won't charge you."

Noah looked at Gethin. Perhaps he was genuinely concerned for the ewe, in spite of being the son of a butcher. Noah felt it was more about challenging his authority. The boy had done this before, asking questions about the running of the farm that were on the wrong side of simply wanting to know. Either way, Noah was irritated by his persistence, and his offensive offer of free vet care.

"I said she'll be fine. I don't want to hear any more about it."

Later that day, Noah went back to check on the ewe. She lay on her side on the bed of hay, as they'd left her. He moved round her, kneeling down to find her beady eyes glazed and staring. She was dead, her throat slit, blood staining the hay beneath. Of course, the boy had denied it, but Noah sacked him, anyway.

* * *

He hadn't spoken to Mandy, the detective, for over a week. She'd said he could contact her any time. He didn't know

95

if she meant it, but he found the card she'd given him and dialled the number.

"It's Noah Robinson," he said.

She was quiet, uncertain.

"My lambs—" he said.

"Oh!" she said. "Hi, Noah. How can I help?"

Immediately he disliked her tone, a polite distance he didn't care for. This was not the way she'd spoken to him when he went to the station, so attentive, then, it had almost been intimate. It put him off what he had rung her to say, but he pushed himself on.

"I wanted to talk to you about something." He paused. "I know you're investigating my lambs as part of these other . . . thefts. I told you I didn't think it was related?"

"I remember," she said.

"This is going to sound strange."

"That's okay," she said. "You never know what might be useful." But her tone was brisk and impatient. *Get on with it, please. I have things to do.*

He took a breath. "There was a boy who worked on the farm, years ago. I didn't think anything of this until recently, but I think he might be involved."

She paused. "Tell me more."

* * *

By the following Friday, Mandy had not come back to him. He wondered if she'd been humouring him when she said she would investigate Gethin. With the long weekend ahead, he rang her again.

"Hello?"

"It's Noah," he said. "Sorry to bother you again. I know you must be busy."

"That's okay!" she said. "How can I help?" That same briskness, as though there was a time limit on her attention. It made him feel like a child.

"I was just wondering if you had anything to tell me?"

96

"Actually, we do have a lead, now you ask. This is related to the gang we've been monitoring."

His heart sank. Increasingly, he felt that the police were not only ignoring his view that the two crimes were unrelated but had a policy of talking to him as though they were in the hope it might eventually convince him. It felt like brainwashing, but too subtle to be challenged.

"Did you talk to Gethin?"

She was quiet. "I did, actually."

He felt himself go still. "What did he say?"

"He doesn't seem to have any information."

Noah wanted to laugh. "I never thought he had information," he said. "I said I thought he was involved."

"There's no evidence to suggest that. And he wasn't able to provide any other information."

"Well, he's not going to provide information if he did it, is he?" He tried not to sound angry. "Did you ask him where he was that night?"

She sighed. "I can't disclose what was discussed, I'm afraid. But we have no reason to believe he was involved."

"You mean because he didn't admit it?"

There was silence. "I was looking at the file today," she said. "I noticed we haven't had a victim statement from you. Have you thought any more about that?"

Noah was confused. "You want me to do another statement?"

"No," she said. "I'm talking about your victim statement. I mentioned it to you at the station. It's where you describe how the crime has impacted you. Some people find it helps them come to terms with what's happened."

He felt a burning of disgust. "Why should I come to terms with it?"

* * *

In the following hours, he turned over his conversation with Mandy, quietly irate. Through the front windows of the house, the sun had nearly vanished behind the mountains, a gloaming over the fields. A crowd of midges fluttered in the driveway. It was eerily quiet. Megan was out, which meant her familiar domestic activity — clattering in the cupboards, the blast of the Hoover, the juddering of the washing machine through the wall — was absent. She had been out a lot, recently. He wasn't sure why. Her Welsh class seemed to be preoccupying her more than it should. Tonight, for example, she was down at the café in Glanllwyd where she had her lessons. Apparently, they were showing some Welsh-language film. Noah couldn't imagine why she wanted to spend her Friday evening doing that, though she'd said she'd be back by eight and would bring takeaway.

He checked his phone. He had a missed call from Aled, who'd rung him twice today already. He considered calling him back now. But he didn't want to get embroiled in some drama involving his sister and the unit. He had missed calls from his father, too, who had been ringing him all week. Almost certainly, he wanted to progress his plan to transfer the farm. He would say there was paperwork to complete. His father was adept at presenting his plans as a fait accompli, documents drawn up by his lawyers, ready to be signed. Avoidance was Noah's main defence. Unfortunately, it was not sustainable. For one thing the anxiety was making him ill. Also, he knew how angry it made his father to be ignored, and that he would eventually show up at the farm, apoplectic, solicitors in tow. Confronted like that, Noah would find it harder to hold his nerve.

He decided to ring him.

"Jesus Christ, Noah. I've been ringing you for a week. What the hell is going on?"

"I've had a lot on my plate," said Noah coolly.

His father was quiet, thrown off by Noah's tone.

"All right," he said. "Listen. I want to get this paperwork dealt with. I want the whole thing over with. The lawyers have done everything. I just need you both to sign."

"Me and Megan?"

"You and your sister."

"She's in the hospital," said Noah. It hadn't occurred to him before now, but surely his father couldn't make Imogen sign legally binding paperwork while she was sectioned?

"Haven't you heard?" said his father. "She's getting out."

Noah remembered the missed calls from Aled. "Is she back on her medication?"

"I didn't ask. But if the doctors are letting her go, that's good enough for me."

"Okay," said Noah. "So when is she out?"

"Monday, if all goes to plan over the weekend. So I'll come up on Wednesday. You'll be around?"

"Can we do it in a couple of weeks?"

"What's different in a couple of weeks?"

"I've got a lot on, Dad. The police still need things. I've got my own paperwork. The insurance. And then there's the farm — I've got to take the last of the lambs—"

"Okay, okay," said his father, unable to tolerate any hint of whining. "Two weeks. No more."

"Okay," said Noah.

"Has she got to work on the cottages yet?"

He considered telling his father what Megan had told him, that she was planning on preparing only Tŷ Gwyn for Christmas. But that could wait.

"Yes," he said. "She has."

* * *

He didn't know where Gethin lived but one place he was sure he would find him was at the film showing in Glanllwyd. He sat in his truck on the driveway, thinking what to do. He wondered, not for the first time since the slaughter of the lambs, if he was going mad. But he just wanted to see the man — where was the harm in that? He was tired of thinking about him, his brain harbouring an outdated image of an insolent teenager. Over the last week he had become tortured by his memory of this boy. Seeing him in the flesh might end the fixation.

He drove down the bypass, still uncertain, even as he headed straight for Glanllwyd, whether to go through with it. By seven o'clock he was outside the café, idling in his truck in the middle of the street. The light was close to vanishing now. Through the rear-view mirror he saw a car behind him, waiting. He drove on, turning into another street to let it pass. Laboriously, he turned back round, reversing his truck into the concrete yard of a pub then driving back to the corner. Looking down the street, he noticed a space where he could park with a view of the café, far enough from the door that he was unlikely to be noticed. He parallel parked in the space and sat in his truck, watching the doorway in the dying light. The café itself was closed. According to Megan, the film was being shown in the room at the back where she had her lessons. Still, it was unsettling that the lights in the front were off.

Shadows gathered. There was movement through the glass, behind the café door. A man emerged into the street. Noah sat up, squinting through the near-darkness. He didn't recognise the man, who was perhaps forty or so. Noah wondered, suddenly, if he would recognise Gethin. More people came out. Noah watched closely. The streetlights had come on now, as had a light inside the café, glowing through the façade. A younger man appeared, followed by several others. This was Megan's class, Noah thought, adults awkward and unfamiliar with one another, diverse in age. Megan wasn't with them. Neither was Gethin. The group dispersed, splitting in three directions.

Noah watched the closed door. Eventually, a woman stepped into the closing dark. It was Megan. She wore her long sheepskin coat, as she had when she left the house. It was by far her most glamorous coat, a fur trim lining the neck and cuffs. Her hair was loose around her shoulders. There was a man behind her. Noah could see straight away that it was Gethin. He looked very similar to eight years ago, just more mature, thicker in the arms, better dressed. His face was imprecise in the vanishing light but Noah could see that he had grown into himself.

Standing on the pavement beneath the streetlight, Megan turned back towards Gethin and smiled, pulling her handbag to her front. Even in this poor light, Gethin was looking at her in a way that provoked Noah. Then he did something shocking; leaning forward, he placed his hand on Megan's shoulder and whispered in her ear. Megan stayed very still, listening. When Gethin pulled away, Megan was smiling. They turned and walked, side by side, towards the high street. Noah turned his key in the ignition, engine rumbling, and pulled out of the space, following them. By the time he reached the high street, they had crossed the road. Vaguely, Noah could make out Megan's Land Rover in the car park. He watched as Gethin escorted her to her car.

Noah knew he should go home now; he had seen him, he had no more reason to stay. But he lingered at the junction, no cars behind him to move him on. His headlights had come on. If she looked across the street, Megan might notice his dallying truck, wonder what on earth he was doing here. But she wasn't paying attention. She was talking to Gethin, holding open the driver's door, talking to him over the top. She wants to go home, Noah thought. Leave her alone.

Finally, she climbed into the driver's seat. Gethin went to his own car. Noah could see Megan's figure, hunched over, looking at her phone. This was his opportunity to drive away, Megan none the wiser that he was ever there. But something stopped him. He looked at Gethin, in his little black Corsa. His headlights came on, the car rolling out of the space and down the ramp, turning left on the high street. Noah glanced at Megan, still staring at her phone. He pulled out, turning in the same direction as Gethin, hoping Megan didn't notice as the truck moved quietly past.

* * *

He followed Gethin out of Glanllwyd and on to the lanes, keeping as far back as he could. There was nothing between

101

them but the glare of headlights. The lane was endless and winding until it finally reached the roundabout connecting to the bypass. Gethin sped up. Noah did, too. Out on the big open road, Noah felt paranoid. It was much lighter here than on the lanes, tall streetlamps flooding the cars with white light. There were boy racers, overtaking his truck, separating him from Gethin until they sped round the Corsa, too. At the next roundabout, Gethin turned left. They had skirted town; Gethin was heading in from the north.

They moved past the industrial estate, with its tall trees and high metal fences, warehouses and concrete yards. Gethin indicated left and turned on to a quiet residential street, lights shining through the front windows of terraced houses. He stopped to let a car through then went ahead between the parked cars. Noah hung back, watching as Gethin manoeuvred into a space and got out of his car. He opened a wrought-iron gate and bounded up steep steps to a high row of terraced houses. Quickly, he unlocked a red-painted front door and disappeared inside.

Noah watched from the end of the street, strangely empowered to know where he lived. Everyone knew the farm; he and Megan lived there, exposed, while he knew nothing about anyone else, including the people who wanted to hurt him. He checked his phone. It was almost eight. He wondered what Gethin would do. There was no movement on the street. Noah was ready to leave when the red door opened again and Gethin appeared. No more than five minutes had passed since he went inside. He had on the same jeans and jacket as before but he carried a rucksack and wore a dark beanie on his head.

Gethin walked lightly back down the steps and turned left, moving quickly along the pavement. He walked straight past his Corsa. Noah sank low, turning his head away as Gethin passed on foot on the far side of the road. There was something purposeful in his gait, like he had somewhere to be. After passing Noah's truck, he turned left, his figure fading into the darkness. Hastily, Noah reversed, trying not to rev the engine, turning to face the same direction Gethin was walking. For a moment he thought he had lost him. Then he spotted his fast-moving figure. How did you follow someone who was on foot if you were in a car? Noah had never done anything like this. He turned off his headlights and moved painstakingly slowly, leaving as much distance as he could. A dip in the road allowed him to coast, keeping the engine quiet. But he thought Gethin must be aware of a car behind him.

At the next corner, Gethin went left again. Noah coasted as he turned the bend. But as the road levelled, his truck slowed. He came to a stop, watching. The street in front of him was lined with slightly bigger semi-detached houses. Gethin turned through a gap in the wall, seeming to disappear between two pairs of houses. Tall hedges shielded him. There might have been a path between the houses, in which case Noah had lost him. But abruptly Noah heard the bite of an engine. A motorbike emerged, gliding over the dropped kerb, the rider wearing a wide gleaming helmet. Noah recognised the jeans and jacket. Before he had a chance to grasp what was going on, the motorbike circled and shot away.

Noah jammed the accelerator and sped after him. Within minutes, they were back on the bypass. Gethin was moving much more quickly on the bike than he had in his car. He overtook several cars, hurtling round the next roundabout and disappearing between trees at the third exit. Noah was stuck behind the cars and felt he had certainly lost him now. He circled the roundabout, anyway, taking the same exit. After a couple of bends in the lane, he came to the long stretch of road overlooking the quarry. He saw the bike, parked and driverless, a few hundred metres ahead. Nearby, Gethin stood, opening a field gate. When it was halfway ajar, he turned his head to look back down the road. He might have been looking directly at Noah's truck, moving slowly towards him. Either way, he hopped back on the bike and charged through the opening.

Noah slowed as he approached the gate. If he turned into the field and Gethin was there, he would be exposed — if

Gethin hadn't already known Noah was following him. He turned in, anyway, angling his truck through the open gate, finding himself on a track that rose towards the night sky. The stars were thick and clear. Open fields lay on either side of him. He reached a peak and found himself looking down at a cluster of trees, the track disappearing among them. He couldn't see the bike, nor hear it. It was very dark, only moonlight illuminating the track and fields. He stared through his windscreen. Over the tops of the trees at the bottom, he made out the low roof of a building, a dark yard surrounding it. He noticed a figure moving from the trees towards it.

He released the clutch and coasted down the track. Reaching the bottom, he went into gear to move along the flat ground between the trees. Ahead, he saw the empty yard and outer edge of the building. The bike was parked alongside a truck and a car. If he emerged into the yard, he would no longer have the cover of the trees. On the left he saw a clearing and pulled in, giving him a partial view of the building. It looked, through the thick dark, like a derelict farmhouse of some kind. There was no light from the building. He couldn't even tell if it had windows: they might have been boarded up. He wanted to stay and find out more. But he had pushed his luck far enough. He felt frightened by now, unsafe in the vicinity of something covert. His heart was thumping. It was deadly quiet all around him. He pulled out, turning back up the track until he reached the safety of the road.

* * *

Back home, he felt more shaken than he had during the pursuit, as though, as the adrenalin left his body, all his fear collapsed in on him. His hands trembled. He felt dizzy and sick. He stayed in the truck for a while. The lights were on in the house, Megan's car on the drive. It was nine by now. What would he tell her? He never went out on a Friday night. He had no plausible excuse for where he'd been. He found his phone, which had slid beneath the passenger seat during the chase, and saw several missed calls from her. He remembered the takeaway she was bringing home.

"Where have you been?" she said when he walked into the kitchen.

"Just driving around," he said. "Sorry. Did you get takeaway? I forgot all about it."

She looked at him. "You were driving around on your own this whole time?"

"Yeah," he said, wishing he'd thought of something else. "I just needed to clear my head. I lost track of time."

She watched him. "Are you okay?" She reached out and touched his sweaty cheek. He pulled back. "What's wrong? You're all pale and shaky."

"I'm fine," he said. "Have you eaten?"

"I was waiting for you. I'm starving."

"Sorry," he said again.

"Do you want a drink?"

He nodded. There were so many things he wanted to tell her. Everything he'd just seen, for one thing, how it surely confirmed his view that Gethin had been involved in the lambs. How strange it was that he was right about him, given it had been such a tenuous theory to begin with. He wanted to tell her he didn't think she should go to the Welsh class anymore. He longed to share the content of his meeting with Iwan, tell her about the letters his father had written to his mother. For different reasons, he couldn't bring himself to tell her any of it. Besides, he was exhausted and famished. He wanted to eat, have a lager — maybe two or three — and forget everything.

Then he remembered one thing he did need to tell her.

"My sister," he said.

Megan turned, peeling the lid off a foil container packed with rice. "What?" she said. "Is she okay?"

He nodded. "They're letting her out."

CHAPTER NINE

Megan

"Are we there now, Auntie Megan?"

"Hari," said Aled, looking back from the passenger seat. "Don't ask that again."

The boy was wild with excitement to see Imogen. Perhaps it was a sign of her naivety and inexperience with children, but Megan found herself constantly surprised by the endlessness of Hari's devotion to his mother. It had been three months with no physical access at all. But through the rear-view mirror, Megan watched him, lifting himself in his booster seat, craning his neck to scan the bypass for any glimpse of the hospital. Perhaps, in his four-year-old imagination, he was looking for the figure of his mother on the side of the road, bags at her feet.

They were not yet halfway but the journey felt long and fraught. The tension was coming from herself as much as Aled or Hari, though she didn't know why. Hari looked very smart, a red check shirt over his clean white T-shirt, his dark curls damp and washed. Hari had wanted to look nice for his mother, according to Aled. At the same time, he seemed a little disturbed. Megan wondered, again, what Aled had told him about why Imogen had been in the hospital.

Hari had gone quiet now. There was no sound at all for a while except the rush of wind outside the windows, pushing gently against the car. It was raining lightly. She turned into the hospital grounds, finding a space in the staff car park outside the unit. Aled said it was fine to wait there, given they were collecting someone. While Aled went in to meet Imogen, Megan stayed in the car with Hari. As they watched him, head bowed against the weather, Megan had an abrupt sense that Aled was afraid to take Hari inside the unit not simply because it could upset him but because, if Hari carried some gene containing his mother's illness, exposure to the psychiatrically ill would somehow awaken it. Megan didn't know if this was fairly reasonable or itself a kind of madness.

While they waited, Hari was not his usual chatty self. He sat quietly, staring through the rain towards the closed doors of the unit. Finally, Aled emerged, bags in each hand. Behind him came Imogen, frowning against the elements, her bob of dark curls whipped over her face. She had the look of a soldier who had been through great adversity and intended to keep going. In the backseat there was an audible intake of breath.

"Mam!" shouted Hari. Startled, she fought an urge to tell him off. "Can I get out, Auntie Megan? Please? Can I get out now, please?"

He was tugging the door handle, as though he could override the child lock by the urgency of his will.

"Wait!" said Megan. She looked through her window, hesitated, then got out to open his door. The second she released his belt, he scrambled from the car like a wild animal, sprinting across the car park.

"Hari!" she shouted. "Wait!"

She watched in horror as Hari bolted behind a reversing car. It did not hit him but the driver, outraged, opened his window and shouted something at Megan. Oblivious, Hari kept running towards Imogen, who was on her knees, arms spread wide, equally blind to the dangers of worldly things like cars. She wrapped her arms around Hari, closing her eyes tightly. Megan went to the boot, opening it for Aled, who drifted over and placed the bags inside.

Imogen and Hari came after him.

"Lovely weather!" said Imogen. She hugged Megan, holding on to her tightly, too. Megan had almost forgotten, amid the strain of it all, how relieved she was that Imogen was finally leaving this place. When they separated, Imogen held her gaze long enough for Megan to see that talk of Megan being a "replacement" was in the past for now.

The wind was blowing hard. Hari, holding his mother's fingers, began to tug at them. Imogen didn't notice at first. She was looking at Aled. Then she glanced down at Hari, blinking. "Don't do that!" she said, snatching her hand from his.

He stared at her for a second. His lip trembled, tears welled in his eyes.

"Oh, I'm so sorry, darling!" Imogen cried, crouching to face him. "I didn't mean to snap. I'm so tired, darling. I didn't get much sleep in the hospital. Please don't be upset with me. Mummy loves you so much." She opened her arms again and he went to her willingly.

"Shall we get going?" said Aled. "Instead of standing in the rain?"

"Can I sit in Mam's lap?" said Hari. He was speaking English to his father, Megan noticed, perhaps to accommodate a mother he didn't dare risk alienating for a second.

"What?" said Aled. "Don't be silly, Hari."

Hari's eyes filled again. He looked pleadingly at his mother.

"Oh, just let him," said Imogen. "Just this once."

"Imogen," said Aled warningly.

"He just wants to sit on my lap," she said. "What's the harm?"

"The harm is it's illegal."

"No one is going to see!"

"It's also not safe. And there's no need for it! He can sit in his own seat, like he always does."

"Let's ask Megan what she thinks," said Imogen. "She's the driver."

"That's enough," said Aled. "I said no. Get in the car — both of you."

There they were, back to their old, practised dynamic. Imogen was like a child, pushing limits in the knowledge that Aled would enforce the boundaries that kept them safe. Imogen sat beside Hari in the back, the two of them chatting happily. After a lull, Imogen leaned forward, saying to Aled, "Remind me to take my you-know-what when we get home."

Aled pulled down his visor, looking at her through the mirror. "Why didn't you take it this morning?"

"I forgot."

"Didn't they remind you?"

"Oh God, no," she said. "You know what it's like there. I'll be surprised if it isn't shut down by the end of the year." Imogen said this every time she came out of the unit.

Aled closed the visor, turning quiet.

Imogen sighed. "I am so happy to be going home."

* * *

"I've had a thing for you since I was sixteen." They were in bed, his breath warm on the back of her neck.

"Really?" she said. "I hardly saw you, back then."

"I saw you," he said. "What are these?" He was lifting his head now, running his fingertips over the faded marks on her thigh.

"IVF."

"Oh." His body turned still.

"Are you still doing that?" he said.

"No."

"Sorry to bring it up."

"It's fine," she said. "I'm over it."

It had happened like before. They went to his car after class without any discussion. This time he took her home. She didn't know why, and she didn't ask. When they walked inside his slim terraced home, she was relieved to find he didn't live in a filthy house share. In fact, he lived alone in a surprisingly domestic, house-proud way. The rooms were tidy. The furniture was not expensive but matching and tasteful. His clothes hung neatly on a drying rack in the kitchen.

"Does your mother come here?" she said when they were downstairs afterwards. Gethin was moving around the kitchen in his boxers, making coffee. It was a complex process. In contrast to Noah, who drank instant, Gethin had weighed beans from a paper bag — Megan recognised the label of the local roaster in Nantlle — and tipped them into his electric grinder. Now he pressed the button, unleashing a shockingly loud noise for such a small machine.

"Sorry," he said after it stopped. "Does my mother come where? To this house?"

"Yeah."

"Not if I can help it."

"So you hung your own clothes on that dryer?"

"Of course," he said, raising his eyebrows. "What do you take me for?"

He came towards her, pressing her against the counter. Through his boxers she could feel him getting hard again. But she didn't want it. She was tired; she wanted to go home. When they got back here, she'd been deranged with desire, as though she was on drugs. His bed smelled intoxicatingly of him. When he had moved his fingers inside her underwear, she'd found it too much, pushing his hand away.

"What's wrong?" he had said.

"Nothing," she'd said, and pulled him towards her, tugging at his T-shirt. It had all been breathless and hurried. But she had felt disturbed, too, sick with guilt, images of Noah flooding her mind far more than they had the first time. Now, in the kitchen, the guilt weighed on her like a rock. Any reckless feeling of desire had evaporated in the wake of their orgasms. She didn't even want the coffee he was offering her in a steaming mug. The smell of it turned her stomach. She placed it on the counter and walked barefoot across the kitchen, going upstairs to the bathroom. She needed a break from the intensity of the two of them together in the same room; she had forgotten how tiring it was to be around someone you couldn't ignore.

There were books everywhere in his house. This had surprised her more than anything. Among the domesticity and neatness, his shelves were packed with them and there were piles on the coffee table and living room floor. They were serious books, from what she could tell. Academic-looking, as though he were a student. Many were in Welsh, most were not.

"Are you having a book sale?" she said when she came back to the kitchen.

"I need more shelves," he said ruefully. He didn't just need more shelves, she thought — he needed a bigger house, and she felt a tug of guilt about her sprawling farmhouse.

"Have you read them all?"

"Yeah."

"All of them?"

"I like to read."

"Are you a nationalist?" she said. She had seen a few titles that suggested an interest in not only Welsh independence but Irish, Catalan, Tibetan, Palestinian.

He laughed. "Don't hold back, will you?"

She waited. "Are you?"

"Most people round here are nationalists, you know." He paused. "Also, it doesn't have the same connotations as it does in English."

"What do you mean?"

"I mean it's not about being intolerant of other cultures. It's about wanting the independence most of the rest of the world won after the fall of colonialism. That's very different to hating immigrants."

"I see," she said.

He looked at her. "In Welsh, we use the word *cenedlaetholwr*. It means nationalist, technically. But it doesn't carry the same meaning. It's gentler. More dignified, somehow."

111

She nodded. "*Cenedlaetholwr*," she said. She pronounced it badly but he didn't seem to mind. "Do you go on the marches?" she said.

"No."

"Really? Why not?"

"I don't see the point."

"Well," she said. "That we can agree on."

She picked up her mug and sipped her coffee. It was too strong, strange-tasting compared with the cheap coffee they drank at home.

"You know the police came to see me?"

She stared at him. "What? No, I didn't know. Why?" It didn't occur to her that he meant anything to do with the lambs and she was panicked for a moment, wondering what he'd done.

"It was about your sheep," he said.

"Are you serious?"

He nodded. "A detective came to my house. I thought someone had died."

"Oh God," she said. "What did they say?"

"She asked if I knew anything. Asked me where I was."

She put a hand to her face. "Noah has this insane idea that you were involved. I have no idea why."

"Does he know about us?"

"I don't think so," she said. "But I did mention that you were my teacher. I think he's become a bit fixated. Something about how he upset you when you had to leave the farm."

Gethin laughed. "He's got an ego on him, hasn't he?"

She sighed. She felt the need to defend Noah but she wasn't sure how. Admitting she thought he might be having a mental breakdown would be more of a betrayal than saying nothing. "He's not himself at the moment."

"Understandable. I wasn't involved, though. I had nothing to do with it."

"Oh God, I know that," she said. "I would never think you would do a thing like that."

"It was a bit barbaric, I suppose."

She looked at him. "You suppose?"

112

"Well," he said. "If you think about it, it's only what you were going to do to the lambs, anyway."

She stared at him. "What?"

He watched her over his mug, lifting it to his lips and taking a sip.

"It's nothing like the same," she said. "Farmers are very humane. I know no one believes that but it's true. And it wasn't going to be us who slaughtered them, was it? We're not an abattoir."

"I know that," he said. "Half my family are farmers — and the other half are butchers. I'm just saying the whole thing is kind of strange, isn't it? I know it's upsetting, what happened to you. But it's hard to know why. You were going to have those lambs slaughtered. And you got the money back from the insurance, presumably — so what's the big deal, when you think about it?"

"For one thing, we didn't get the full value of the lambs — not even close. More importantly, that's not the point. It was our field. They were our lambs."

"So it's about property?"

She stared at him. "Gethin. These men came on to our land in the middle of the night, butchered our lambs, and left a mess of limbs and skin for us to clean up. We found bin bags full of severed heads! How can you act like it was nothing?"

She found herself becoming tearful. She was stressed by the conversation, hurt by Gethin's nonchalance. She considered leaving, as she had wanted to, anyway. But she didn't want to come across as hysterical.

"You're right," he said. "I don't know why I said that."

She folded her arms. "So why did you?"

"I don't know," he said. "I really don't."

"It's because it's us, isn't it?"

"What do you mean?"

"People think we deserved it. Because of who we are."

He shook his head. "I don't think anyone thinks that."

* * *

They began meeting several times a week. The weather was miserable, day after day of wind and rain, rumbling thunderstorms overnight. The days were gloomily dark, the sun shut out by thick grey cloud. The small windows of Gethin's house let in little natural light, anyway, and when they were in bed the landing bulb flickered off and on. Rainwater tunnelled along the gutters and washed over the bedroom window, creating a liquid view of the backs of the houses.

It wasn't difficult to hide the affair from Noah. She told him she was at the cottages or running errands, or else doing something with her Welsh class. She never saw Gethin in the evening; he was often teaching online classes, anyway, but mostly it was just harder to find a cover, then. She never went out at night except those rare occasions she and Noah went for dinner. Having an affair in daylight hours felt more sordid, somehow. When they were finished, dull light slipping between his pleated curtains, she felt she had fallen out of time. Almost always, she wanted to get away, slip back into her legitimate life, which was imperfect, lonely, but at least made her feel contained. When she was with Gethin, it was like she was freefalling, cut loose from the bonds that held her, and the disorientation hardly seemed worth whatever it was she was gaining.

* * *

The tension gathering in her Welsh class came to a head one Saturday in early October. It had surely been inevitable, given Roger had become more petulant and outspoken with every lesson. More or less every time Gethin explained anything, Roger commented. Gethin ignored him, or smiled and went on with the lesson. God forbid he should inadvertently reveal an inconsistency, an exception to a grammatical rule.

"You would think so, wouldn't you?" Gethin would say, nervously. "But that's not quite how it works."

Roger would laugh knowingly. "Of course that's not how it works — it's Welsh!"

It was becoming tedious for everyone. Young, timid Rhys now routinely threw dirty looks in Roger's direction. Even Sally clearly saw how unhappy her husband was making everyone, though she never managed anything more than to tut quietly and mutter, "Roger." It was Denise who eventually confronted him. Gethin had been talking them through the changing first letters of place names, why it's "*ym Mangor*", not Bangor, "*i Gricieth*", not Cricieth, and "*o Bwllheli*" instead of Pwllheli. Roger asked if, in that case, whenever it's "in", "to", or "from" a place, the start of the place name changes? Gethin looked hesitantly at Roger, considering his options. Finally, he said, "It's not quite that simple."

Megan felt bad for Gethin, having to endure this man.

"Should've known," said Roger. He leaned back in his chair, as though he had really proved his point this time.

"We'll come back to this later," said Gethin. "Try not to worry too much about it now." He pointed to the flip chart, clearly wanting to move on.

Roger interjected. "Oh, but I do worry!"

Jim, sitting next to Megan, was looking at Roger with the sad confusion he reserved for behaviour he didn't understand.

"You know, Roger," said Denise. "I have to tell you something. I was listening on radio about how is better learning language not with rules but organic, like child. You are thinking too much. Try just relax and speaking Welsh."

Everyone stared at Roger, whose folded arms turned from a posture of triumph to defensiveness.

"I think that's a really good point, Denise," said Gethin. "We'll learn the rules as we go. But the important thing is just trying to get used to speaking Cymraeg."

"How can I feel comfortable speaking it if the rules don't make sense?" asked Roger.

"English doesn't make sense, either," said Megan.

Roger looked at her in surprise. "It makes more sense than Welsh!"

"How would you know?" said Megan.

"Pardon?" said Roger.

"You won't be able to compare the two until you're fluent in both. And even then, not really, because English will always be your native language. You learned it without thinking about it. Like Denise just said. You'll probably never see the contradictions, because it's so natural to you, like water or air."

Roger stared at her.

Beside her, Jim nodded supportively. "That's true, Megan."

"Well," said Roger, laughing. "We needn't worry about what will or won't happen when I become fluent in Welsh — because that's never going to happen!"

* * *

Meanwhile, Megan was concerned that Noah was losing his mind. He had been deeply affected by the attack — that was obvious — but the more time passed, the more she worried it wasn't temporary. She hadn't seen much of him lately. When she did, it was usually while eating a late supper or watching television in bed before they went to sleep. He had become preoccupied by supposed noises in the field, the apparent flash of a light.

"What kind of light?" she would ask.

"I don't know that, do I? Just a light."

"It was probably just the reflection from the television."

He would shake his head sadly, like she could never understand such things. Sometimes, if it wasn't too late, he went outside, wandering the perimeter of the fields, shining the white light of his torch on the wet grass. He seemed agitated always, snapping at delivery drivers, workmen, strangers on the phone. She had always felt he repressed his anger. Maybe this explosiveness was a good thing, a healthy expression of long-held rage. Maybe everything his father had not allowed him to feel was emerging now. But what was she meant to do with his paranoia, his dark moods, his sudden need to control everything, including her? Like when he said, out of nowhere: "I don't think you should go to your Welsh class anymore."

She was undressing in their bedroom. She'd been with Gethin that afternoon and had hoped to sneak into the house and shower before she saw Noah. In the aftermath of sex, she felt so physically appalled with herself that all she wanted to do was wash the whole thing off her. It was an urgent moral need; but she was equally worried Noah would smell it on her clothes, her skin.

"What?" she said, looking at him, clutching her clothes against her. For a horrifying moment, she thought he must know about the affair, that he was addressing it directly by telling her she was no longer allowed to see Gethin.

"I just think he's bad news," he said.

She understood, then, that he was just fixated, still, on Gethin and the lambs.

"Noah," she said, sighing. She didn't want to go over it yet again. She disliked being forced into a position of defending a man she was sleeping with behind Noah's back, which seemed an unnecessary humiliation for Noah, even if he wasn't aware of it.

"I know you don't believe it," he said. "Fine. He's your teacher."

She crossed the room to the door, taking her dressing gown down, slipping it on. She dropped her dirty clothes in the wash basket.

"Don't you think it's a bit unlikely?" she said. "Someone who happens to be my teacher? It's too much of a coincidence."

"Someone has to have done it."

"I know that."

She sat on the bed, aware of her body, sullied, beneath her dressing gown. She felt that her hair and skin must smell of Gethin. Noah came towards her. He sat down, their bodies touching. He took her hand.

"Don't you think there's a good chance it was connected to the cottages?"

"Maybe," she said. "But then — why go to all the trouble of butchering lambs? It seems a bit . . . random."

"To cover themselves? Make it look like a straightforward crime? Gruesome and upsetting for us, but not an obvious retaliation for the cottages."

"So then what's the point? Why send a message if the message is unclear?"

"Just to unsettle us. Make us feel threatened and on edge."

She sighed. He had an answer for everything, but none of it made much sense to her.

"Even if that's true," she said, "it doesn't mean it's anything to do with Gethin."

He was looking at her in a way she recognised. He let go of her hand, brushed her hair back from her face with his rough hands.

"I need a shower," she said.

He put his hand between her knees, teasing them apart. Her dressing gown slipped open. In spite of her fear of being caught, desire stirred in her. She had come to believe their sexual bond was broken. But she wanted him now.

* * *

On his bedside table, Gethin had a volume of poetry by R. S. Thomas. Megan had noticed it the first time she came to his house. She remembered studying Thomas in school, some miserable old priest who either hated Wales or thought it was wonderful, she couldn't remember which. She picked up the book one day and opened it to where Gethin had left a cinema stub as a bookmark. She read the first lines aloud, then twice more in her head. "That's not very nice," she said.

She was unclothed, Gethin's red and ochre check duvet clutched under her armpits. Gethin was at the other end of his narrow bedroom, turning down the handle on his window. He pushed open the frame and stood, naked, cool air rushing in. He was not self-conscious about his body, perhaps because he was young and good-looking — and male.

"You can get arrested for that," she said.

"Sort of true, though, isn't it?" he said.

"What is?"

"What he said in the poem."

"Is he talking about Welsh people?"

"I suppose so," said Gethin. He moved away from the window and jumped on to the bed, crouching beside her like an oversized child. She slipped her arms beneath the duvet and pulled it to her chin, cold now the window was open. Gethin climbed beneath the covers, too.

"Is he anti-Welsh?" she said. "Or pro? I don't remember."

"It's not Brexit," said Gethin.

"You know what I mean."

"He's both."

"I see," she said. "I think I'm the same."

"Me too," he said.

"Really?" She looked across at him, his elbow on his pillow now, hand propping up his head. "I thought you were a . . . *cenedlaetholwr.*"

He smiled. "Well remembered."

"Thanks."

"One of the reasons I like R. S. Thomas is the mixed feelings he has for his country. I'm a nationalist because I want independence, not because I think everything is wonderful here and we don't have any problems. In fact, one of the reasons I want independence is because I think it would help solve a lot of those problems — or at the very least we would be the ones who decide how to."

"That makes sense," she said. "Isn't R. S. Thomas actually anti-Welsh, though?" She pointed to the book. "Isn't he the one who thinks we're all inbred?"

"I thought you didn't remember?"

"It's coming back to me."

They seemed to be drawn back to these questions. They skirted them jokingly, but she couldn't shake her sense that it was deeply serious to Gethin, his flippancy defensive rather than light. She was confused by her own urge to provoke these

119

discussions. It was as though she was trying to negotiate a problem that had eluded but troubled her since she married into the Robinsons. Similarly, she wondered if Gethin was attracted to her partly because she represented all the things he was defending his culture against, sharpening his position by pushing against its edges.

"So," he said, with a tone of changing the subject. "What are you doing for the rest of the day?"

"Are you trying to get rid of me?"

"Not at all," he said, though she got the impression he did want to get on with things; as did she.

"I have to go to the cottages," she said.

He was quiet, looking at her thoughtfully, elbow propping up his head. His expression had darkened a little.

"You did ask," she said.

"I didn't say a word."

"Exactly."

"Okay," he said. "Tell me about the cottages. What are you doing there, exactly?"

She shook her head. "We don't have to talk about them."

"No, I'm interested. Tell me about it."

"The truth is, I don't even know if I want to go ahead with it."

"Really?" He didn't exactly look pleased. "Why not?"

"It's complicated," she said. She hadn't told Gethin about Ray's plan to take away the farm and she didn't intend to. "Not that it's my choice, anyway."

"Wouldn't Noah's dad agree to just rent them out?"

"I don't think so," she said. She was still holding the R. S. Thomas book in her hands. She reached over and put it back on the bedside table. "It just wouldn't make as much money as a holiday rental. And he thinks tenants are more trouble."

"Yes," he said. "You don't want to be dealing with the natives."

She rolled her eyes. "I don't think he means it like that."

"So when are you going to start letting them?"

"I don't know," she said. "Why do you ask?"

"Just taking an interest, like you wanted."

"Okay," she said. "Sorry. The whole thing just stresses me out. I'm trying to get Tŷ Gwyn ready for Christmas. The other two won't be done until Easter. I won't bore you with the details. Thanks for asking, though."

He put his fingertips lightly on her shoulder, drawing circles. "You know you've never asked me anything about myself?"

She looked at him. "Really?"

"Really."

"Do you want me to?"

"Not especially. But it's strange that you haven't, don't you think?"

She sighed. "I'm not really familiar with the etiquette of extramarital affairs."

He didn't smile.

"That was a joke," she said.

"I know. I just don't like that word."

"Affair?" she said. "What is this, if not that?"

"Something there isn't a word for."

CHAPTER TEN

Noah

He couldn't talk to anyone about this — it would sound so absurd and childish — but he couldn't help feeling the life he'd known since he moved to the farm was collapsing before his eyes. When they came here, his life changed overnight. Of course it changed in the obvious ways, transplanted from a quaint English town to a Welsh wilderness that was harsh and primitive by contrast. The language was different, the people, the food they ate, the smells. But the fundamental shift was that they no longer lived with his father. Eventually, Noah came to understand that this was the true gift his mother had given him, enabling him to live his adolescent years free from the brooding presence of a man who would monitor his transition to manhood with nothing but mockery and malice.

At the time, though, Noah was only vaguely aware this change had taken place at all. His mother had not told them that they were leaving their father indefinitely. The plan in relation to him had been unclear. He and Imogen assumed Ray would follow later, or perhaps, once they were settled, live between Warwickshire and Wales. Having known nothing but the dark shadow of that man, Noah would not have believed, even if his mother had said so, that a life without him was possible. The reality of his freedom was revealed incrementally, almost imperceptibly, attaching itself to the mountains and the sea, the sharp smell of silage, the stretching hours when he and Imogen picked blackberries and waded the cold stream. As he adapted to life on the farm he was, somewhere in his deep subconscious, learning what it meant to exist without fear. As the years passed, these far-flung acres became indistinguishable from his accumulation of freedom.

Nor could he set the place apart from his mother's happiness; how, after they came here, she was more content than he had thought her capable during his early childhood, when he had assumed obedience and nervousness were her nature. At the farm she was light, uninhibited. She sang in the bath, played music in the kitchen, watched films with them under a knitted blanket, fire crackling, popcorn spilling in their laps. She baked crumble, flour dusting the counters, slicing the champagne apples they'd gathered from the shadows beneath the low trees. There was spontaneity and fun, even as his father's letters landed on the doormat, debts accumulated.

Of course, the farm was bitterly hard work, far more than his mother had bargained for. They were isolated, too; notwithstanding the reliable, no-nonsense assistance provided by neighbours if they ever needed help, owning a chunk of land had not embedded them in the community in the way she had envisaged and wanted. His mother complained about their disconnection, sensing they were not trusted, which was perhaps unsurprising given they'd come here as interlopers, their only claim to the land his father's hard cash, which he had used to outbid a local. Still, Joan loved to be out on the farm, wrestling sheep, charging uphill against the wind, shouting orders at Noah, who was technically her apprentice, though she had no wisdom or experience to impart. She would have worked night and day to preserve their tentative independence, as would Noah. School became a secondary consideration, notes from teachers slipped into his bag, his mother summoned to meetings. Joan worried endlessly about the impact of the farm on his education. But she still let him stay home when things were busy, usually fretting with him over the decision the night before. Noah really didn't care about school. More than anything, if working the farm helped protect them from the life they'd led in the Midlands, he would never have gone to school again.

Thinking back over all this now, Noah was coming to understand that a spell had been cast when they came to the farm, an abiding sense of the land and house as a haven from not only his father but all the malign forces beyond the perimeter. Lately this spell had been broken. The farm had been violated, men creeping on to his land at night, butchering his lambs with cold knives. In tandem with this, his father had chosen to lay claim to the land, as Noah should have known he eventually would. Everything Noah had been hiding from, all the cruelty and unpredictability he'd pushed out into the world, was spilling over the periphery into his life, his house. Boundaries were breaking down, becoming permeable. Perhaps it had started with the protests against the cottages, strangers waving placards at the top of his track. Then came the trespassers, scrawling graffiti on the lambing shed. The slaughter of the lambs. His father's violation of a long-held agreement. A series of breaches, each one worse than the last.

* * *

It was October now. There had been endless rain and unexpected storms. It would wreak havoc on his crops, if it carried on like this. He was trying not to fixate on yet another thing he couldn't control, though he had remained preoccupied by the police investigation, ringing Mandy's mobile many times over the last few days. She hadn't been answering. He had the distinct feeling she was ignoring him. When he tried again on a Wednesday morning, two weeks after they'd last spoken, she finally picked up, taking him by surprise.

"Noah," she said. "I haven't got back to you yet."

She didn't offer an explanation or apology, just a statement of what he already knew.

"That's fine," he said. "I have some information."

"Oh yeah?"

"It's about the Welsh teacher."

She was quiet; he could grasp her irritation through the phone, one of the reasons he had been reluctant to share this. He went on.

"This is going to sound a bit — I don't know, hard to believe — but he's been having secret meetings."

Still, she said nothing. He became hot in the face.

"Are you still there?" he said.

"Yes," she said. "What do you mean by secret meetings?"

"He's been meeting people — I don't know who — at night. At an abandoned farmhouse on the road to Llanrug."

"How do you know about this?"

He hesitated. "I can't tell you that. But it's true."

"Okay," she said, "Well, thanks for bringing this to me. I'll make a note."

He waited for her to say more. When she didn't, he said, "Are you going to investigate?"

"How do you suggest we do that?"

"I don't know — watch his house? Find out what he's doing? I thought this was what the police did."

"It would be virtually impossible to get the authority for something like that, based on so little evidence."

* * *

After hanging up, he got in his truck and drove to Gethin's house. He hadn't been back here since that night he followed him. The house looked sad, almost pathetic, in the cold light of the afternoon. It was small and inconsequential, the pebbledash dull and stained, the window frames cheap ugly uPVC. Even Gethin's Corsa, parked in the same spot, looked insubstantial. There was no movement through the windows but the lights were on. Noah wondered about the motorbike, whether it was sitting in a driveway or garage round the corner. Maybe, in the daylight, Noah could find the spot where Gethin had disappeared and work out where that bike was kept. He held the key in the ignition, preparing to pull out. Through the wing mirror, he saw a car approaching. He pulled his hand away, waiting for it to pass. Glancing in the mirror again, he stared at the black Land Rover moving towards him, the eyes of the driver shielded by sunglasses. It was Megan, about to pass him on this back street where neither of them had any business being.

For a long second, he was immobilised by the shock of seeing her here. Then he panicked, throwing himself down across the double passenger seat, the handbrake pushing against his ribs. How ridiculous, he thought, as he hid from his wife. She would recognise the truck, anyway, wouldn't she? She might even look across and see him, lying here like this. He prayed she would keep her gaze on the road, concentrate on manoeuvring her car between the parked vehicles instead of looking across to where he lay hiding like a child. As these calculations flashed through his mind, he stayed very still, though his heart pounded in his chest. Above him, the Land Rover moved past like a shadow. The truck shuddered. He lifted his head and peered over the dashboard, watching the car drift to the end of the street and reverse slowly into a space. No more than a hundred yards away from him, Megan got out, hopping down on to the pavement. She was wearing the knee-high boots she'd left the house in that morning, the false fur of her long sherpa coat almost brushing the ground.

She hadn't seen him. If she had, she would have stopped, asked him what the hell he was doing here. Then he wondered — why was she here? He had been so consumed by his own humiliation, this question only now occurred to him. He watched her open the wrought-iron gate and climb the narrow steps towards Gethin's house, reaching for the doorbell and standing, arms folded, in front of his red door. She must be having extra lessons, he thought. Private tutorials. She had mentioned that the classes were slow and that there was a man who annoyed her. She hadn't mentioned having one-on-one lessons. But he had been so negative about Gethin, maybe she'd decided it was better not to tell him.

He was hurt and betrayed, thinking of her having secret lessons with this man whom he'd asked her to stay away from. He looked up at the sky, an uncertain grey. Sun broke between the clouds, warming him briefly through the windscreen. When Gethin opened the door, he was clearly expecting her. He smiled and stood back, letting her into the shadows. She stepped over the threshold. But she didn't walk past him. She stopped, lifting her face towards his. He bent his head. As their lips touched, he slipped his hand beneath her coat, pulling her towards him. With his other hand he shut the door.

Noah sat in his truck, staring at the closed door. Wind moved through the branches of a nearby tree. There was an unexpected clap of thunder that Noah was sure came from the atmosphere though he would wonder, later, if he'd imagined it. The sky darkened. The shock of what he had seen reverberated in his mind like a long echo. Time slowed. Fine details slipped through his conscious thoughts, evidence collecting itself: Megan's tone when she talked about Gethin, her refusal to consider that he was behind the slaughter of the lambs, her mood, which had been strangely light, even giddy at times. The guilt on her face, which he'd interpreted as a projection of his own. He felt a wave of nausea surging up through his middle. He clutched at the handle, pushing open the door, and leaned out to vomit, liquid sick splattering the street. Dumbly he wiped his mouth, hand shaking, shutting the door weakly and leaning back against the seat. The world felt slow, unreal. His head was light. But his heart thumped hard. He wondered if he might die. He thought of them inside and pictured himself getting out of the truck, kicking down the door, beating Gethin until his blood spilled. But he sat quietly in the truck, waiting for the pounding of his heart to slow. Then he went home.

* * *

Back at the farm he felt bereft, as though someone had died. His phone vibrated as he unlocked the front door. It was his father. He stared at the flashing screen. His hands were still trembling. He tapped the green button, brought the phone shakily to his ear. In a bleak moment, he wanted to tell his father what he'd seen, ask for his help or advice — maybe some comfort. Quickly he realised it was a sign of his despair, to think such a thing was possible.

"It's been two weeks," came his father's voice.

Noah's desperation turned inward, buried itself inside him. He shored up his tone, though he was breathless and shaken.

"Not quite," he said. "Friday will be two weeks. It's Wednesday. Isn't it?"

"What's the matter?"

"Nothing."

"You sound funny. I'll come up Friday, then."

"Dad," he said. A lump rose in his throat. He forced it down. "I'm not ready."

"You don't need to be ready. There's nothing for you to do except sign a few papers."

"I know. But I'm still thinking things over."

"There's nothing to think over. You're not getting out of this, Noah."

Noah held the phone tightly against his ear. "I know. But can we just wait another week? I won't push it back again after that."

"I'm going away next week. I'll be gone a fortnight."

"Let's wait until you get back, then?"

"I wanted to get this sorted before my holiday. It's causing me stress, having this hanging over me."

"Where are you going?"

"Italy. Don't change the subject."

"Look," said Noah, thinking hard. "Imogen is finding it hard, adjusting to being home."

His father paused. "Aled hasn't mentioned anything."

Noah wondered how often his father and Aled were speaking, these days. "Well," said Noah. "He probably doesn't know what Imogen is comfortable with people knowing."

"I'm not people, I'm her father."

"I know. But you know what she's like about her illness. Anyway, she's back on her medication, going through all the side effects. She's not in a state to be signing anything."

His father was quiet. Noah knew what he wanted to say — that Imogen was never going to be in a state for such things. But he would never admit that aloud.

"Fine. When I get back. But that's it. No more excuses. I'm emailing you a date for the meeting. I'm doing it now. And Noah?"

"Yes?"

"Keep an eye on your sister."

The email arrived as soon as Noah hung up. *1 November* was all it said. No sign off, nothing. Noah stared at the email, struck by an old familiar disbelief.

* * *

Later — he had no idea how much time had passed — he heard Megan's car and went to the dining room, watching the Land Rover bump into the drive. It was late afternoon, the sky overcast and drizzling. He checked his phone. It was three hours since he'd watched her go into the house. Had she been there the whole time? Had they made love for hours, like he and Megan used to do? Was that what she wanted, even though she seemed to recoil at the idea of sex with him these days? Did she and Gethin talk? What could she possibly have in common with him? Mixed in with the shock and betrayal, Noah had that feeling of deep denial, that this was a mistake, that his eyes had deceived him. He was aware, all the time, that his feelings were a cliché.

He watched her through the window. For a while she sat in the driver's seat, typing on her phone. She often answered texts and emails in the car before she came into the house but for the first time he wanted to know who she was messaging. Was she telling her friends about her afternoon with Gethin? Describing the details, humiliating Noah in the process? Was she messaging Gethin? Had it not been enough that they'd only just been together? Did she not need a break? Or did she want more all the time? Was she infatuated, in love? Was she going to leave Noah? Would he — Noah — have to leave her?

She got out of the car, her coat flapping open in the wind. Between the lapels he could see her dark knitted dress, sheer tights, black boots. She marched to the front door like any other day, clutching her keys. After she came through the door, closing it behind her, her boots clipped the tiles. She didn't take them off at first, as she moved around the hall. He stayed by the window, in the shadows of the dining room. He heard her sigh. The proximity of her voice, so familiar, made him want to beat his fists against the glass. But he stood quietly, listening as she finally unzipped her boots and padded the house, opening doors.

Eventually, she found him.

"What are you doing in the dark?"

He stayed quiet, like a mouse caught in the open.

"Noah?"

He couldn't look at her. If he did, he would surely convey that he knew. He wasn't ready for that.

"It's cold," she said. "Are there windows open?"

"I don't think so," he said, still looking through the glass.

She walked over to him, touching the radiator near his legs.

"I'm going to have a bath. Try to warm up."

"Okay."

"Are you hungry?" she said. "I'll make us something to eat after?"

She moved towards him, putting her hand on his arm. Inwardly, he shrank from her. He was raw from the pain of it all; he felt that he couldn't take any more. His body was reeling, hot emotions stirring. He felt like an open wound. But he worked hard to present a cool façade, reminded of how often this was demanded of him as a child, looking up at his father, whose eyes dared him to cry so he could swipe a hand across his cheek.

CHAPTER ELEVEN

Megan

She hadn't worn make-up for a long time, not like this. Occasionally, like if they went out for lunch with Imogen and Aled, she dabbed concealer under her eyes, brushed a few strokes of mascara over her eyelashes. Her whole life was this family. She rarely saw her mother, who lived back in the south and whom she visited no more than twice a year. This year she had only seen her once. She almost never saw her father, who was far more interested in his second family, her half-siblings all much younger than her. She didn't see her friends from home much, either. She had been so close with those girls once, sharing clothes, secrets, money. Now she watched their lives pass by across social media, a remote observer of pregnancies, new babies, anniversaries, holidays. You had to stay in the same place as people, that was the problem. Otherwise it was too much work. And what happened when you didn't find friends in the place you lived? Forming friendships in adulthood was virtually impossible, it seemed to Megan. She used to tell herself she would make friends when she had children. And that it wouldn't matter so much, then, because her life would be full. Everything would be different when she had children.

She washed the remnants of blusher and eyeshadow from her fingertips then pulled on a pair of sheer tights, stretching the thin fabric carefully over her waist. She adjusted her breasts, ensuring they were evenly lifted, and slipped on a daisy-print dress with flutter sleeves. Looking in the mirror, she saw that the dress was wrong — too flowy and middle-aged. She went back to her wardrobe and found her black slip dress, looking in the mirror again. This was better, flattering but plain, pronouncing her lined eyes and rouged cheeks rather than her body. She was surprised how effectively the make-up had transformed her. She didn't look twenty-one, but she looked a lot better than she had half an hour earlier. Still, she worried there was something obscene about the amount of make-up on her forty-year-old face. Was she still allowed to paint herself up like this? Would people laugh at her, think she looked an old tart, someone's mother, mutton dressed as lamb?

She slipped on her strappy high heels and went downstairs, quickly reminded that these shoes demanded a certain amount of clutching. Noah was out with the rams. He'd been working flat out the last few days, getting everything ready for tupping. The teasers were in with the ewes, the tups due to go in on Sunday. That was Bonfire Night. It had been a tradition with Noah and his mother, tupping the ewes on the fifth of November then celebrating with a bonfire and toffee apples, sparklers in the cold air. No fireworks, of course, which would upset the animals. Noah had stuck religiously to tupping on Bonfire Night after his mother died but it was a few years since he and Megan had even drunk a celebratory hot chocolate.

She wasn't planning to say goodbye. For one thing, she didn't want to get her heels muddy walking out to the shed. Mainly, though, she didn't want Noah to see her dolled-up like this. Though she'd told him she was going for drinks with her Welsh class, she felt gaudy in her make-up and clinging dress. But as she crossed the drive to her car, she heard him down the track, trudging back to the house. She threw her bag in the Land Rover, hoping to drive away before he saw her. But as she climbed into the driver's seat, he called her name. In the wing mirror she saw his figure, moving towards her under the moonlight. She left the driver's door open, covering her legs with her coat. When he reached the car, he was breathless, clutching the frame of the door. God knew where his hands had been, spending his days worming sheep, checking their teeth, examining their bits. Noah was an expert in the private parts of rams, the correct colour for their discharge, the desired scrotal circumference. In contrast with the muck on his hands, she was excruciatingly conscious of having washed her intimate places, rubbed scented lotion into her skin. As he stood panting gently, belly pressed against his shirt, Megan couldn't help noting the difference between his paunchy figure and Gethin's trim, athletic build. In almost the same instant she was ashamed that the comparison even crossed her mind.

As Noah watched her, she wished she had turned off the interior light, illuminating her made-up face and scant clothing. Her coat had slipped open, revealing her tights, dress riding up her thighs. Her knees looked bony, poking between the lapels. He took it all in, his gaze resting briefly on her legs, then her cleavage. She waited for him to tell her she was overdressed, that she looked like a drag queen. She would have felt better if he did.

"What time are you back?"

"Not late," she said. "I'm driving, so I won't drink a lot."

He nodded, looking over the roof of the car. "Dad's here tomorrow."

"I know," she said. "I'll be here."

He was talking about the meeting with his father — and with Imogen and Aled — when they were supposedly finalising these property transfers. She and Noah were long overdue a discussion. She had no idea what he intended to do. But the weeks had slipped by and here they were.

He looked at her again.

"Do you want me to stay home tonight?" she said. "So we can talk about it all?"

His eyes turned cold. "You go," he said. "Have a good time."

Curtly, he shut the door.

* * *

Any excitement she had felt was soured by her encounter with Noah, imprinted on her mind as she drove into town. He'd been brutally cold with her these last few weeks, even worse than he'd been immediately after the attack. It had crossed her mind that he knew about Gethin — but how? And why hadn't he said anything? More likely it was everything else, especially the meeting tomorrow.

She wanted to forget all that tonight. She was tired of thinking about it. There was nothing she could do, anyway. Every time she asked Noah if there had been an update from the police, or whether he wanted to talk about his father and the farm, he said the same thing: no need, he was handling it. What was the point? If he wanted to shut her out, that was his choice. She wasn't going to beg. She was aware of the selfishness of it, but right now she just wanted to escape. She had no release but this — Gethin. Who knew how long it would last — probably not long — but when they were together she felt an uncoiling of everything inside her that was knotted and tangled and too much to bear.

Tonight was Halloween. There were children on the streets, fairies and superheroes and Harry Potters shrieking as they clattered through gates and held out their buckets in the soft light of porches. Gethin had joked that he was looking forward to seeing Megan's costume. Though she'd told him she didn't agree with adults wearing fancy dress, she was worried, now, that she would show her age by failing to. She opened the window, letting in the cool air. She felt hot suddenly, anxious. It was busy in town, though she had little to compare it with, having rarely been in on a Tuesday night. Most people were costumed, she noticed, as she pulled into the harbour. Behind her the castle walls loomed in the dark, track lights in the grass lighting them from below. Small boats were scattered, sunk in the muddy banks or bobbing on the moonlit water.

As she walked up the hill towards the maes, a gang of men and women passed, their laughter echoing. One of the men wore a screaming mask and hooded cloak. A short woman had a chalk-white face and blood-red lips. Megan felt a chill. She was starting to regret coming, thinking longingly of her warm bed. She considered turning back, telling Gethin she was unwell. But she was here now. She'd gone to the trouble of dressing up. The castle walls followed her as she reached the top of the hill and turned down the pebbled lane. Her heels clacked and echoed.

She had been to this pub a couple of times but never at night. In the dark it looked Gothic and menacing. Inside there were endless corridors and unmarked doors. She became anxious walking among them, trying to remember what Gethin had said about where to meet him. Had he said anything except the name of the pub? She had a sensation of dropping out of time. She shouldn't be here, she thought. Glimpsing rich mahogany and gleaming beer taps through the glass of one of the doors, she pulled it open and walked into a small, enclosed bar. The chatter quietened. The room smelled of lager and salty chips. A fire burned behind a black-iron grate. Dipped lights and red carpet created a rosy glow. People were looking at her. The barmaid stared from behind the taps. Gethin was not here.

Megan considered going back to the corridor. But she needed a drink. She hoisted herself on to a cushioned stool at the bar. The barmaid recognised her as an outsider and spoke in English. Megan asked for a vodka and lemonade. She was too warm with the fire behind her and wanted to take off her coat. But she was aware of the cut of her dress, how people had stared when she walked in. The barmaid placed the drink on a coaster in front of her. Megan drank it quickly. The vodka was warm and acidic but she felt better as it slipped down her throat.

"Can I have another, please?"

The woman raised her eyebrows only a little before taking the empty glass. Megan reached into her handbag and pulled out her phone, writing a quick message to Gethin. *I'm here. Where are you??*

She had been at the bar for twenty minutes — and finished her third vodka lemonade — when the door opened and Gethin wandered in. He smiled, opening his mouth to speak before a man shouted, "Gethin!" and walked over to him, slapping him on the shoulder. Megan watched, irritated as they chatted and she had to wait even longer. Finally, Gethin broke away and came up to her.

"Here you are," he said.

"Here I am? I've been here for ages! Where have you been?"

"In the back."

"You could have mentioned this place was a maze."

"I thought you'd been before?"

She didn't reply. Gethin was keeping his distance, standing a couple of feet back from her. He hadn't kissed her, even on the cheek. He glanced at her empty glass. "How many of those have you had?"

"Sorry, are you the vodka police?"

"I was just asking."

"Haven't you been getting my messages?"

He pulled his phone from his pocket, holding it up to show the empty screen.

"Typical," she said. "It's one of the worst things about this place. No bloody signal."

His eyes were wary. The barmaid was eyeing her, too. She shouldn't have come. But she didn't know how to leave without causing a scene.

"The quiz has started," said Gethin, putting his hands in his pockets.

"Oh, the quiz!" she said. "What am I thinking, sitting here all by myself when the quiz has started!" She rolled her eyes, finishing her drink.

"What's wrong with you?" he said. "You're not yourself."

She sighed. "I just need to go home."

"Suit yourself."

"I will. Thanks."

"I told you which room we were going to be in."

"Did you?" she said, looking at him. "Funny, I don't remember that."

"I don't know why you're being like this."

"I'm not being like anything. This was a bad idea, that's all. I want to go home."

To her dismay, tears welled in her eyes. She looked down, fiddling with her bag, and tried not to stumble as she got down from the stool.

He looked at her evenly. "I'd like it if you stayed."

She sighed.

He took her hand and leaned towards her, brushing her hair away from her ear. "You look amazing."

* * *

The room at the back was dark and loud, tables full of rowdy groups in costume, laughing and talking or else heads bowed, scribbling with yellow pencils on their quiz sheets. Megan was thankful that Gethin was not in fancy dress. He led her to one of the booths, a semi-circular high-backed bench encasing a round table littered with empty pint glasses and stained quiz papers. There were two men sitting down, looking up at a woman standing on the other side of the table, talking to them. As Megan and Gethin approached, the woman stopped talking and stepped back. The men looked up at them. The woman was roughly Gethin's age with naturally black hair, plaited in pigtails that were clearly meant, along with her white collar and long-sleeved dress, to look like Wednesday Addams. Her legs were bare, her pale thighs showing beneath the hem of the dress. She wasn't wearing make-up, but she had pretty eyes and thick lashes, framed by her dark fringe. Megan was immediately jealous, feeling that this woman's costume — both in the spirit of Halloween and lacking any obvious effort to look attractive — could have been intended to show Megan up as both vain and old. There was something about her stance, too, the way she had been talking to the men and the way she was standing now, that made Megan wary.

The woman said something to Gethin in Welsh that Megan assumed was deliberately quick. Gethin smiled uncertainly.

"I found her in the end," he said. "This is Alaw," he added.

He pointed at the men, introducing them as Huw and Llion. They nodded, the one called Huw raising his hand. Gethin nodded towards the quiz master on the other side of the room, a man in a sequinned jacket and Elvis sunglasses.

"It can't be finished already?"

"*Brec bach,*" said Alaw. "I was just getting some pints in."

She looked at Megan, who panicked a little. She didn't drink lager, nor did she want to ask for a girly drink like vodka lemonade. If she said she didn't want anything, wouldn't it be more evidence she was refusing to join in? But why did she care what this woman thought?

"I'm okay, thanks," she said.

Alaw looked at her. "Suit yourself."

* * *

The quiz master picked up his microphone, voice cutting unpleasantly through the speakers. Alaw came back gripping four pints, spilling lager on the table and over her fingers as she put them down. Huw and Llion had moved round the bench to allow for Megan and Gethin. The only space for Alaw was on the end, next to Megan. Alaw glanced at Huw.

139

Megan knew — everyone knew — she wanted him to shift back the other way so she could sit next to him, instead. But no one moved, and she couldn't ask. In the end she sat down next to Megan.

To be fair to Alaw, the seating arrangement turned out to be awkward. The quiz was entirely in Welsh and no one was translating, partly because there wasn't time. Given Alaw was clearly the team leader, and given Gethin was not particularly interested in participating, Alaw kept having to lean across Megan and Gethin to confer with Huw and Llion, occasionally snatching the pencil from one of them to correct their answer. Megan considered offering to swap places with her so that at least she — Alaw — would only have Gethin in her way. But Megan wanted to stay next to Gethin, the only familiar fixture in this strange experience. She liked being pressed against him, smelling the aftershave on his neck. And she didn't want to give Alaw the satisfaction of separating them.

When the quiz finished, several tables left. The room was suddenly arrestingly quiet. The four friends chatted, an occasional companionable silence falling over them. Every now and then, one of them — usually Huw — switched to English to politely ask Megan a question. She would answer, trying to sound in some way interesting to these people half her age. Quickly, they would revert to Welsh. Even if she could understand what they were saying, Megan guessed she would have connected with very few of the things they were talking about. They were close childhood friends. None of them were married or had children. Megan could see this without asking; she could see it in the carefree way in which they were sitting here on a Tuesday night. She could also see that they were like family to each other, clinging together as they navigated that bewildering terrain between leaving their parents' home and finding their own. She remembered what it was like to be their age, to stay out all night talking with her friends. It felt a long time ago.

She sat quietly and let them get on with it, resisting the urge to take out her phone. Though it was hard to complain — they were only speaking their natural language — Megan had never experienced anything quite like this in the thirteen years she'd lived here. When she was with a group of Welsh speakers, they tended to speak English to include her. Unthinkingly, they would slip to Welsh, but someone always moved the conversation back again. It had always impressed her how adept north Walians were at this. Living in a mostly Welsh-speaking area, she didn't believe she was entitled to this level of accommodation. At the same time, she couldn't help feeling it was the immaturity of this group that caused them to leave her out in this way. Ultimately, though, it was Gethin she blamed. She couldn't fault his friends for carrying on as though she wasn't there, whereas he must have known they would do this. In which case, why had he invited her?

* * *

It was ten thirty when she went to the bathroom and found Alaw at the sink, wiping her hands on a paper towel. She dropped the towel into the bin, the stainless-steel lid slamming closed, then gave Megan a reluctant smile as she walked straight past her. Megan was suddenly outraged. Even taking into account Alaw's obvious animosity, Megan couldn't quite believe she was going to refuse her the smallest crumb of female camaraderie when they were alone in the toilets.

"Have I done something to upset you?" she said.

Alaw paused in the doorway, turning back to look at Megan.

"I don't know you," she said.

"Exactly."

Alaw hesitated. Then she walked up and stood in front of Megan, the ultraviolet lights above giving her pale skin an artificial blue tinge. She looked suddenly absurd in her Wednesday Addams costume.

"I just don't think it's right," she said.

"What's not right?" said Megan.

"What you and Gethin are doing."

Though she had asked for an explanation, Megan was shocked to have her marriage brought into the open by a stranger.

"That's none of your business, is it?"

"You're making it my business."

"Gethin invited me here. But you don't seem angry with him, strangely enough."

"Gethin can do what he wants in his own time. I don't want to be part of this."

She opened out her hand to indicate that Megan was the "this" to which she was referring.

"So you're saying it's fine if we have an affair as long as you don't have to see us together?"

Alaw shrugged.

"I don't believe you," said Megan.

"Excuse me?"

"I don't believe that's what you're upset about."

Alaw considered her coldly. "Believe what you like."

* * *

Megan was shaken. There was no way she could stay now. Leaving the toilets, she noticed Gethin at the bar, talking to a skinny older man with an oversized denim jacket and bald patch on the crown of his head. She looked over at their table and saw Alaw, sitting down again with Huw and Llion. She was giddy from booze, humiliated by Alaw. Humiliated by the whole thing, really. She was an overdressed forty-year-old, fraternising with twenty-somethings who not only had no wish for her to be here but looked down on her.

She moved towards Gethin. But there was something about the way he was talking to this man that made her pause. Their heads were close. There was none of the light-heartedness he'd shared with other people he'd bumped into this evening. The two of them were serious, deep in conversation. The other man was doing most of the talking. There was something in Gethin's facial expression that Megan disliked. Noticing Megan, the man sat up, smiling sheepishly, picking up his drink. Gethin turned and saw her, too. For a second he looked annoyed, as though she'd been eavesdropping. But she hadn't heard anything. He didn't introduce her to the man, who got off his stool and nodded at Megan before walking away.

* * *

They shared a taxi with Alaw and Huw. Alaw, quietly seething, sat in the back with Megan and Gethin. Huw was in the front, talking politely in Welsh with the driver. Alaw was dropped off first, leaning forward to shove a five-pound note in Huw's hand before she got out and slammed the door.

"What's the matter with her?" said Huw, glancing back at Megan.

In spite of everything, Megan appreciated this. Sitting to her right, Gethin was deep in thought, looking out of the window. Megan didn't think it was anything to do with Alaw. He seemed oblivious to all that. It was the man at the bar, she thought, plunging him into hard reflection.

His house was cold when they got back and Megan wasn't in the mood. She wasn't sure Gethin was, either. As they stood in the bedroom, kissing, it was like they were getting on with a necessary chore. Megan pulled back, looking into his pale eyes. She could see he was a little drunk.

"Were you and Alaw an item?" she said.

"Why are you asking that?"

"So yes, then."

He sighed, closing his eyes. "A hundred years ago."

"You're twenty-four," she said. "How long ago can it have been?"

"We were in school."

"What happened?"

"Nothing much. We were lonely. We've been mates since we were two. It was like sleeping with my sister."

"Who finished it, you or her?"

"Bloody hell," he said. "Why do you care so much?"

She waited.

"I did," he said.

"Thought so."

"Why are you asking?"

"Just how she was with me tonight."

She sat down on the bed. She felt tired, drunk, inexplicably angry. Gethin knelt behind her and put his hands on her shoulders, resting his forehead wearily on the back of her head.

"You don't need to worry about Alaw," he mumbled.

"I'm not worried about Alaw," she said. "I would just appreciate knowing in advance if we're going out with one of your ex-girlfriends. Who was that man?"

"Which man?"

"The one at the bar."

"Oh. No one."

"He seemed like someone to me."

"He's just a mate."

"Okay," she said. "Don't tell me."

Gethin sighed, rocking back on his heels into that crouching position she had come to dislike. This had run its course. She did have feelings for him; she'd grown fonder of him than just the visceral attraction they'd started with. But the whole thing had already taken on a stale flavour. The shame and self-loathing was now overwhelming. Trying to do something normal, as they had tonight, had only made it worse.

"I shouldn't have come tonight," she said.

He fell back on his pillow, closing his eyes. "Why do you say that?"

She stared at the wardrobe in front of her. The doors hung open. Why had he left them like that, like a child? Who did he think was going to close them?

"I don't know," she said. "Your friends weren't very nice to me."

144

"Weren't they?"

"Not really."

"You mean Alaw?"

"Not just her."

"Who else?"

"All of them. Hard for me to know, though, wasn't it? I couldn't understand anything they were saying."

"Oh," he said. "I see."

"What does that mean, you 'see'?"

"This is about people speaking Welsh."

She turned to face him, still lying back on his pillow, looking down the bed at her.

"No," she said. "It's about basic decency. I didn't know anyone in that pub. The four of you knew everyone, and each other. You could have included me, at least a bit."

He shook his head, looking at the ceiling. "The narcissism of privilege."

She stared at him. "Did you read that in one of your books?"

"It just occurred to me."

"Well," she said. "You sound like an arsehole."

He sat up, suddenly. "I invited you to the quiz because I thought you were capable of not doing this."

"Not doing what? What is it I'm doing?"

"Being like them." He brought his hands melodramatically to his chest and did a crude impersonation of an English-speaker. "*I don't understand what they're saying. I've been left out. I feel excluded.*" He shook his head in disgust. "You're not a victim, Megan."

"Who said anything about being a victim? I'm just saying — I'm just telling you, because it's the truth — that your friends treated me like shit tonight. I'm telling you because I thought you cared about me. Clearly, I was wrong."

"It's not rude for people to speak their own language."

"Well, it depends on the context, doesn't it?"

He shook his head. "You've been here for what, ten years?"

145

"Thirteen."

"Haven't you got used to being in a minority by now?"

She stood up. "Yes!" she said. "That's my point. It's not about being in a minority. I don't care about that. I've never minded it. I'm talking about something else."

He sat up, placed his palms together and brought his fingertips to his chin. "We're not going to agree on this."

"Do you think they'd have refused to speak English with me if it wasn't my first language?"

"What?"

"Say you brought a Ukrainian refugee to the quiz. Or — I don't know — a French person. And English was my second language, like it's yours. And theirs. Do you think the four of you would still have behaved that way, only speaking Welsh?"

He considered this. "No," he said. "Probably not."

"So that's my point," she said. "It's not about speaking Welsh. It's about not speaking English with an English person. Or not speaking English with me, anyway."

"I thought you considered yourself Welsh?"

"I am Welsh. But it's all the same to you lot, isn't it? I don't speak the language so I might as well have gone to Eton."

"I don't think you're any less Welsh than me."

She laughed mockingly. He gave her a look to say he wasn't finished.

"Fine," she said. "Carry on."

"I don't think you're any less Welsh than me. But I do think you have no idea what it's like when the language you love — the language that is your whole identity, and your family's, that's in your blood — is dying in front of your eyes and there's nothing you can do about it. I don't think you have a clue about that."

"It's not dying," she said. "People are learning it all the time."

He shook his head. "Not enough. It's at its lowest point in history, Megan. You must know that? There are 300,000 of us, speaking it as our first language. At most. And that's after

146

thirty years of government policy promoting it. It's hanging on by a thread. Meanwhile, millions of English speakers flood in every year and treat the place like a theme park. And do you know what they say? Exactly what you just said. Why don't they just speak English? But we've been speaking our own language for over fifteen hundred years. We're not going to stop now because it makes people like you uncomfortable."

When he finished, she found she was crying. She looked away from him, wiping the tears from her cheeks.

"I didn't say anything about being uncomfortable," she said quietly. "I like hearing Welsh. But tonight it was different. Tonight it was rude. If you can't see that, I don't know what else to say to you."

She stood up. Through the bedroom window the dark of the night was disturbed by a bright round moon. She looked back at Gethin, who was hunched forward now, head bowed between his knees. His breathing sounded ragged and strange.

"Are you okay?" she said.

He took a breath, his back heaving. "Yeah. But I think you should leave."

She nodded, walking out of the room. She went downstairs, looking for her coat, finding it near the front door, folded over her bag and shoes. It was after midnight now. Her car was still parked at the harbour. She would have to walk back to town, heels sliding off like they had been all evening, the streets cold and dark. She was miserable at the thought, and a little frightened. She would never walk alone at night by choice these days, though she'd done it without fear when she was young. Opening the front door, she heard Gethin on the stairs. She turned to see him in the shadows, pulling on his hoody.

"What are you doing?" she said.

He looked at her. "Driving you home."

CHAPTER TWELVE

Noah

The morning of the meeting, Noah woke feeling as if he had flu. There was an ache in his legs that was deep and painful, a shivering inside him. He felt loose at his core. Megan was asleep, naked as a baby under the covers, dark make-up smudged around her eyes. When he and Megan met, she was twenty-seven, he was thirty. They drank too much and made love uninhibited, slipping into boozy sleep. In the morning, she'd often looked like this — stripped bare, make-up staining her face and pillow, hair mussed and wild. It struck him, then, that through her affair with Gethin she was crawling back in time, trying to disentangle herself from the pain of recent years by getting drunk and sleeping with a man half her age. In spite of everything, he felt sorry for her.

She had come home late, as he knew she would. He hadn't heard her car on the drive, just the sloppy tread of her heels as she approached the front door. She must have taken a cab, the driver dropping her at the top rather than traversing the dire potholes of the track. Or perhaps — far more sickeningly — Gethin had brought her home, daring to bring his car on to their land. He had lain in bed for hours wondering whether she'd come back at all, as though coming home to him, rather than staying overnight with Gethin, would mean something. It was after one when she got back. He had pretended to be asleep. She was drunk, making a clumsy show of trying to appear sober. He had sensed, from her uneven breathing and loud sniffing as she moved around the room, that she'd been crying. Lying in the dark, he'd wondered if she'd fought with Gethin, a stranger notion to him than the thought of them sleeping together. Even stranger was his quick defensiveness — his impulse to protect her — when he thought of Gethin hurting her. He laughed inwardly at himself for this, and almost as quickly the protective feeling turned to a wish to hurt her himself.

When she got into bed, she had smelled of booze. Though repulsed by her drunkenness, and the sloppiness of her betrayal, he'd wanted to move towards her, find his way inside her. He had found himself wanting her more since discovering the affair, his desire strangely awakened. At the same time, he wanted to demonstrate that he was the one with a right to her body, no one else. All these thoughts shamed him, seeming only to illustrate that he was no better than her.

Now, in the still morning, the room was quiet, curtains closed against the rising day. Megan had begun shutting them at bedtime, accusing him of being fixated on light and movement outside the window. Initially, he had resented having them closed; last night he'd shut them himself.

He pushed himself up like a sick animal, hanging his legs over the side of the bed. He felt dizzy, weak. He looked at Megan again, snoring lightly, then got up and took his flannel dressing gown from the back of the door. Crossing the landing to the bathroom, his legs were just as painful. Being up made him feel even more ill; he should be in bed. But people were arriving in a couple of hours. He needed to tidy up a bit, think things through one last time. He had to speak to Iwan once more before his father arrived.

* * *

An hour later, he had done little but rush to the toilet every few minutes to empty his bowels. He wasn't vomiting, at least, and he hoped the diarrhoea would pass. He made sure not to eat anything; he couldn't stand the thought of it, anyway. Feebly, he got dressed, becoming anxious about what he should wear. The smallest decisions were causing him worry. Should he dress smarter than usual? His father would wear chinos and a polo shirt, like he always did. He looked at Megan, still dead to the world. She had sprawled on to his side of the bed, spreadeagled on her front. It was after nine now. He knew he should wake her. But her being asleep was somehow calming. He walked out to the landing and stood at the window, staring at the fields. Everything was wet from the perpetual rain. He'd been forced to delay things lately, like levelling the track and chopping up the tree, adding to his accumulating sense that he was behind.

* * *

His father arrived early, which Noah should have expected. He went out to the drive, watching as Ray got out of his Range Rover and walked to its boot. Standing under the hatch, he rifled through his briefcase, pulling out a bending stack of clean white documents, licking the tip of his finger to flick through and check them. He slipped the papers back inside and slammed the boot, carrying the briefcase with him.

"What's the matter with you?" he said, approaching. Noah was taller and, when Ray came close to him, Noah found himself looking down at his father's rough face and small angry eyes.

"Nothing," said Noah. "Why?"

"You're pale as a fish."

"Oh. I just ate something that didn't agree with me, I think."

His father eyed him with familiar distrust, like he was working out how Noah might have brought it on himself.

"Where's your sister?" said Ray.

"Not here," said Noah. "It's not even ten, yet."

"She been behaving herself?"

"Haven't seen much of her."

This was the truth. Noah had seen his sister twice since she left the unit five weeks earlier. He knew he should have visited her more, especially in these early weeks when she was getting used to being home, taking her medication again. There was always a difficult readjustment period. Perhaps that was why he'd been avoiding her.

His father was considering him. "You can't be that busy, Noah," he said, as though Noah had mentioned that he was.

"It's always busy. It's a farm. We've had terrible weather. I've been finding a ewe on her back every morning. The tractor's been playing up. Plus the insurance, the police—"

His father waved his hand. "That's life. Get used to it." He looked at Noah. "You can't still be sorting the insurance?"

Noah shrugged. "It's more or less dealt with now."

"They're paying?"

"The least they can get away with."

"Well, that's their job. Shall we go in?"

Noah was relieved to be out in the fresh air, which was taking the edge off his nausea. But he turned towards the house, his father behind him.

"Where's Megan?" said his father when they got to the kitchen.

"She'll be down in a minute."

Noah didn't want to admit that she was in bed at ten o'clock on a Wednesday. His father looked at his watch, anyway. Noah went to the kettle, lifting it from the base, and took it to the sink. Looking across the kitchen, he thought his father looked small, standing alone on the terracotta tiles, glancing around at the walls. Noah disliked the appraising expression on his face, as though the house was up for sale.

"I never did like this house."

"I like it," said Noah. He turned on the tap, water thundering into the empty kettle.

"What's to like?" His father shouted over the rush of the water. "The place is falling apart!"

Noah waited for the kettle to fill before answering, shutting the lid, turning off the tap. "It needs some work. But it's got character. That's the important thing."

His father lifted his briefcase on to the table. "If you like that kind of thing."

Noah did like that kind of thing. His father, on the other hand, liked sweeping modern houses with high ceilings and marble floors, American-style fridges.

"Is Megan coming down, then?"

Noah sighed. "I'll get her in a minute."

"Is she in bed?"

How he knew this, Noah didn't know. Maybe it was the quiet, the fact there was no noise from upstairs. Plus, it wasn't like Megan not to come down when his father arrived. Noah looked at his father, who was smiling strangely at him, as though he knew something about Megan. Noah had a sudden horror that he had found out about the affair. But surely there was no way he could.

He heard a car, out on the driveway. He walked into the dining room and looked through the window. Aled's truck was crunching into the yard, slowing down behind Ray's Range Rover. Aled got out and squinted at the sky, stretching his arms as though he'd been driving for hours. For the first time since Noah had known him, he found Aled's harmless demeanour insincere. He wondered if it had been a cover all along.

Imogen was taking her time getting out of the passenger side. Finally, she appeared, stepping over the shallow brown puddles of the drive, her arms tucked under a leopard-print shawl, fastened at her neck with one of their mother's brooches. On her feet she wore garish cowskin boots and on her fingers there were heavy enamelled rings. Plastic red cherry earrings hung from her lobes. It struck Noah that his sister's apparel was armour, his mother's brooch a badge of loyalty.

He watched closely as they moved towards the house. He was particularly focused on his sister, whom he usually didn't have to study for long to have some idea of her mental state. But as she moved towards the front door, he felt there was a block between his perception and whatever was coming from her. He couldn't read her.

* * *

"Hi, Daddy," she said as she walked into the kitchen, her voice light and clipped. She kissed their father on the cheek then walked over to Noah, who had returned to the counter to finish making the tea.

"*Ga'I helpu efo'r te?*" she said.

Noah looked at his sister, unsure whether she was using Welsh with him to get on his nerves or exclude their father. Her eyes were gently pleading, and he understood that, either way, she meant not *can I help with the tea* but *please let me help with it*. He told her to get milk from the fridge and fill a jug. Meanwhile, he took six mugs from the cupboard, placing them on a tray. Staring at the mugs, he realised he'd miscounted. Imogen watched as he tutted and put one back.

"I do that kind of thing all the time," she said supportively. He winced at the comparison. The kettle was slowly heating, Noah having forgotten to switch it on at first. His legs were still weak, his bowels delicate. He needed to visit the toilet again. Their father stood at the table, spreading the papers from his briefcase. He had made copies of the same document and was positioning one at each place setting.

Aled came through the door, the noise of the flush following him.

"Ray," he said, walking over to Noah's father, shaking his hand like they were old friends. Imogen and Noah stared at them for a few seconds, then went on preparing the tea. Noah was looking for the big teapot, trying to think where they kept it. He was distracted by Aled, asking Ray about his various businesses, commenting on their relationship to the economy in a way Noah would not have been able to. Noah felt he was under water, unable to emerge into the room. Imogen looked as removed as he felt, withdrawn inside her bulky layers.

The kettle beeped loudly, startling him. Staring at the steam rising from the spout, he realised he needed Megan here. There was no one else from whom he could derive the strength he needed, including his sister, though he was glad she was here. He exited the kitchen quietly and went upstairs. In the bedroom, the curtains were still closed and the room smelled more rancidly of alcohol. He pushed up the sliding sash window, cool air drifting through, carrying the bleating of a ewe.

Behind him Megan stirred, lifting herself on to her elbows in a panic of waking, slurring when she spoke. "What time is it?" Her smudged make-up looked comically panda-like now she was awake and speaking.

"Twenty past ten," said Noah.

She shielded her eyes with the back of her hand. "Are you serious? What time is everyone coming?"

"They're here."

"Oh God, Noah. I'm so sorry. Let me get dressed."

She stumbled naked from the bed and went to her drawers, tottering as she pulled on her pants. She found socks and a vest, sitting down on the rattan-mesh chair on which she slung her clothes at bedtime. Half-dressed, she slumped, head in her hands, the effort of all the sudden activity overwhelming her.

"Just give me a minute," she said. "I drank too much last night. I'm not used to it, these days." She looked up at him, wincing with the misery of her hangover. "I don't know what I was thinking."

"I'm making tea," he said. "Do you want paracetamol?"

"Oh God, yes. Please."

"See you downstairs," he said, making clear he wasn't going to bring it to her. As he crossed the room to the door, she watched him with that guilty look he had come to despise.

* * *

A strange thing had happened since discovering his wife's affair; he'd been thinking all the time about his mother. He saw her in flashes, kneeling by the television, reaching behind to fiddle with the wires and try to make it work. He saw her out in the field, blouse flapping in the wind, curls gathered at the back of her neck. Walking back into the kitchen now, he looked at Imogen and saw his mother clearly in the strong cut of her jaw, the slope of her shoulders, her tight curls, cut off decisively at her chin. Imogen turned to him, smiling in relief. Aled and his father were sitting down at the table now, waiting for everyone else.

Noah sensed that Imogen wanted to sit next to him. In normal circumstances he would avoid indulging her childish attachment to him. When they were children, he had taken a hard line against it. His mother used to chide him. "Oh, let her hug you, Noah. Don't reject her. That's very hurtful." But it was his way of protecting her. Imogen's clinging dependency was abnormal, Noah felt. She had to learn some basic boundaries. Nonetheless, he let her sit with him now. Selfish and hypocritical as it was, he needed Imogen on his side. Their father was at the head of the table, the oak dresser a backdrop to his hunched figure. Aled sat at a right-angle to him. Noah directed Imogen to the chair opposite Aled, so that she too was next to their father, and sat down next to her. This left only one chair, opposite Noah and next to Aled. Noah wasn't sure Megan would be happy with this, in the circumstances. Just then she appeared in the doorway, hair brushed, face scrubbed clean. She glanced at the empty chair. Noah leaned across the table, dragging it round to the end so she could sit next to him. His father watched, frowning, but said nothing.

Noah decided to pour the tea, standing up again. Imogen had poured soya milk into a mug for herself. He topped that one up first, placing the warm mug in front of her. He lifted the teapot again and filled the remaining mugs, leaving room for milk from the jug. Everyone watched silently. When he was finished, no one moved to take their tea. So he lifted the mugs off the tray, one at a time, handing them out. He removed the jug and sugar bowl, placing them on the table. Left on the tray were the two paracetamol tablets, which he scooped up and handed to Megan.

"Not you as well?" said his father, looking at Megan. She stared at him, glancing at Noah.

"I wasn't feeling well when Dad arrived," said Noah.

"Oh," she said, blushing. "It's just a headache."

Megan looked away from Ray, who was busy now pushing his fat fingers through the dainty handle of the jug. He splashed milk sloppily into his mug, spilling tea on the table, bundled in a spoonful of sugar then dropped the dirty teaspoon on the table. Aled was staring at the sugar bowl, reluctant to put a used spoon back in. Noah went to the counter, taking a handful of clean spoons from the drawer, bringing them to the table.

For a while there was no noise but the dinging of teaspoons and slurping of tea. There was an air of not only tension but self-consciousness. They felt ridiculous, Noah thought; because it was ridiculous. This meeting was a charade, a pantomime. Even if Noah had been planning to sign the papers, they could have been sent by post, or even email. This was purely for his father to demonstrate both his power and supposed generosity.

"Okay," said Ray from the head of the table. He looked around at the four of them. "Everyone ready?"

Noah felt a surge of something chemical inside him that seemed to charge his limbs and override the systemic weakness of his body.

"You all know my wishes," his father was saying. "You two will take on the cottages." He gestured towards Noah and Megan. "Imogen and Aled will take over the farm."

"But I don't want the farm, Daddy," said Imogen.

His father looked at Imogen. "I asked you to listen."

She stared blankly at him. Their father went on. "This is what I've decided. I know some of you have objections. But this is in your interest. Megan is already making progress on the cottages. Aled has a lot of ideas for making this farm profitable."

Aled went very still, refusing to look at Noah.

"Neither of you should need anything else, if you run things properly. You won't be lacking an income, if anything should happen to me. Your mother would be distraught if she thought I was leaving things a mess."

"Why do you keep talking about leaving things?" said Noah. "Are you ill?"

"Not exactly."

"What does that mean, not exactly?" said Megan.

"It's nothing," said his father. "They found some pre-cancerous cells during my last surgery. And a couple of other things. I'll be fine. But I want things sorted. I'm seventy-nine it's about bloody time."

Megan opened her mouth to say something but Ray cut her off. "I don't want to talk about my health! This is about the farm and cottages. That's all."

Noah was thrown off by his father's admission. It made him look more ruthless now. But Noah couldn't be sure it was true. This was the kind of casual admission that could have been designed to knock him off his game.

"Splitting the farm and cottages makes sense," said Noah. "There's no reason Megan and I should have both. But you're doing it the wrong way round."

His father shot him a look. He went on.

"Farming is very insecure. We all know that. I'm sure Aled knows it, too. You don't do it for the money. That's not why I do it."

He felt a lump in his throat. He was thinking about his mother again, what this farm had meant to her. What it meant to him. These papers before him, his father staring him down; he felt she was being taken from him all over again. The farm was their shared endeavour, their last connection.

He told himself to get a grip. This was not the time to show weakness. To his irritation, Megan put a sympathetic hand on his arm. He pulled away, placing his hands in his lap.

"Noah," said his father. "This is exactly what I'm talking about. This is the problem."

"What's the problem?" he said.

"You're too attached. You've always been like this. It's just a bloody farm! It means too much to you. You don't make the right decisions. It needs fresh eyes — and you need to move on."

Noah glanced at Aled, still refusing to look at him. He felt exposed by his father's words, which were both true and deeply unfair. It also occurred to Noah, for the first time, that his father was in some way trying to divide him from his mother, as though, by taking the farm, he could finally sever the bond.

"What is it you're going to do?" he said, looking at Aled.

Aled looked up. "What?"

"What are these plans you have for the farm?"

Ray held up a hand. "We're not here to discuss that. Now listen — this is what I'm proposing. I'm going to sign over the deeds." He looked between Noah and Imogen, both on his left. "But I need you to sign some additional paperwork first."

"What additional paperwork?" said Noah.

He turned his head and looked at Imogen, sitting quietly on his right between himself and their father. She was looking at Ray. Noah couldn't see her face, but her posture was defensive, arms folded beneath her shawl.

"I don't want you both agreeing to one thing now then changing things around. I know how Imogen is influenced by you, Noah."

"Can't you leave anything up to us?" said Noah.

His father slapped his hand on the table. Megan jumped, gripping Noah's hand beneath the table. Noah looked at Megan. Her eyes were wide, blinking at his father. He looked at Imogen, still blank and shrunken away. He cleared his throat, coaxing himself to say what he needed. First, he wanted to make clear that he was not trying to deny anyone. He did not begrudge his sister anything. His way was better for them. He was not the difficult one here; he was none of the things his father would call him.

"Aled and Imogen should have the cottages," said Noah. "They have Hari to think about. Imogen might get ill again.

You can't run a farm and raise a child alone. But Aled could run the cottages and look after Hari, if it came down to it. They're easier to manage. And the income is more reliable. Aled may think he knows what he's doing with the farm. But he doesn't have a clue." He looked at Aled. "You don't know until you do it."

"I've listened to your objections, Noah," said his father. "More than once. But I've made up my mind."

Noah looked at his father. He had promised himself that, when he had his own children, they would not be afraid to look him in the eye. He would not be a god in his house, exploiting their vulnerability to exercise power. But there had been no children. Noah would not correct the past with a family of his own. As he faced his father, he tried to feel emboldened. Finally, he had the means to assert himself. Through the case Iwan was building, Noah was being offered the gift of justice, not only for what his father was doing now but everything he'd done in the past. He felt the walls close in when this man entered his home, returning him to the bitter enclosure of his childhood. But he had to overcome this now and use the power in his hands.

"No," he said.

His father looked at him. "What do you mean 'no'?"

"I'm not signing anything."

"Noah," said his father. "I'm doing this the nicest way possible. There are other ways."

"Threaten me all you want. I'm not signing anything. I have other ways, too."

He could feel Megan's gaze, the dumb fear emanating from her. Imogen and Aled were watching, too. His father smiled.

"No, you don't, Noah."

"Yes. I have my own solicitors. And they're going to stop this."

As soon as he said it, his heart began to beat very fast. A sensation of falling overcame him. He dropped his hands, gripping the seat of his chair.

"Now you listen to me," said his father, pointing a finger. "I don't know what anyone has told you — but they're wrong. You haven't a fucking clue what you're talking about. Now don't make a fool of yourself."

Noah stood up, trying to hold his legs steady as he walked to the dresser, opening the top drawer. From inside he pulled out the letter of claim, a clean sheet of paper with Iwan's letterhead. He placed it in front of his father then went back to his chair. He didn't sit down.

"That's from my solicitor," he said. "They'll be expecting your response. If we can't resolve out of court, we'll go to trial."

His father stared at the letter, his chest rising and falling sharply with quick shallow breaths. After a moment, he picked up the letter and ripped it in half. His eyes were murderous. "You have no rights here," he said.

"In fact, I do. This farm was intended for me. You know that. Everyone here knows it. That means something in court, even if it means nothing to you."

He went to the door, his vision blurring. By the time he reached the hall, he could hardly see a thing and had to feel his way upstairs. His legs were quivering and loose as though he'd run a long distance. He felt he would collapse. He thought maybe he would die, as though his life had led to this point and, in the end, it would be too much for him. He held on to the thin banister and half-dragged himself to the top. On the landing he gasped, like breaking through the surface of water, and he pushed his way into his bedroom, collapsing on the bed. His body was pulsing. He closed his eyes, unable to think about what he'd done. There was a part of him that had been certain he wouldn't go through with it. He knew he would be glad, in the end. But for now the experience was so physical that he could only lie still and let his body absorb the shock.

Downstairs he could hear his father shouting and yelling. A moment later there were soft footsteps on the stairs. The door opened. It was Megan, aghast.

"He's gone nuts," she said.

"I know. Don't worry about it."

Megan sat on the bed, placing a hand on his leg. He sensed she was about to speak.

"Can we talk later?" he said. "I can't now." He looked at her. "I really can't."

She nodded. He turned away from her, lying on his side, closing his eyes. In his mind he imagined the torrent of abuse from the kitchen rising through the house and dying outside the bedroom door.

CHAPTER THIRTEEN

Megan

Once Ray had calmed down, Aled and Imogen made their excuses and left. Ray went soon after them.

"Tell him something for me, will you?" he shouted to Megan through the driver's window as he jammed his key in the ignition. His hands were shaking, jowls quivering. It was nothing like as bad as he'd been in the kitchen, when an uncontrolled rage had taken over his ageing body and Megan worried he would end up on the floor. "Tell him I won't hold this against him if he'll just stop it now. Tell him that for me, okay?"

She nodded, willing him to leave, watching his car tear round the shed and disappear. Of course she wouldn't tell Noah any such thing.

* * *

She felt dire and it wasn't just her hangover. It wasn't the family meeting, either, though that wasn't helping. Last night's fight with Gethin was like poison in her blood, along with the booze that her body could no longer tolerate. How had it become so unpleasant between them? They'd been fine one minute, bitter the next. But maybe they'd never been fine. The day they met, Gethin had made his disapproval of the cottages clear; his disapproval, basically, of her. She'd been naive to think that had been set aside. He wasn't in love with her. She didn't know how he really felt. She didn't know anything except that it was better it was over.

In the dull light of day, she was aware that, if she wanted to repair her marriage, she'd have to tell Noah about the affair. That was the golden rule. A therapist, or even just a friend, would say that this was the only way to restore any trust or intimacy to their relationship. Then again, when she imagined trying to rehabilitate her marriage — if Noah would even agree to that, after what she'd done — she felt tired. Surely they were both too worn out, too thwarted and cynical, to embark on something requiring so much energy and hope?

She was also upset to remember that her car was still parked at the harbour. Gethin had driven her home, a stony silence between them as they moved along the quiet roads and he deposited her at the top of the track. She would have to get a taxi — or worse, the bus — to collect her car from town.

In the bedroom she found a pair of pyjamas in her drawer, keen to take off her jeans and get back into bed. She needed to nurse her hangover, try not to think, maybe even sleep. She went down to the kitchen. Noah had gone out to the farm. When she'd found him in the bedroom earlier, he looked so pale she'd wondered if she should take him to the doctor. But he told her he was fine, he just needed to go outside. She was glad he was still out there. She didn't feel she had sufficient reserves of sensitivity to deal with him right now. She was depleted. If any emotions could be stirred, she thought they were unlikely to be nice ones.

One thing she did feel was hungry, not having eaten since yesterday. She opened the cupboards, mulling her options. She would have liked porridge, if she could be bothered to make it. She settled on Noah's low-sugar muesli. Pouring it into a bowl, she looked over at the table where the sugar was abandoned along with legal papers and half-drunk tea. She set about emptying cold tea, stacking mugs in the dishwasher. She ripped Ray's documents into small, unreadable fragments and buried them in the recycling.

She got in bed with her tea and cereal, feeling heavy and dark. Something was wrong, a terrible foreboding in the air. A butterfly flitted near the window, her attention drawn sharply to the sudden movement. She was surprised to see one in November. She disliked its chaotic energy but couldn't be bothered to get out of bed and guide it from the room. The wrongness was in her bones. Was it Gethin? The fight had stirred something up in her, yes; but there was something else. Maybe it was the meeting. Ray Robinson was a frightening man. He carried power in ways she didn't even understand. Surely he had the means to take everything from them, not only the farm and cottages but deeper, more valuable things. He could annihilate them, if he wanted to. Clearly Noah had a plan. But she wasn't exactly reassured given he'd told her nothing about it.

There was something else. She slipped down under the covers, pulling the duvet higher. The fluttering creature was unmoving on the wall, its wings tightly closed. Her eyes were heavy and painful. The muscles in her back were sore. Her breasts were tender. It must be her period, she thought. It would explain this dread-feeling, this sense of standing alone at the edge of a cliff. She was relieved. She got out of bed and went the bathroom. The period feeling was so strong and familiar now that she expected to find blood in her underwear already. It wasn't there. It would come later today, if not tomorrow. Emptying her bladder, she began to mindlessly calculate when she was due. It would have been helpful, by her age, if she'd adopted a better means of keeping track. She could have done what her friends did, put a mark in her diary or downloaded an app. But she had resisted deference to her cycle since she was eleven, refusing to give it the satisfaction of planning for it. Of course, when she and Noah were trying, she was forced to pay better attention and for a while she was fanatically attuned to her body. Then, when they gave up, she lost track again with an almost vengeful disregard.

She sat on the toilet, knees apart, working through a familiar mental maze. She combed back through recent events — meetings with Gethin, Welsh classes, collecting Imogen from the unit, the lambs — trying to locate her last period. Usually, it didn't take long. She would bring an experience to mind and remember how she had woken that day to blood-stained sheets or found herself stranded somewhere without a pad. But this time there seemed to be a block to finding such an occasion. She couldn't recall a single recent time when she'd been on.

Then she realised something, her body becoming still as she turned her attention to the thought: she couldn't remember having a period since starting her relationship with Gethin. Going back through it all, she couldn't think of a single occasion when she'd cancelled plans or asked herself whether he'd be okay with a woman bleeding. She stared at the closed bathroom door. Her mind twisted and somersaulted but seemed to throw itself against a wall. It couldn't possibly be that she hadn't menstruated this whole time — how long was it?

She got off the toilet, rushing into the bedroom, emptying her handbag chaotically on the bed. Her diary wasn't there. She went to the bedside drawer and found it there, seizing upon it, riffling through the pages. She found the entry for her first Welsh class: the second of September. She flicked forward to two Saturdays later, the day she and Gethin had been in his car. That was the sixteenth. She said this to herself aloud, aware, with coursing dread, of what she was going to find when she flicked back to today — the first of November. If she was right about this, she hadn't had a period for six weeks. At least. She sat down on the bed and went back over it all, determined to be wrong, willing her brain to find a time she'd discovered blood on Gethin's sheets or told him she wasn't up to seeing him tonight.

There was no such occasion. She was sure of it.

She touched her breasts, their soreness taking on a new meaning. She felt suddenly sick and ran back to the bathroom, retching into the toilet. There was nothing to bring up. She hadn't touched her cereal or tea, which stood undrunk on the bedside table.

* * *

Downstairs she heard the front door open and Noah's footsteps in the hall. The sound had an air of unreality as she pushed herself away from the toilet, wiping her mouth on her pyjamas. She washed her hands then went to her chest of drawers, getting dressed for the second time that day.

She found Noah in the kitchen, pouring hot water into a mug, the jar of instant coffee open beside it. Megan had gone off coffee in recent weeks and now wondered if this was part of it, if there had, in fact, been a hundred signs she'd ignored. She was carrying her mug of cold tea, which she tipped in the drain. Noah was a few feet away, his back turned as he faced the counter.

"Can you get another mug out for me, please?"

He hesitated, as though he might say no, then opened the cupboard.

"You want coffee?" he said.

"Tea," she said.

He nodded, opening the teabag caddy in front of him. She couldn't tell, anymore, if he was angry with her or just angry. What was the difference when you'd lived with someone for thirteen years? A bad mood was a bad marriage, if it went on long enough.

"How are you feeling about the meeting now?"

"Great," he said. "Just great."

"I was proud of you for standing up for yourself. He deserves it."

He shook his head, irritated.

166

"What?" she said.

"You don't really know anything about it, do you?"

She stared at him. "Only because you haven't told me anything!"

He looked over his shoulder. "Why do you think that is?"

"I have no idea, Noah. I really don't know why you're so angry with me."

He looked back at the counter, taking the spoon from his mug, stirring the teabag floating in hers.

"Megan," he said. "I don't want to do this now."

"So when are we going to do it? I don't know about you but this is not my idea of how people should live together. We used to talk to each other."

He sighed, leaning over the counter, putting his head in his hands. She wanted to go to him, put her hand on his back. She loved him very much. But she was angry with him, too.

He walked to the fridge, taking out the milk, slamming the door so the glass inside rattled. He splashed milk into his coffee, placing the bottle beside her unfinished mug of tea, and walked out of the room.

* * *

Waiting for the bus, she was amazed — and angered — by her stupidity. She had been careless with Gethin. There were times they hadn't even used a condom. They'd never discussed contraception, Gethin probably assuming she was on the pill, if he'd thought about it at all. But the truth was she hadn't taken contraception since before she and Noah started trying.

The thing was, no one had ever been able to explain why they couldn't conceive. Tests showed two reproductively healthy adults. A doctor had told Megan once that the medical understanding of fertility was more limited than people realised, that it was still, in many ways, a mystery. Megan found no comfort in this but she came to see it was true. She had a friend from school, told she'd never have a child, who went on to have three. She knew women who couldn't conceive for years, were successful with IVF, then had another child naturally. She'd met a couple who'd taken so long to conceive their first that they got pregnant again by accident, weeks after it was born. She knew couples with secondary infertility, who had one child with no issues then couldn't get pregnant again. Imogen and Aled were one of them.

Megan should have known this could happen; that anything could happen. But the truth was she had convinced herself she was not capable of having a child. She believed that, in some fundamental way, her body was broken, frequently thinking to herself that Noah would be better off with someone else.

Her car was there at the harbour, thankfully without a ticket. The sun was out, boats brightly lit, grey water sparkling. She paid for parking then walked up the hill to the maes. A bell tinkled as she entered the pharmacy, an impatient-looking queue of mostly elderly people turning to look at her. At the front a tall, slightly stooping man came through from the back. It was Gideon, Aled's best friend. Megan had known he was a pharmacist but was somehow shocked to find him here.

Panicking, she looked around for something innocuous to purchase, deciding she would go elsewhere for the pregnancy test. But then she found herself indignant at the prospect. She was entitled to buy a pregnancy test, wasn't she? And Gideon wasn't allowed to tell anyone he'd sold her one, was he? She didn't know if confidentiality rules were followed round here. But even if he did say something, Aled surely wouldn't mention it to Noah? They weren't that close, especially not since all this business over the farm. And wouldn't it just be uncomfortable for them both, if Aled randomly mentioned to Noah that Gideon — who was not a friend of Noah's — had sold Noah's wife a pregnancy test? And of course Gideon wouldn't say anything to Aled in the first place. It was private, and not worth mentioning, and pregnancy tests were routine, like sanitary pads and other things men preferred not to discuss.

Under the bright pharmacy lights, her mind went into meltdown. She was not making sense. Or she was making too much sense, overthinking everything in minute detail. Gideon was talking with a girl behind the counter, muttering as he handed over a bulky package of medication. The overweight woman at the front of the queue watched them with urgent eyes, awaiting the transfer of her drugs.

As Gideon turned to retreat into the back, he noticed Megan, nodding silently at her. He didn't smile or speak. He was being professional. That was good, she thought. That was better. She picked up a box of ibuprofen, clutching it like a weapon. Thankfully it was the young woman — bony and pale-skinned, her hair slicked back in a bun — who was doing most of the serving.

"I need a pregnancy test," Megan said quietly when she reached the front. The girl's face was impassive, her eyes dull. She moved from behind the counter into one of the aisles. Megan followed her, confused at first then remembering, embarrassed, that the tests were not kept behind the counter. She already knew this, having taken dozens of pregnancy tests from the shelves of pharmacies and supermarkets. The girl humoured her, though, selecting a few boxes and clutching them between her slender fingers, nails gleaming with pale polish. She talked Megan through the different options, from the old-fashioned strip — a fiver for a box of five — and the rapid-result digital option that was ten times the cost but as accurate as an ultrasound.

Megan chose the expensive one.

"Just one?" said the girl.

Megan hesitated. "Yes," she said. "And a box of the cheap ones, too."

The girl nodded, taking both to the counter. Megan followed her, trying not to lock eyes with any of the customers who probably thought she had wasted their time making the girl do what Megan could have done herself. The girl scanned the boxes, placing them on the counter. Gideon came through from the back again. Megan stuffed the boxes in her handbag. Gideon nodded again, not seeming to notice or care what she was buying. The machine awaited payment, its contactless sign glaring. She pulled out her purse, shoving the tests down to the bottom of her bag, and nudged her card against the machine before dashing back into the open air.

* * *

When they were trying, Megan was always advised — by doctors, friends, faceless online personae — to wait until her period was due. The result wouldn't be reliable until then. But as the days had crawled excruciatingly towards her due date, she felt she would lose her mind. Every month she had tested early, putting herself through the double disappointment of a negative result followed, days later, by the occurrence of her period. It had become expensive to keep buying digital tests so she switched to the sticks. It was all the same, in the end. She was never pregnant.

Back at the farm she went straight upstairs, clutching her handbag against her as though it contained illegal drugs. Locking the bathroom door, she had a stricken, breathless feeling and when she glanced in the mirror she thought she was pale. She pulled the boxes from her bag and ripped open the digital test, tearing off the thick crinkly packaging to reveal the bulky stick. She found an old toothbrush holder in the cupboard, washing it at the sink before sitting on the toilet and angling it beneath her. She was jittery and it took a moment to summon her bladder. Eventually urine came, splashing the bottom of the pot.

She placed the pot carefully on the counter, washing her hands before removing the cap from the test and resting it, tip down, in the ammonia-smelling liquid. She counted to twenty then extracted the stick, placing the cap back on, laying it flat on the counter.

She waited.

Outside the window the branches of a tree rustled in the wind. She watched the ewes in the field, munching grass with their single-minded purpose. She thought about Noah, the two times they'd been together recently. If she was pregnant, it was technically possible that the baby was Noah's. She knew this was wishful thinking, though, given everything.

She didn't know how long she'd waited — probably not the length of time she was meant to — but she looked down at the test, expecting it to be blank. Like magic, it had transpired a word on its impossibly tiny screen. Pregnant. Directly beneath the result — which was 99 per cent likely to be true, according to the manufacturer — was the number three, followed by a plus sign. She picked up the box and read the back, reminding herself that the test offered four possibilities: Not pregnant. Pregnant 1-2. Pregnant 2-3. Pregnant 3+. Hers was the last one, which meant she was at least three weeks gone but the test could be no more specific than that.

CHAPTER FOURTEEN

Noah

He disliked visiting his sister's house. It made him feel like an intruder. But he needed to talk to her. Slowly, he manoeuvred his truck along the hedge-lined lane that sloped down to the village. At the bottom, he was confronted by the cottages, silent on his left with shallow front gardens whose tangled weed and wildflower flourishes contrasted against the pruned enclosures further up. Tŷ Gwyn was stark white between the grey of the other two. The school on his right was wide and taupe with a dark slate roof and red-brick chimney, partitioned by green-painted metal railings. The pub was imposing at the top of the lane, the church spire opposite a nineteenth-century rebuild of the medieval original, skirted by a cemetery with flat slate graves. On the rare occasions he came here, Noah felt how pleasant the village was, hills rolling gently to the sea. He did understand the local impulse to protect it from people like his father.

He turned down the tight lane where Imogen and Aled lived, parking outside their house. Left here, his truck would block anything wider than a small car. This gave him an excuse not to stay long. He stood on the doorstep before the arched blue door, its handle round brass, and pressed the bell. Aled came to the door, shambling as ever and surprised to find him there. Before either of them could speak, Hari popped up in the shadows.

"Uncle Noah!" The boy turned and ran upstairs, shouting for his mother.

"Come in," said Aled. Noah stepped into the dark hall, taking in the familiar scent of must and damp. The clutter made the small cottage oppressively cramped but the smell of structural decay filled Noah with despair.

"Sorry to disturb," he said. "I just wanted to speak with Imogen."

He didn't mean it to sound threatening but that was how it sounded, in the circumstances. The memory of the meeting, which had taken place only that morning, was surreal as a nightmare in Noah's mind.

"She's upstairs," said Aled. "She's been up there since we got home. God knows what she's doing."

Hari ran back down, stumbling at the bottom then picking himself up. Excited wasn't the word; he was disturbed.

"Uncle Noah? Uncle Noah?"

Noah smiled, worn out already by his nephew. How did people with children do this all the time?

"Mam said — Mam said—" The boy took a big breath then enunciated carefully. "You can go to see her. She's up at the top."

* * *

Noah mounted the first flight of stairs in trepidation then crossed the small landing, climbing the spiralling passage to the attic. The only window in the vaulted room was a skylight, pointing at the white sheaths of cloud above. Laminate floor stretched under the sloped ceiling towards a jumble of taped boxes. There was a frameless, sheetless double bed, the bumpy grey mattress atop a boxy ottoman with sliding drawers.

This attic conversion had been intended as a guest room. But no one would want to sleep in here now it had deteriorated into what could only be described as an exhibition of his sister's illness. It looked to Noah worse than the last time he was here, the sloping walls more opaquely plastered with printed emails, handwritten lists, appointment letters, and bright Post-it notes with scrawled reminders — *Take tablets! Go outside! Breathe!* Because the walls were sloped, documents often came loose, fluttering down and collecting at the edges of the floor like fragments of Imogen's jumbled mind.

From his sister's perspective, this disarray was an earnest attempt to function. She wasn't monitoring the government or unravelling conspiracies. But the effect was almost as unsettling. Most dismaying for Noah were the letters about owed tax, overdue library books, unpaid parking fines, over many of which she had scrawled in black marker *Discuss with Aled* or *Don't pay this!!!* Some time ago, Noah had asked Aled to stay on top of higher-stake paperwork. Aled said it was harder than you'd think. He often knew nothing about the parking tickets, for example, until she was being summoned to court.

Stepping over fallen debris, Noah was not convinced Imogen was up here at all. Then he noticed her beyond the bed, squatting like a child over an open box, items emptied on the floor around her.

"Hi, Imogen."

She turned her head, frowning. "I don't want to come down."

"I know," he said. "That's why I've come up."

He moved round the bed, ducking under the slanted ceiling. He knelt beside her. They were directly beneath the skylight and it was surprisingly warm, the glass collecting phantom heat from the translucent veil of cloud above. He looked at Imogen. She was staring at an old school badge, held between her fingers. She turned it over, moving the pin with her thumbnail.

"Oh, look!" she cried suddenly, discarding the badge. From the box she lifted a twinkling gold watch. As she examined it, chain strap slipping through her fingers, she seemed to be working to awaken the memory attached to the item.

"Daddy gave me this?" she said doubtfully, looking at Noah, who nodded.

"How old was I?" she said.

"Your twelfth birthday, I would say."

Noah remembered the extravagant gift box delivered to the farm, and how petulantly jealous he had been, not because he liked or wanted the watch — which anyone could see was ugly and gaudy, especially for a child — but on account of the expense which, in his adolescence, he had interpreted as symbolic of the affection his father withheld from Noah but occasionally lavished on Imogen.

"I don't know why he bought gold when he must have known I only wear silver."

Noah could see there was no point discussing the court case. It would have to wait. He decided to sit with his sister for a minute, though, which seemed the least he could do. The laminate was becoming painful against his knees so he slumped sideways on to his thighs.

"Is there anything you need?" he said.

She was still staring at the watch. Suddenly, as though it had bitten her, she threw it back in the box.

"Noah," she said. "I have to tell you something."

"What?"

She didn't say anything else. She was looking beyond the open box, staring at nothing.

"Imogen?"

She looked at him. "What?"

"What is it you need to tell me?"

She considered him. "You mustn't tell Daddy I told you."

"He and I aren't really on speaking terms."

"Why not?" she said.

He looked at her. Had she forgotten the meeting? Or had she misunderstood what had happened there, blocked out

175

its implications? She was up here, he thought, at least partly because it had upset her.

"Doesn't matter," he said. "Tell me what you wanted to say."

There was a thumping on the stairs, the quick muffled thud of footsteps. Hari appeared, breathless, in the doorway.

"Mam!" he cried. "You told me you and Uncle Noah were coming downstairs!"

His eyes brimmed with tears. He looked around the room, as though trying to locate the source of his mother's betrayal.

"Oh, darling, I'm so sorry. I don't remember saying that! Don't be cross. Come and give Mummy a hug."

Hari clambered round the bed. Imogen opened her arms, letting him bury his wet face in her neck.

* * *

Noah went downstairs, finding Aled in the kitchen.

"She's off her meds."

Aled looked at him. "I know."

"When did this happen?"

Aled sighed. "I'm not sure. I was keeping a close eye for a while and then, I don't know."

Noah felt a stab of irritation — the man who thought he could run a hundred-acre farm with no experience but couldn't keep his wife on her medication for a month.

"What are you planning to do?"

Aled looked through the window at the overgrown garden. "I can't force her to take them."

"So you're just going to wait until she goes missing again? Or worse?"

Aled looked at him. "What is it you think I should do, Noah?"

"I thought the doctor released her on the condition she was taking her tablets?"

"He did."

"So why not contact the unit and say she's not doing it?"

Aled stared at him. "It's not that simple, is it? She's only just come home. Hari's so happy to have her back."

"He seems pretty anxious to me."

Aled looked at him. "Hari?"

"Yeah."

"What do you mean 'anxious'?"

"I mean, the kid seems anxious. Worried. He was calmer when it was just the two of you."

Aled looked devastated. "She's his mother."

"I know," said Noah. "So it frightens him when she's not well, doesn't it?"

Aled shook his head. "I can't send her back. We'll just be at square one again as soon as she comes out. I can't keep doing it to her. I can't keep doing it to any of us."

* * *

When Noah got back to the farm, he noticed a missed call on his mobile from a withheld number. It was bound to be the police, calling with some pointless update. He rang Mandy. It went straight to voicemail. He turned his ringer on and put his phone in his pocket. When he felt the vibration a while later, he was on the quad. Jerking to a stop, he turned off the engine and pulled out the phone. It was almost five. If he missed this call, they wouldn't ring again today.

"Hello?"

It was Chris, who Noah hadn't spoken with since he came to the farm on the day of the slaughter. Mandy was probably just not on shift. But he had a sense of her having cast him aside.

"We just wanted to let you know we made some arrests," Chris was saying. "The men are in custody, they've been charged."

"Who are they?"

"The gang we've been monitoring. We caught them at it."

177

"Caught them at what?"

"Stealing livestock."

Noah paused. "Have you asked them about my lambs?"

"They haven't admitted to any of the previous crimes yet. But they will."

"Okay," he said. He didn't have the energy to argue. As he hung up he realised he hardly cared, anymore, what the police did or didn't do.

* * *

The next morning, Noah opened the curtains to find a thick fog had settled overnight, shrouding the fields.

"God," said Megan, sitting up in bed. "What is that?"

Noah was quiet, staring at the ominous vapour blotting out the land.

"I've never seen it like that," Megan was saying. "Except — do you remember that time when we were driving home from your dad's?"

Noah nodded. "Yeah."

"Will you be able to tup the ewes?"

"It'll clear." He looked at her. "I need some help, though. I've been meaning to say."

She looked put out, as he'd expected. He was annoyed all the same. Not long ago, he wouldn't have had to ask for her help. She would have just known.

He watched as she got out of bed, slipping her dressing gown on and hurrying to the bathroom. With the door ajar, he heard her vomiting. He went out to the landing, standing near the door. She hadn't been unwell in the night, as far as he'd been aware. He thought back to the night before. He didn't remember her drinking. They'd spent the evening together — deliberately together, for the first time in months. Megan picked up takeaway from their favourite Chinese. She was lavish in her order, bringing home hot trays of sticky meat, thick noodles, crunchy spring rolls, salted fish, as though they were celebrating something. Indulgence characterised more than the food. They talked intimately, unguardedly. Noah confided in Megan how hopeless he had come to feel about Imogen, a despair that he felt went beyond his usual cynicism. He told her about the case against his father, the legal details, the evidence gathered so far. He felt close to her again, as though they had slipped, temporarily, out of the mess of their lives. For a while he even forgot about Gethin.

"What's wrong?" he said to her when she emerged from the bathroom, pale-faced, moving carefully towards the bed.

"Just a bug," she said, sliding back under the covers. She closed her eyes. "I just need to rest."

"Okay. Do you want anything?"

"Water, please." Before he left the room, she added, wearily, "What are we going to do about Imogen?"

He looked at her. "Just wait and see. There's nothing else we can do."

* * *

While Megan stayed in bed, Noah skulked around the house, willing the fog to clear. He had a lot to do outside. But the fog stayed where it was, a silver-white sheet catching his eye through the sash windows as he moved between rooms, as though he was seeing it for the first time. It was just as well, really. There was a mess of paperwork on the dining table that had been piling up for weeks into an administrative hell. Stuck inside, he was forced to confront it.

He was angry when he started then fell into a rhythm and wondered why he had let it become bigger in his imagination than it was in real life. Still, he felt a certain blackness on him, a blanket he couldn't shake. It was on his shoulders all the time lately, and he worried that soon it would be over his head, suffocating him. He thought uneasily about death, an abyss at the back of his mind. Now and then, a more direct image intruded; he pictured himself out in the field with his shotgun. He would never do a thing like that. But it was a relief to know he had the option.

Around teatime, there was an urgent knocking at the door. The bell rang. Noah looked through the dining room window and saw Imogen, alone in the grey light. She looked at the window and saw Noah. Her eyes widened. She mouthed something to him.

The front door was unlocked. She could have let herself in. But it was more dramatic this way. He sighed and went to the hall. As he opened the door, she pushed past him.

"Close it," she whispered, looking back through the glass. He shut the door calmly and turned to her. Her eyes were wide and frightened but also vacant, as though the substance of her was missing.

"Did you walk?"

"I have to talk to you," she said. "Is Megan here?"

"She's asleep."

Imogen nodded. "She's not well," she said. "I noticed it yesterday." She presumably meant at the meeting, if she meant anything that existed in reality.

"She's fine," said Noah.

Imogen nodded again. "So there's no one else here?"

"No one else."

"Are you sure?"

"Yes."

"Shall I check?"

"If you want."

He wandered into the kitchen and filled the kettle while she rushed through the downstairs rooms. She came into the kitchen.

"Why did you walk?" said Noah.

She looked at him. "Walk? Oh, walk. Yes. I did walk, didn't I? I don't like to drive."

She went to the kitchen window, fingering the glass. The fog had dispersed a little by now, the vapour more sparse, though it still clung to the fields.

"Don't you?" said Noah.

"Don't I what?"

"Like to drive?"

She moved away from the window. "Cars are dangerous. It's only going to get worse, too. All these cars driving themselves. Do you know about this? We're not going to have any control at all."

"Hmm," said Noah. He turned back to the counter, reaching into the tin, taking out two pyramid-shaped tea bags, dropping one in each mug. He poured steaming water over them until they bobbed at the surface.

"Walking is better," said Imogen. "It's good for you. You walk a lot, don't you? Because you're a farmer."

"I suppose I do. Though I use the quad a lot, these days. More than I should, probably."

She came up to him, standing close so that he glanced over his shoulder and saw how her cheeks were blotched and red from her long walk, her nose was pink at the tip, dark hair damp at the scalp with sweat and condensation.

"The fog," she said.

"What about it?" said Noah.

"It's a sign."

"Of what?"

Imogen had always read meaning into the weather. This was surprisingly common round here. Farmers monitored the climate constantly, of course. Sometimes their appraisal bordered on superstitious. There were moon-worshippers, too, women who organised their lives around the lunar calendar, attributing the moods of themselves and their children to its cycles. Imogen took it further, believing, like the Greeks, that nature was communicating directly with her, conveying secret messages, issuing instructions.

She was still wearing her coat, which she removed now and hung, wet, on the back of a chair. Rubbing her hands together, she sat in the leather armchair that was wedged between the dresser and the wall. Noah turned up the radiator before bringing her tea, placing it in her hands, putting his own mug on the table. He turned a chair to face her.

"I'm sorry," she said, staring at the tea in her hands. "I do try. But it's getting harder all the time. I can't do it anymore."

"You are doing it, Imogen. It's not easy when you have a child. I understand. Megan and I would like to help more."

She looked at him. "I love him so much."

"I know."

"But he wants so much from me. My God — who would ever believe a child could want this much from their mother?"

He nodded.

"I wish Mummy was here. I can't do this without her."

"You said that when Hari was born. But you've been doing it for five years."

"She was the one person I didn't have to worry about."

"What do you mean?"

Imogen looked up at him, her dark eyes serious. "She never got replaced. She was always herself. Always."

He watched her. "Are there replacements around now?"

She nodded.

"Who?"

"Aled," she said. "And Daddy."

He nodded. "Okay. Do you want to stay here tonight?"

She stared at him. "Noah, I have to tell you something."

"So you keep saying."

She looked at him. "When did I say it?"

"Yesterday. When I came to your house."

She frowned, putting the end of her thumb in her mouth, chewing on it.

"It doesn't matter," he said. "What is it you want to tell me?"

"It's hard to say it. Especially to you. But I have to. It's poison, Noah. Do you understand? But you need to know first. Before anyone else."

He felt suddenly nauseous. He was trying to be patient, reminding himself that this wasn't her fault. But he didn't have the strength for it. He was hanging by a thread as it was. Imogen was the last thing he needed.

"Whatever it is, you can tell me," he said.

She bent her head, hair falling in her eyes, chewing her thumb again. He had an urge to go over and pull it from her mouth, as he had when they were younger.

"Do you remember our bedrooms when we were children?"

"I can't hear you with your thumb in your mouth, Imogen."

She pulled it away obediently, putting her hands in her lap.

"Do you mean in this house?" said Noah.

She shook her head. "Our old house."

"Oh."

"Do you remember how we shared when we were little? The bunk beds?"

He nodded. "Yes."

"And then you didn't want to share anymore?"

"Well, I was eleven. It was a bit odd, sharing with my sister."

There had actually never been any reason to share at all. They lived in a big house, five bedrooms. But Imogen had been afraid of the dark and their mother indulged her for years.

"I would have shared with you forever," Imogen was saying. "But Mummy said you needed your own room. You were getting bigger, starting comprehensive school."

He had become relentlessly resentful at having to share with his baby sister for no good reason. Yet he felt guilty when they finally separated. She must have been nine, then. They moved to the farm no more than six months later so the whole thing had been pointless, in the end.

He looked at Imogen. She was looking him dead in the eyes. "Mummy shouldn't have done that," she said.

"Done what?"

"Let us have our own rooms."

"Why not?"

"It wasn't safe."

Before he could say anything, a dull droning erupted like a swarm of insects in his ears. He scrunched up his eyes, waiting for it to pass. When the noise subsided, Imogen was talking.

"Noah? Are you okay? I know it's upsetting. And I know he didn't mean it. It was his replacement. I understand that now."

He held up his hand. "Give me a minute."

But she went on. "After we came here, I thought I'd imagined it. But when we were having the meeting, I saw he'd been replaced again. It all made sense to me."

"Imogen," said Noah. His voice came out a whisper, whereas hers thundered in his ears. "Just stop for a minute, please."

"Then I was looking at the watch and I was thinking how Daddy would send presents, after we moved to the farm. But I didn't go back. Mummy didn't want me to go back. Because she knew, Noah. That's why she brought us here."

He closed his eyes again. He wanted to stand. But he felt his legs wouldn't work if he tried. He placed his palms flat on his thighs, staring at the tiles.

"Imogen," he said. "This is extremely serious."

"Oh, I know," she said. "And Noah, this is why I had to tell you first — I'm going to the police."

"You're what?"

She shook her head. "All these things that have been going on. With the farm and everything. And how you stood up to him, after all these years. I was so proud of you, Noah! I'm going to be brave now like you."

His body turned cold. He stood up, holding on to the table as he moved to the counter.

"Noah?"

"Please, Imogen," he said. "Just be quiet for a minute."

She did as she was told. He stood at the counter, facing away from her, thinking. The room was quiet. He turned everything over. Would the police take such an allegation seriously when she was psychotic? When she was talking about people being replaced and cars taking over the world? Could they process a complaint like this in those circumstances? Maybe they had to? He thought back to his childhood. Wouldn't he have known if something like that had happened in the house he lived in? Hadn't he known it about Stuart's father, sensed it every time he was in that house? But he couldn't deny the possibility. His father was a bully. He manipulated people, including his children. Especially his children. Megan had said once that she thought he was a sociopath. Was it conceivable that he would do this? Either way, he couldn't let Imogen set off a bomb like this — with irreparable consequences — when she was delusional.

"Have you told Aled about this?"

She shook her head. He remembered she'd just said that Aled had been "replaced", which was actually helpful. Noah didn't want her telling Aled this.

"Imogen?" he said, going to her. He knelt on the floor in front of her. "How long have you been thinking about this? Talking to the police, I mean?"

"I decided last night. After you left. I couldn't sleep. I was so relieved to realise I could do this. Be free."

He put his hands on hers. "We need to wait. Just a few days. This is not something you can rush into. There will be very serious consequences. A police investigation. Dad may be arrested, put in prison. If it goes to trial, you will be questioned by a top, top lawyer. They'll tear you to pieces, Imogen. They'll make you look crazy and call you a liar."

"I'm not crazy," she said. "I'm not a liar."

"But that's how they'll make it look. How they'll make you feel. Is that what you want?"

"I want to tell the truth. It will get the demons out of my head."

"Will it? Or will it make things worse?"

"Please, Noah. Don't stop me. If you don't want to come, that's fine. But don't stop me. And please can you drive me there? Or can you ask that officer to come and get me? I can't ask anyone else."

He looked at her. "I'll take you."

"Really?" she said. "Oh, thank you, Noah! Will you stay with me, too?"

"Yes. I'll stay."

* * *

He led Imogen to his truck, opening the passenger door, helping her climb in. Mai raced from the shelter of the work shed, barking like they were intruders.

"Quiet," said Noah. Mai had not been herself today. It was the fog. The haze still hung over the fields, swallowing the lambing shed from view. He nodded for Mai to get in the truck. She hopped on to Imogen's lap, licking her face. Imogen giggled, turning her head.

"Wait here a minute," said Noah.

"Where are you going?" said Imogen, looking out at him.

"I just need to get something. I'll be two minutes."

As he walked to the front door he glanced up at the bedroom window. The curtains were closed. There was no sign of Megan. He should check on her but he didn't want her involved in this. He went back in the house and found a shopping bag in the kitchen drawer. Quietly, he moved around the house, placing items in the bag. He found a blanket in the living room, soft wool with tassels and a floral pattern, and took an unopened box of raisin biscuits from the pantry. He saw Megan's slippers in the hall and put them in the bag, too. Finally, he went to Megan's handbag, slouched open on the hall table, and rummaged for the keys to the cottages.

He went back to the drive, pulling the front door quietly closed behind him. When he got in the driver's seat, Imogen was humming absently to herself, stroking Mai's head.

"I need to drop something at the cottages," he said.

"Now?"

186

"I promised Megan. It won't take long."

The fog persisted beyond the farm, hanging low over the thick trees, obstructing the sweeping view of the village. Noah drove slowly, even on the wide stretch of main road. The visibility wasn't helping his nerves, which were raw. He didn't know what he was doing. Imogen was quiet. Parked on the lane outside Tŷ Gwyn, he turned to her.

"Why don't you come in and see the cottage? Megan has been working on it. I haven't seen myself, yet."

"Do you want me to see it?"

"Of course."

"Oh, then, I'd love to."

She unclicked her seatbelt, unsure what to do with Mai. Noah pulled the dog on to the seat, telling her to stay. It was almost dark, the fog fading from sight in the dying light. Noah went to the boot and got the bag, carrying it with him as he held the gate for Imogen. Finding the keys, he thought of Megan discovering them gone. She was unlikely to notice until tomorrow.

At the door he hesitated, thinking over what he was doing. How was this going to work? He should have woken Megan and discussed the situation. She was good in a crisis. But she might say they had to let Imogen go to the police, and he wasn't ready for that. He was on his own.

Inside Tŷ Gwyn it was cold. He flicked the switch near the door, lighting the cosy entryway. There was a narrow pine table and a jute doormat that he was sure Megan must have installed. The light in the hall was bright and he remembered that Megan had been hunting for bulbs at the farm to replace the missing and broken ones at Tŷ Gwyn.

While he looked for the thermostat, Imogen wandered into the living room, finding the light switch and brightening the low-ceilinged room with more exuberant light. The room was in a state of being worked upon, a bucket full of cleaning products on the floor, a cardboard box on the couch filled with recycling and broken knick-knacks.

"It's lovely, Noah!" exclaimed Imogen, though he wasn't sure what Megan had been doing here.

He stood at the window beside Imogen, looking across the darkening lane at the low shape of the school.

"It is a shame, isn't it?" said Imogen. "It should be a family that lives here. They could send their children to the school. That's one less family using a car to get to school, isn't it? It's not right what we're doing."

Noah went back to the kitchen, inspecting the door to the basement. A long silver-coloured key stood in the lock. Megan had decided to offer the basement as another bedroom. Maybe children would like sleeping down there, she said, like camping. She was planning to remove the key, which she thought gave the impression of the flat being separate. But for now it was still there. Noah turned the key, checking it worked. Imogen came to the kitchen.

"What's that?" she said, looking at the staircase leading down into darkness. Noah stepped through the doorway and flicked the switch on the wall, illuminating the passage with light.

"The people who lived here before had the cellar converted," he said. "Come and see."

He let Imogen go ahead of him down the steep staircase, taking the bag from the hall, and following her. At the bottom they were met with soft carpet and an extravagance of whiteness and mirrors. Megan was right; it was nicer than you expected. It was a studio, essentially. There was a bed — double — with a swirling white metal frame. There were no sheets. A kitchenette ran along the far wall, with a stainless-steel sink, curved tap, neat black microwave and white plastic kettle. It was all basic but the effect was modern and clean. A window overlooked the back garden. This was not a terrible place to leave his sister. It was far nicer — and considerably more private — than the unit she was routinely locked inside.

Still, he felt a heavy sickness in his gut.

"Imogen," he said. "Sit down for me."

She went to the bed, and sat on the bare mattress, staring up at him.

"What is it? Are you okay?"

He sat next to her. "I can't take you to the police station today."

"Why not?"

"I just don't think you're well enough."

"But Noah—"

"Listen to me. I know you think you're well. But you always think that when you're off your meds, don't you? You always think everything is fine. Even when things are really not fine."

"Noah, please."

"I'm not saying I don't believe you. But we need to wait until you're feeling better. And because you're so unwell, I want you to wait here. Just until the morning. I need some time to think. I'm worried about what you'll do if I take you home. Do you understand?"

"You want me to stay here?" She looked around the room. Noah did too. For a horrible moment, the bare whiteness appeared clinical, hospital-like.

"You'll be completely safe and comfortable."

"Can't I just go home?"

"You might talk to Aled about this and end up going to the police. I don't want that to happen. Not while you're in this state."

"But I'm fine."

"You're not fine, Imogen."

"But what if, when I'm feeling better, I don't want to go to the police anymore?"

He looked at her. "Then maybe that will be for the best."

She looked doubtfully at her hands.

"I have another idea," he said. "What if I get your tablets and bring them here later? Then once you've been back on them a few days, we can see how you feel about going to the police?"

She looked at him. "I can't go back on my tablets, Noah."

He sighed.

"They're controlling my brain," she said.

"In a good way, Imogen."

"They make me think things are okay when they're not. They make me numb to everything that's wrong in the world. I can't live like that."

"Imogen — you have to live like that."

"What if the medication makes me think it didn't happen? What if I only remember it when I'm off them?"

He looked at her. "Is that the case? That you only remember it when you're off them?"

She stared at the empty shelves against the wall. "I don't remember."

"Look — this won't be for long. I brought some things for you. Blankets. Food. I'll bring supper for you later."

"Aren't you going to stay with me?"

"I wish I could. But I can't. Megan will wonder where I am."

"Aled's probably wondering where I am, too."

"I know," he said. "Imogen, I need you to give me your phone."

Dutifully, she took it from her pocket and handed it to him.

"Where's your handbag?"

"I left it in the truck."

"Okay," he said. He got up and checked the cupboard above the sink. The glasses worried him. He looked at Imogen again. Maybe later he could stay with her until she went to sleep, if he could think of something to tell Megan. He sat back down on the bed, frightened, unsure of himself. Maybe this was insane. But the alternative seemed worse.

"I wouldn't do this if I didn't have to," he said. "You know that, don't you?"

She nodded. As he shut the door to the basement, he decided against locking it. He couldn't bring himself to lock her in. Anyway, it wasn't necessary. He knew her well enough to know that she would stay there, simply because he had asked her to.

* * *

Back at the farm, Megan was wandering around downstairs, her dressing gown flapping open, long hair unwashed. She still looked pale, but better than she had this morning.

"Who was at the door?" she said.

"When?"

"Earlier. Someone was banging."

"Oh. Delivery driver. Did it wake you?"

"I went back to sleep. I'm so tired, I haven't been able to wake myself up all day! Where did you go just now?"

"Town," he said. "I needed something from the garage."

"Oh," she said, frowning. "Are you okay?"

"Fine. I just need to lie down."

CHAPTER FIFTEEN

Megan

It was seven in the evening and still Thursday, only a day since discovering she was pregnant. Time had slowed like a scene in a film. She'd spent the day in bed. Through the morning she rushed to and from the toilet, Noah downstairs, quietly working through his mass of paperwork. Occasionally he'd brought her tea and tablets. After lunch she fell into a hot sleep, languishing under the duvet, waking panicked to find Noah gone. There had been a strange banging. She had thought she might have dreamed it. Noah had come home, looking anxious and harassed, telling her an unconvincing lie about where he'd been. He was a terrible liar, so flustered within his stillness. He'd gone out again an hour ago, saying he was going to see Iwan. Why was he deceiving her, now, when the night before they'd been open and easy with each other for the first time in months?

Then again, she was still lying to him. Last night had been a perfect chance to tell him about the pregnancy — and the affair — but she couldn't bear to ruin it.

She lay in bed, feeling her body had shut down. Maybe this was nature's way of protecting the baby from the stress of discovering it. Baby. Embryo. Pregnancy. What was she supposed to call it? Was it an embryo or a foetus? She didn't know. There it was, though, a tiny secret planted within her, like the house wrapped in fog. She wanted to stay like this: under the covers in the quiet house, the grey mist at the windows a veil guarding her from the shame. She wanted to let the pregnancy take its course. Maybe it would go away on its own, vanish as unexpectedly as it had come. But there was a small, persistent voice insisting that her options were diminishing, that this would only get harder.

She got out of bed and found her phone, noting, as the screen flashed, that Gethin had not tried to contact her. She opened the browser and searched. She walked to the window, making sure Noah's truck was still gone from the drive. She tapped the number, bringing the phone to her ear. There was an automated message. Music played. She placed the call on speaker and lay the phone on the bed, sitting beside it and staring at the rising seconds on the screen. The music stopped. The call connected. A man was talking. She grabbed the phone, her heart beating wildly. Fumbling, she dropped it on the floor, scrambling to pick it up, and took it off speaker, bringing it to her ear.

"Hello?" the man was saying.

"Sorry!" she cried. "I'm here."

"How can I help?"

His accent was northern Irish, soothing.

"I've found out I'm pregnant."

"Okay," he said lightly. "How can we help?"

"I don't know what to do. I need to talk to someone first, I think."

He knew what she meant by "first" and he took on a delicate tone.

"Do you happen to know how many weeks along you are?"

"More than three, according to the test."

"I understand. What I can do is we can have a quick phone consultation now. When I've taken some more details,

I can book you in for an assessment at one of our clinics, where you can talk through your options and they'll do a scan to determine gestation?"

"That sounds like a good idea."

"You'll be free to speak with one of our counsellors, too. They can't advise you what to do but they can provide information and support."

"Okay."

"What's your postcode there, please?"

* * *

The man got her an appointment in Llandudno the following day. She was relieved not to have to wait through the weekend. However she thought about it, she couldn't see any other option except to terminate. It was almost impossible that the baby was Noah's. Before she met Gethin, they'd been trying for eight years and never conceived, naturally or otherwise. Whereas now, two months into a new relationship, she was pregnant for the first time in her life.

When she woke the next morning, the fog had resumed its original position, stubbornly guarding the house. Getting out of bed, she felt bereft. She reminded herself she was not actually having an abortion. It was an assessment. She didn't have to go ahead with it. But she felt the loss was imminent and beyond her control. No one had actually said she had to get rid of it; no one even knew. But wasn't that what they would say? If she told one of her friends, wouldn't they say: *well, you can't keep it, Megan — it's not Noah's!* Wouldn't Noah say the same thing?

She got dressed with trembling agitation, rattled by the injustice. She didn't want Noah to see her like this, all these violent emotions churning. Hurriedly, she went out to the drive and got in the Land Rover. As she pulled on to the main road she was weepy, her driving erratic. A car honked her at the first roundabout, the driver gesticulating irately as he moved around her. She took a breath and turned on the radio, trying to calm herself down. But it all seemed so deeply unfair. Years of wanting and despair were rising to the surface, stinging her eyes, swelling her throat. Her skin felt scratched and raw. The tiny life swam inside her, oblivious to the calculations that might blot it out like an insect. How could she go through with an abortion? She would never forgive herself.

No one could make her do this. It was her decision. But it didn't feel like it. At the fertility clinic a few years ago, there was a woman on her second cycle of IVF. She told Megan that her stepchild, a jealous ten-year-old boy, was upset with her for wanting a child. "It's none of his business, though," Megan had said. "It's your choice." The woman had looked at her. "You know that's not really true, don't you?"

Megan tried to think clearly now, amid the swamp of feeling and complication. What was the worst thing that would happen, if she kept it? Noah would leave her. He wouldn't raise a child conceived like this. She wouldn't ask him to. His family would despise her, too. People she'd never met would judge and disapprove. None of it was important except losing Noah. That was the choice in front of her.

The drive took her along the coastal road, the sea vast and glittering to her left. Wind turbines looked like they were rising from the crystal water. She thought about Noah. When she came downstairs the evening before, she had wanted to tell him everything. He had always been the person who helped her solve problems, seeing things clearly when she couldn't, defending her interests even when they conflicted with his own. When had that changed? Their long struggle to conceive had exhausted them. But that wasn't the only thing. It was this year when things had really soured. She wondered if it was the cottages that had broken them. Either way, she knew she had done an unforgivable thing, inflicting on Noah the double humiliation of not only cheating but becoming pregnant by it.

At the same time, she wondered if she had somehow pursued this. Not consciously, but deeply and powerfully.

Perhaps her body, better attuned to her needs than her mind, had sought out a man who would give her what she wanted.

* * *

The chairs were low-backed and grey with curved metal legs, making Megan think of giant insects. She felt better in this listless waiting room, temporarily safe from the imagined forces trying to coerce her. There were people here who would help, in spite of what she'd done. They had no personal attachment or interests. Presumably, they kept their moral judgements to themselves. A woman called her name and led her down a speckle-floored corridor into a windowless room. The badge pinned to her midwife uniform said "Samira".

"How are you feeling?"

Wide-hipped with soft skin and full lips, Megan thought Samira was the perfect specimen of how a midwife ought to look. The only problem was her age; surely she had not yet had children.

"I'm fine," said Megan, holding her wild emotions tightly in her chest. Samira seemed to know she wasn't fine, smiling with the restrained empathy of a healthcare professional. Another day, another pregnancy crisis. She gestured for Megan to sit on another insect chair, pushed back against the wall beside a dark-wood desk. Samira sat down at the desk, giving Megan a profile view of her face.

"We'll fill in some paperwork first, okay?"

Megan nodded. Samira picked up a biro with an elegant, manicured hand, her skin warm brown on the back and pale underneath. She didn't wear a wedding ring. Megan reached for her own, twirling the band between her fingers, pushing her thumb against the stone. Samira asked a series of questions about Megan's medical history, marriage, whether she'd been pregnant before, if she'd ever had an abortion. Megan relayed these private details impersonally, as though Samira was not a human but a mediator between Megan and the service being offered. Samira listened with particular attention to Megan's experience of infertility and IVF, writing careful notes, scribbling in the margins.

When the paperwork was complete, Samira lingered, staring at the forms before she pushed herself back from the desk and wandered to the far side of the room. Snapping on blue gloves, she went to the rolling cot bed at the back and pressed a lever. The bed lowered.

"You can lie down now, please."

Megan went to the bed and sat, lifting her legs, lying against the raised head. Feeling suddenly hot, she removed her jumper, putting it behind her neck.

"Should I take off my shoes?"

"No need," said Samira, wheeling over the ultrasound machine, positioning herself on to a stool in front of it. Pausing, she looked down at Megan. "You know how it works? I won't tell you anything about the pregnancy except the number of weeks. You won't see the screen. Lift your top, please."

Megan rolled up her vest.

"Could you roll down your trousers a bit, please?"

Megan folded down the waistband of her leggings, her blue underwear showing.

"A little more, please?"

Megan lifted her bum, lowering the leggings more.

"Cold gel coming now."

Samira held out a grey tube and clenched, leaving a quivering blob on Megan's bare skin. She was right; it was cold. Megan had never had an ultrasound. Even in these awful circumstances, she felt strangely exhilarated. In fact, she did want to know about the pregnancy. She longed to know everything. She wanted the screen facing her, like ultrasounds on television.

Samira picked up the probe, its thick wire uncoiling, and moved it over Megan's belly, spreading the cold slippery gel. As the probe scanned her uterus for signs of life, Samira looked at her. "How many weeks do you think you are?"

Megan didn't know if this was a routine question or Samira making conversation. The Irish man had explained that she could only take the pill if she was under ten weeks. Perhaps Samira was trying to gauge the extent to which Megan was relying on this.

"I don't think I can be more than a few weeks."

Samira glanced at her. "Pregnancy is dated from the first day of your last period."

"Oh," said Megan, remembering that she had told Samira a few moments ago that her last period was around 30 August, two months earlier. This was the date she had come up with the night before, looking through her messages, finding a reference to her period in a text to Imogen. Megan's mind hadn't yet squared the circle but technically, if she hadn't had a period since the end of August, she was closer to eight weeks than three. But how was this possible?

"So I have to be under ten weeks, I can take a pill?"

Samira nodded. "Two pills, forty-eight hours apart. The first is uneventful. The second breaks down the uterus wall and causes it to contract, expelling the pregnancy. There is bleeding, it can be painful. You must ask someone to bring you home."

"Okay," said Megan, unable to imagine who that person might be. Samira was digging the probe hard into her flesh now, as though trying to expel the pregnancy herself. Megan wondered exactly what Samira could see on the screen. She thought of ultrasounds on television, the grainy big-headed foetus swimming in and out of blackness. She closed her eyes, trying to stop thinking. Abruptly, Samira stopped, rattling the probe back into its holder.

"You can get down, now, please."

She handed Megan a wad of paper towel to wipe the sticky gel from her belly. Businesslike, she squirted hand gel into her palm from a dispenser on the wall, rubbing her hands vigorously together, rinsing them at the sink.

Back in their chairs, Samira looked at Megan.

"How are you feeling now?"

"Fine," said Megan. She watched Samira, awaiting the crucial information.

"I can tell you the length of your pregnancy now, if you'd like?"

"Yes. Please."

"From my readings, you are at nine weeks gestation. Nine weeks and two days. I did several measurements, to be sure. They were all the same, and they match when you date your last period—" she glanced at the forms, "30 August."

Megan looked at her. "Nine weeks?"

Samira nodded. Megan thought about the fact she had met Gethin no more than nine weeks earlier, sleeping with him two weeks after that. Though she was vaguely aware how the dating worked, it was hard to get her head round the idea her pregnancy had started before she met the father.

"Explain to me why it's dated from my last period?"

Samira placed her hands together, teacherly. "Think of it like this — when your body started preparing for a pregnancy — getting itself ready to release a new egg — that is how we're dating the start of the baby's life."

Megan registered the word "baby" with hidden shock. Was Samira allowed to call it that at an abortion clinic? She probably hadn't meant to; but it was more powerful, somehow, when a professional uttered the word. Now it rang in Megan's ears.

"So when was the pregnancy conceived?" said Megan.

"About two weeks later. When you were ovulating."

That took her to the day she and Gethin had been together in his car. If Samira was right, she and Gethin had conceived a child the first time they'd had sex. She had been pregnant for the entirety of their affair. She didn't know what to make of this, except she felt someone was playing a series of cruel jokes.

"Is there any way it could have been conceived later?"

"It's possible," said Samira. "But ultrasounds are very accurate. And, of course, your period."

Megan nodded. The evidence was fairly incontrovertible but Samira impressed it calmly, perhaps accustomed to the stupidity and denial that accompanied unplanned pregnancies.

"Nine weeks," said Megan. "That's nearly a trimester. Can I still have the abortion pill?"

"The cut-off is nine weeks and six days. So it depends how soon we can get you an appointment."

"What happens if you can't find one in time?"

"I will try hard. The other option, up to fourteen weeks gestation, is vacuum aspiration."

"What's that?" said Megan, not liking the sound of it.

"It's gentle suction that removes the pregnancy from the uterus. You have local anaesthetic. No need for putting you to sleep."

Samira said this like it was a good thing. But Megan did not want to be awake while a machine sucked an embryo from her uterus.

"Can I ask you something?"

"Please," said Samira.

"What does a nine-week pregnancy look like?"

Samira made a small gap between her thumb and forefinger.

"That's tiny," said Megan. The smallness made it worse, somehow.

"Two and a half centimetres," said Samira. "The size of a strawberry."

"What does it look like?"

"It's still an embryo. Organs are developing. Head is forming. It has hands and feet. No fingers or toes."

* * *

She didn't wait to see the counsellor. It wasn't going to help. She had all the information she needed — nine weeks, strawberry-sized, vacuum aspiration, no fingers or toes. What was the counsellor going to do? Predict Noah's reaction? Help her decide whether a baby was worth her marriage?

200

She got home in the early afternoon, utterly shattered, lacking motivation to do anything but collapse into bed. She turned on the television, letting the sounds drift over her as she slipped into sleep.

* * *

She was woken by the doorbell, opening her eyes painfully, unable to place herself in time. She went downstairs, clutching her dressing gown. Aled was at the door, his face drained and stricken.

"What is it?"

"Imogen," he said. "She's gone."

"Oh, Aled. Let me get Noah." She glanced beyond Aled's slouched figure at Noah's truck on the drive. "He must be outside. I'll find him. Sorry. I just woke up."

"Oh," said Aled. "Right. Sorry to turn up like this. I tried ringing him but—"

"Don't apologise. We'll sort it out." She looked at him as she pulled on her wellies. "How long has she been gone?"

"Since last night. I've been out looking all day. I need to ring the police, I think. I wanted to talk to Noah first."

Since last night? Why had he waited this long to tell them? As she hurried down the track, she shouted back to him, "You go inside, Al! I'll be two minutes!"

She didn't know why she was running. Imogen had been missing for nearly a day. She found Noah in the shed, crouched behind a ram, his hand between its hind legs.

"Aled is here."

He glanced up, taking in her white towelling dressing gown, wellies pulled hastily over her bare legs. "Yeah," he muttered. "He's been ringing me."

"Why haven't you answered?"

"I've been busy."

"Imogen is missing."

He nodded. "Yeah."

"What do you mean 'yeah'?"

"I guessed. How long?"

"Since yesterday. If you guessed, why haven't you spoken with him? Come and see him, Noah. He's waiting!"

He sighed and pushed himself up, giving the ram a comradely pat on its back and brushing his hands over his trousers.

When they got back to the house, Aled was still on the drive, the front door hanging open.

"Didn't you invite him in?" said Noah.

"Of course I did!" she hissed.

When they reached the door, Noah gave Aled a sympathetic pat, as he had with the ram.

"Come in, mate," he said, bending down to untie his boots.

They went to the kitchen. Noah washed his hands at the sink, pumping out handfuls of liquid soap, scrubbing between his fingers. Megan felt starving. Having been sick all day yesterday, she hadn't eaten breakfast today, either, too upset before she left for the clinic. She thought protectively of the pregnancy, how she needed to eat if she wanted to sustain it. Whatever her mind told her, she couldn't help acting as though she was keeping this child.

Either way, she didn't want to start making food in front of Aled. For now, she made a pot of tea and looked for biscuits in the pantry.

Noah and Aled were at the kitchen table, opposite one other.

"Well, you were right," said Aled. "I should have contacted the unit. Now she's gone. I blame myself. I didn't think we would be here again so soon."

"It's not your fault," said Noah.

"The strange thing is, she hasn't taken her car. Unless she called a cab or someone came to get her, she must have gone on foot. I've been driving around near the house. How far could she have gone without a car? She's been gone all night."

"That is strange," said Noah. "And worrying."

"Where's Hari?" said Megan. She had a vague inkling that it was autumn half-term.

"He's with my mother. I took him there this morning, when Imogen still hadn't come home."

"She was here yesterday," said Noah.

Megan stared at him.

"When?" said Aled.

"Around teatime. She'd walked."

Megan watched Noah from the counter, wondering why he hadn't mentioned it. Then she remembered the strange banging, Noah saying it was a delivery driver. Had it been Imogen? In which case, why had Noah lied?

"What did she want?" said Aled.

"She was manic. Talking nonsense. I offered to drive her home. She said walking back would clear her head. I assumed she came home. Sorry. I should have rung you."

Aled sighed.

"You can't blame yourself, either," he said, though he looked a little annoyed.

Megan looked at Noah again. If Imogen was psychotic and had walked here alone, in the fog — why hadn't Noah insisted on driving her back? In Megan's experience, the one person who could influence Imogen, whatever her mental state, was Noah.

"Should we call the police?" said Megan.

Noah looked at her. "It's only been twenty-four hours."

"It doesn't hurt to report it now, though, does it? And isn't it different with Imogen? Won't they look for her straight away, because she's classed as vulnerable? I thought they told us that?"

Aled nodded. "That's right."

Noah shrugged. He seemed detached, Megan thought, almost indifferent. She couldn't blame him. This had happened so many times now, maybe he was becoming immune.

* * *

Before she left the clinic earlier, Samira had told Megan to ring them today if she wanted to get an appointment for the tablet abortion. She mustn't leave it until Monday. It was nearly six o'clock now. Their phone line was open until eight. She knew her window was rapidly narrowing. But she couldn't make this decision alone. Noah and Aled were out looking for Imogen. She'd told them she would do the same but instead she got in the Land Rover and drove towards town. It was raining, her wipers hectically clearing water. Dark had fallen, the tall lamps of the bypass flashing bleary white light. The yellow headlights of the oncoming cars were smudged. She turned into Gethin's road and parked, staring at the blurry red door. They hadn't spoken since that awful fight, three nights earlier. In the interim, she'd had the family meeting, discovered she was pregnant and been to an abortion clinic. Imogen had gone missing. She wondered what Gethin had been doing. Teaching classes. Going to the pub. Living his normal, uncomplicated life.

She'd made no effort whatsoever with her appearance and looked abysmal from two sleepless nights, pregnancy sickness, the intolerable stress of everything. She didn't care. If such concerns had not evaporated with the fight, they certainly had with everything since. Life was happening now. Was Gethin mature enough for it? She didn't think so. She didn't want a child with him, anyway. She would never have chosen him for this. She wanted Noah. But she couldn't have it with Noah. Her mind had run through this a hundred times, as though, if she thought about it hard enough, she might find a way to change the fundamentals.

She was certain that, left to his own devices, she would never have heard from Gethin again. But she hadn't texted him before coming here. The thought of asking his permission to see him just made her angry.

She got out of her car and climbed the steps to the terrace, ringing the bell.

"What are you doing here?" he said, peering round the door. He kept it close to his body, as though hiding himself.

"That's nice," she said.

He smiled, not warmly. "I wasn't expecting you."

"Why would you be? Can I come in?"

"It's not a good time."

"Are you still upset about that silly fight? I have something more important to talk to you about."

He shifted his weight, glancing back over his shoulder.

"Oh God," she said. "You've got a woman here."

This hadn't occurred to her. But that was how he was acting. Why wouldn't he? He was young, they'd broken up, it was a Friday night.

"It's not that," he said. "But I am in the middle of something."

"What can you be in the middle of that means I have to stand out here in the rain?"

He didn't say anything. She felt suddenly furious.

"Forget it," she said. "You're a bloody child."

She turned on her heel and stalked back down the steps, outraged that he was sending her away from his home for the second time in a week?

"Hold on," she heard him shout. He came after her. "Okay," he said, catching up. "You can come in."

"Oh, don't do me any favours!"

He took her arm roughly, turning her round to face him. "Will you just give me five minutes? To deal with something? Can you just do that?"

He sounded a little crazy, she thought. He wasn't wearing shoes, standing on the street in his socks as rainwater ran along the ground. She nodded, walking back with him to the house, waiting at the door while he disappeared inside. She couldn't imagine what was so secret and important that she had to stand on the street in the dark, rain wetting her head. When he opened the door again, he stood back, letting her in. She hadn't come here for sex but the minute she walked in he was taking her coat, his hot breath on the back of her neck. Her nipples were stiff from the cold when he brushed his fingertips over them. But it wasn't the same between them. The urgency coming from him had little to do with her. It was in his state of mind, dark and frantic as he pulled off her clothes and groped her body. When he tried to push inside her, she clenched.

"What's wrong?" he said.

"Nothing."

"What is it?"

"Don't worry about it."

He pushed himself off and lay on his back. He wasn't one of those men turned on by a woman not wanting it. She looked at him, arm flopped against his forehead, panting gently. In the quiet intimacy of his bedroom, it was fleetingly the right time to say it. She could tell him the whole thing. Maybe, if she was lucky, he would prioritise her situation, understand the severity of it, what was at stake for her. But how likely was that? What if, instead, he wanted the baby? What if he wanted her to leave Noah and be with him? Worse, what if he insisted she have an abortion? Or what if he didn't care, either way? That might have been the best thing for everyone, but it would make her feel more worthless than she already did.

"What were you doing earlier?" she said.

"Nothing."

"So secretive."

She meant it playfully but it came out like she was angry. Maybe she was. He was angry, too. And far away from her. Rain splashed the window. The room was cold. There were shadows around them, moving against the wall. She wanted to go home.

CHAPTER SIXTEEN

Noah

Imogen had been in the basement of Tŷ Gwyn for twenty-four hours. This was the last thing Noah had intended. Last night — a couple of hours after first taking her there — he'd gone back and lain with her on the sheetless bed, watching a sitcom together on his tablet. He stayed until she slept, guarding her like a parent as her breathing became rasping and deep. He turned off the lights as he left, leaving the basement door unlocked again. He set the heating timer, ensuring it would come on early, and pulled the front door of the house closed behind him.

He'd returned early this morning, taking fresh coffee and croissants from the bakery. He'd planned to take her home then, naively hoping her plan to go to the police would be forgotten, or her resolve weakened. But when he'd got to Tŷ Gwyn, she was even more adamant. He'd tried to persuade her again that it was a terrible idea, that she needed to be in her right mind before going ahead with something like this. But she had insisted, with even stronger conviction, that she was most reliable — most authentically herself — when free from the distorting effect of her medication. She had to do this now. She was so passionate as to be almost convincing; until Noah reminded himself of the nonsense and delusions, the fact she still believed Aled and their father to be replacements, and all the rest of it.

They had the same argument at lunchtime, when he took her sandwiches and fresh milk. He became tired and distressed by the repetition, her stubbornness and refusal to listen. At the same time, he was questioning his own motives and state of mind, wondering if he was being hysterical and controlling rather than cautious and caring. One minute he would decide this had gone on long enough, that he needed to take her home and let things unravel. Then he would change his mind, thinking about the alternative, deciding, for the hundredth time, to keep going. The more he thought about it, the more it wasn't his father he cared about but Imogen herself. Even if what she was saying was true, she had no idea what she was letting herself in for. He had heard how these things went. Police officers who belittled and disbelieved victims. Defence lawyers whose sole job was to publicly eviscerate them in the witness box. If what she was saying was true, maybe he had to let her endure all this. She was a grown woman, it had to be her decision. But letting her set that in motion if it wasn't true? That seemed to him like another thing entirely, not least because, if it was false, she was all the more likely to be humiliated and destroyed.

He needed to protect her from herself. Aled and Megan would not understand this. As soon as you said the word "abuse", people lost their reason. He had seen it for himself with Stuart's father. Noah had to be the one thinking clearly. If he just kept a lid on things a little longer, there was a good chance she would run out of steam. This had happened before. When she was a student — only a year or so before she was diagnosed, when her symptoms were getting harder to ignore — she got it in her head that her professor was trying to kill her. She went to see Noah, asking him to come with her to the police. Noah persuaded her to stay for a few days, go back when she was feeling better. By the time she left, she had forgotten all about it. The professor didn't kill her. The world went back to how it was. Noah wanted to give this a chance to happen again.

But everything was getting out of hand. The police were involved, looking for her, posting appeals on social media. Aled was driving around in the rain, his mother watching Hari, who must know by now that Imogen was missing again. Megan was out looking, too. He had told both of them that he was doing the same. Instead, he was taking her tea, having collected fish and chips from town, jittery the entire time that someone would see him. Word was bound to be spreading already that Imogen was missing again. By tomorrow, the whole village would know.

The chips were on the passenger seat, sweltering in fat-stained paper. His truck smelled of vinegar. He'd had to get chips because the electric cooker at Tŷ Gwyn wasn't working. But Imogen liked fish and chips, anyway; it was a treat. He couldn't leave his truck outside the cottage in case someone noticed it. So he parked at the pub, instead. He could say he'd gone in to ask if anyone had seen anything. Did it matter that he hadn't actually gone inside? He was second-guessing everything he did.

He tried to remind himself that he wasn't committing a crime. He hadn't forced Imogen to stay at the cottage. He had persuaded her. It wasn't a crime to persuade someone to stay in a certain place, if you believed it was better for them, was it? Even if they were classed as vulnerable. People did this all the time, didn't they? When someone was drunk and wanting to do something foolish, you got them in bed and out of the way until they slept it off. Sometimes you had to protect people from themselves. Noah had spent his life protecting Imogen. This was just an extreme version. It wasn't like he was doing this for himself. In fact, it would probably have benefitted him if his father was being criminally investigated, a fact that had crossed his mind more than once.

This wasn't about him. He was trying to help.

So why did he feel so guilty?

It was pitch dark on the lane, the lights from the pub glowing yellow through its tall sash windows. The school was a huddled shape opposite, the playground black with shadow. The cottages at the top of the row exhibited light, signs of life, while the three at the bottom, belonging to the Robinsons, stood empty and dark. You couldn't see the basement from the front of Tŷ Gwyn. Imogen's studio was only visible from the back garden. And you could only get to the garden through the house.

Every time he came to see her, he was tense, imagining she'd vanished and gone missing in reality or, perhaps worse, gone home and told Aled where she'd been, what Noah had done. He imagined her breaking a glass above the sink, finding her covered in blood. Or that she'd removed the pull from the blind, which was surely too thin to hold her weight, but still. These things were always a risk with Imogen. The only difference now was that everyone would blame him. If she hurt herself in these circumstances, people would say she'd done it because he was keeping her there, that she'd been isolated and scared. They would be wrong. She was not distressed by this voluntary confinement. In fact, Noah had probably given her more quality, focused attention in the last twenty-four hours than in their adult lives to date. Certainly it was no worse than what the doctors did to his sister as a matter of routine. He wasn't a medical professional, but he knew he cared about her more than they did.

While he turned all this over, he knew for sure that either tonight or, at the very latest, tomorrow morning, he would have to take her home. If she still wanted to go to the police at that point, he would have to let her. There was nothing else he could do. And whichever way he thought about it, he knew he would have to tell Aled and Megan.

* * *

The cottage was deathly quiet. But at least it was warm as he walked through the dark rooms clasping the handles of the carrier bag emitting the wet heat of fish and chips. He turned the handle to the basement, looking down the steep staircase. At the bottom it was dark.

"Imogen?"

There was silence. Then he heard her voice from below. "Noah? Is it you?"

He sighed in relief, turning on the light on the stairs, walking down. "It's me."

At the bottom he stepped on to the soft carpet, looking around. The light escaping from the stairs, combined with the moonlight through the window at the back of the basement room, illuminated the scene. Imogen had taken the blanket from the bed and draped it to create a den. She had used the base of the swinging mirror to fix one end to the dressing table, draping the other end generously over the back of the rocking chair.

At the entrance to the den she sat, crossed-legged, a second blanket covering her shoulders.

"What are you doing, Imogen?"

She put her finger to her lips. "Someone is out there." She was whispering, wide-eyed. She pointed at the window. He felt a chill.

"What?" he said. "Who?"

He went to the glass and looked out at the sloping grass, the black sky punctured by the full white moon.

"Who is out there, Imogen?" he said again.

She beckoned him to the den. He walked back to her, crouching down, looking her in the eye. She sat unmoving under the sagging roof of the shelter, her eyes wide with vacant wonder, perhaps a little fear.

"Did you actually see someone?" he said.

"Shh!" she hissed. "They'll hear us."

"There's no one out there."

She looked at him. "Noah. You have to take me to the police now."

"It's too late now."

"What?"

"Too late in the evening, I mean."

"Oh." She frowned. "Which day is tomorrow?"

"Saturday."

She nodded. "Saturday. So we'll go tomorrow?"

He sighed. "Imogen. We've been over this. Don't you remember everything we've discussed? You need to go back on your medication. Then I'll take you."

"I'm not going to change my mind," she said.

"Okay. Well, let's just see how you are tomorrow."

"Is Hari okay? Does he miss me?"

"Of course he does," said Noah.

"I miss him."

"I know. Are you hungry?"

She nodded. They ate in the den, pulling apart the battered fish with their fingers.

"Did you get it from the place by the castle?" said Imogen.

Noah looked at her. "That closed down, remember?"

She nodded. "I think you're right."

They were silent, eating their chips.

"Noah?" she said.

"Mm."

"I think Daddy should give these cottages back to the village."

"How would he do that?" said Noah.

"Sell them to people who will live in them," she said.

"He's not going to do that."

"We're never going to be free, are we?"

"Free from what?"

She stared over at the window. He opened his mouth to ask her again but her finger flew to her lips. "Shh! Did you hear it then?"

"There's nothing there, Imogen."

He looked at her, thinking about the noises he'd been hearing outside the window at the farm. Maybe he and Imogen were more similar than he thought.

"There was definitely someone out there earlier," she said.

* * *

212

He left her for a second night, manic and alone, phantom noises outside the window. As he drove up the track to the farm, the sky big and dark above him, he had a stark image of himself as one of the monstrous men he had known, heard of, read about. A sociopath, like his father; maybe it was in his blood. The image came with such clarity that he stopped the truck dead, bringing his hands together at the top of the wheel. He saw himself how others might if they knew about this, a callous man keeping his mentally ill sister in a basement to protect his abusive father. He heard himself explaining how it was for her own good. The justification bounced back, hollow and unconvincing.

Then he thought again about the alternative — letting her take this to the police, blow up her life and their father's over what might be nothing more than a delusion. Tomorrow he would have to let her do that. But at least he would have tried to contain it. He would tell Aled, and Megan, that he had done what he thought was right. They would have to make their peace with it, whatever they thought of him. Maybe — and this was his only consolation when he thought about taking her home in the morning — he could convince Aled that Imogen shouldn't be allowed to go to the police until she was back on her tablets. Between them, they might be able to make sure of this, even if they had to threaten to have her sectioned again.

Megan's car was on the drive, lights on in the kitchen and hall. As he took off his boots and wandered the house, he thought about the routines of marriage, ingrained even at times of bitter distance and crisis. His future with Megan was more uncertain than he could remember. It was possible they wouldn't survive this. Maybe she was going to leave him. If she didn't, it was possible he couldn't forgive what she'd done. In spite of all that, he still looked for her when he came through the door.

He found her sitting up in bed, duvet over her legs, staring at the television screen. Her bedside lamp was on and her face looked puffy, like she'd been crying.

"Here you are," he said.

"Here I am," she said.

Her phone was face down on the bedside table. She had an air of detachment as she stared at one of the sitcoms she streamed when she was feeling sorry for herself. The characters moved on the screen, expressive and physical in their comedy, the laughter of the audience echoing. Megan glanced over at him.

"I'm going to go back out and look again soon," she said defensively. "I just need a break."

"I would leave it to the police, to be honest. We're not going to find her driving around in the dark."

She shrugged. "You never know." She looked at him again. "Where do you think she is?"

He sighed. "I really don't know."

He hated lying to her, especially about this. It made him feel as worthless as he could imagine, letting his wife fear that his mentally ill sister might be dead in a ditch when he knew perfectly well she was safe.

"Megan?" he said.

She looked at him. "What?"

"Doesn't matter."

She looked back at the television, not bothering to press him.

"Have you eaten?" he said. He had brought her some fish and chips, too, though he had the problem of explaining why he'd eaten his, and why hers were cold.

"I'm not hungry," she said.

He turned to walk out of the room.

"The police were here," she called after him.

He turned back, holding the door frame. "When?"

"Twenty minutes ago?"

His heart jumped. He pictured officers at the farm, asking about Imogen while he was at the cottage with her a mile away.

"What did they want?" he said.

"They want to speak to you."

"Why?"

She frowned. "What do you mean 'why'? You were the last person to see her."

"So?"

"So they want to ask you how she seemed and everything. Don't be dim, Noah."

"I really don't remember much."

She shrugged, looking back at the screen. "Just tell them what you can."

He walked out of the room.

"So are you going to ring them?" she said.

He went back, put his head round the door. "Do you think I should do it now?"

"Yes!" she said. "Why wouldn't you?"

It was a fair point. If Imogen was actually missing, out alone in the dark and cold and rain of early November, and had been for over twenty-four hours, wouldn't he try to help the police as urgently as he could? He needed to act as though this was really happening — and not just because of how it looked to Megan.

"You're right," he said. "I'll do it now." He paused. "Why are you in bed, anyway?"

"I don't feel well."

"The tummy thing still?"

"Something like that."

* * *

He tried to think back to how he had behaved when his sister was missing in the past. Had he been frantic, frightened? Somehow he couldn't remember. He wanted to get his tone right with the police. Even if telling her to stay in the flat wasn't a crime itself, he was pretty sure that wasting police time by reporting someone missing, when he knew where she was all along, was not something they'd be pleased about. But as he took his mobile from his pocket, he was sickened by the thought of it. What if his voice gave him away? What if he said something incriminating? What if they already knew? Wasn't it possible someone had seen him taking her into the cottage yesterday? What if this was what they actually wanted to talk to him about, and were looking to catch him out by pretending they didn't know?

Something else occurred to him, then — wouldn't the police search the cottages? Given they were Robinson property, and given Imogen had supposedly gone missing on foot, wouldn't they wonder if she might be hiding there? What if they were there now, had passed right by him as he came back to the farm? What if Imogen was in the process of telling them he had taken her there, told her she had to stay there? Should he go back?

And if they weren't there, shouldn't he just send her home now, anyway? This had become too much of a risk, too many people involved. He couldn't cope with all this lying and deceit. He felt ill from the stress of it. But even if he did take her home now — and he hadn't thought of this until now either — wouldn't the police want to speak with her? Once Aled told them she was home, wouldn't they come to check she was okay? And what if she told them she'd been at the cottage, that Noah had been with her, that he had encouraged her to stay there and let his brother-in-law report her missing? She would tell them the whole thing innocently, not even considering that it could get him in trouble.

With his thoughts in turmoil, he felt a sudden loosening of his bowels. He rushed to the toilet, emptying them. After washing his hands and splashing cold water on his face, he gripped the sink, trying to catch his breath. He felt a lightness all through him, a gaping black hole all around him. He felt utterly alone. In the mirror above the sink he looked drained and sick. His forehead shone with sweat. He didn't know how to calm down. Out of nowhere he remembered how his mother used to sit cross-legged on the floor of the living room, breathing deeply through her nose, her shoulders rising like bread. He did the same, sitting on the cold tiles of the locked bathroom, breathing air into his lungs, puffing it out through his mouth. He felt idiotic. But it was working, bringing him slowly down from his towering fear.

Once he was calmer, he called the police, speaking to an officer he didn't know. After all, they just wanted to ask how Imogen had been when he saw her, if there were particular places she might have gone. Noah tried to answer clear-headedly, aware of what he was omitting, how he was lying with every word. He felt his panic rising again, desperate for the call to end. When it did, it was almost ten. He knew he would not sleep. He thought about going back to the cottages. Even if he didn't take her home, he could stay with her for the night. He might feel better if he was actually with her. And wouldn't it look better, if the police did come? If he was with her, rather than having left her there alone again?

But what would he tell Megan?

Maybe he should just take Imogen home. But he couldn't take her now, late in the evening. It was better to wait until the morning. Everyone would handle it better in the light of day. Plus, it gave him one more chance to talk her out of going to the police in this state, another night's sleep after which she might have changed her mind. Imogen's illness was prone to sudden change. One night could be transformative. She might wake up feeling entirely differently about this, or with a new delusion or obsession. If so, this whole terrible ordeal might have been worth it.

* * *

He went to the bedroom to check on Megan. She was asleep, turned to face the wall, knees bent. He decided to go outside. The evaporated fog had left a sheen of wet on the fields. He walked up the track. The ewes were all around, most of them asleep. After two days of fog, the sky appeared majestically clear. The moon hung, white and luminous against the blue-black of the night. The clouds were thin and high, passing wispily over its bright face. Noah stood at the top of the track, looking up at the sky then down across the fields and the dark mountains. Behind him, the invisible owl hooted. Apart from that it was quiet, the wind still, nothing to disturb the silence of the land.

He thought about his mother. Working the farm together, they had developed certain routines, like having a break mid-morning to sit on the low crumbled wall under the oak, looking down at the woods and lake. They had done this every morning for years. The day after she died, he made sure to sit on that wall again, knowing that if he stopped for even a day, he may never do it again. Thinking of his mother brought him back to his sister, and he thought of the two of them, mother and daughter. It was a different relationship to his own with his mother. Though she doted on them both, she saw Noah as the capable one. Long before Imogen was diagnosed, Joan had understood her vulnerability and strived to protect her, relying on Noah to help. Thinking about his mother's protectiveness, guilt tunnelled through him. What would she think about this? When she was dying, even as the powerful drugs treating her cancer made her delirious, she told him, unambiguously, that she needed him to look after his sister once she was gone.

His mother had been naive to think he could maintain his paternal position indefinitely. Noah had always known that if Imogen got married, or settled into any serious, long-term relationship, his role in her life would naturally diminish. Then again, Aled had never really resented his involvement. Though they sometimes, at certain points of crisis, exchanged harsh words, Aled generally welcomed Noah's support, finding things overwhelming on his own.

Noah walked further up and sat on the wall, under the wide branches of the tree. During all of this, he had tried hard not to think about Imogen's allegations. Given he could not know for sure either way whether what she was saying was true, he had felt it best not to think about it, to focus instead on delaying her complaint until she was more lucid. But maybe he should have been thinking about it, maybe he owed Imogen that. He looked up at the sky through the branches of the oak. The longer he stared, the more stars transpired, until there seemed to be thousands, multiplying across the deep blue. Then a coldness passed through him. To his left he heard a scuttling, a creature scrambling at the foot of the tree and vanishing in the grass.

* * *

When he got back to the house, it was close to midnight. He didn't go to the bedroom. Instead, he took a thick blanket from the window bench and lay on the couch, trying to reconcile himself with the strong possibility that Imogen would not have changed her mind by the morning. He imagined the police at his father's house, looking through his things. He thought about how everyone in the town where his father still lived would know about it, as they had with Stuart's father. People would decide for themselves. The truth wouldn't matter. It mattered to Noah. But each time his mind brushed against the possibility, he could not contemplate it. He couldn't make room in his head for the idea that he — a selfish, petulant eleven-year-old boy — had worn his mother down asking for his own bedroom, leaving his sister to fend for herself against the most monstrous thing imaginable. How could he live with that, if it turned out to be true?

A square of moonlight illuminated the rug and something else came to him. His father's letter; his mother's accusation. He was amazed he hadn't thought of this until now. But as he lay there, he wondered for the first time if this was what she had been referring to. Was it the reason his father had bought the farm, after denying it to his mother for so long? Why had it all happened so quickly, his mother leaving her job, tearing the children so abruptly from their friends and school? Why had his father stayed behind, allowing them to live here without him? Had his mother told him that unless he did what she asked she would ruin him? It would have been characteristically pragmatic, removing his sister from the situation while using the circumstances to negotiate what the three of them needed.

* * *

At some point he fell asleep, facing away from the stretching moonlight, exhausted from turning everything over in his head. He was woken by Megan, shaking him awake. Groggily, he opened his eyes, aware of the darkness still outside the windows. He felt a stab of fury, being woken after so little sleep.

"What?" he said, his voice slurred.

"Noah," she said.

Her tone irritated him — so serious. He didn't want to know. Whatever was wrong felt distant enough that he could ignore it. He turned away from her, closing his eyes. But she turned on the lamp, leaning across him, her hand on his shoulder. He looked back at her, squinting in the painful light. Her face was stricken, her T-shirt flapping away from her body.

"What is it?" he said.

She had a strange look on her face, one of shock and fear but resignation, too, like she knew this would happen in the end.

"Is it Imogen?" he said.

"No," she said. "Come on. We have to go."

* * *

The village was only a mile away but the drive was surreally, painfully slow. He wanted to tell Megan to hurry, drive quicker, but looking at the dashboard, she wasn't driving as slowly as he thought. Anyway, he couldn't speak. All he could do was stare ahead at the moving lights of the Land Rover, cutting through the dark.

"I knew something like this would happen," she muttered.

He didn't reply.

"At least it wasn't the farm," she said. "At least no one has been hurt."

Still, he didn't reply.

* * *

As they approached the village, he felt himself turn cold, his fear blacker than the night. He could see the smoke billowing in the sky ahead. As they descended the hill, he saw the commotion. Fire engines blocked the lane, police cars, an ambulance. There were people in the street, a crowd gathered beyond the hectic blockade of emergency vehicles and rushing fire fighters. He had not asked Megan which cottage it was. Somehow, he had known. And there it was, right in front of them. Tŷ Gwyn was ablaze, hot orange flames strutting in the moonlight. On one side of the cottage, the fire had been extinguished, leaving a charred frame. The moon hung above, the trees in the back garden silhouetted through the burned hollow. Firefighters pummelled the lingering flames, which looked wild and hungry to spread. He couldn't believe the number of people, the thick crowd of villagers and emergency services, like a scene of urban mayhem.

"Why is there an ambulance?" said Megan. "Is that just in case?"

She looked across at him in alarm. He stared ahead, eyes fixed on the cottage. Megan slowed the Land Rover, searching for somewhere to leave the car given the chaos ahead. He couldn't wait. He tugged the handle, door opening, car still moving.

"Noah!" Megan shouted.

He stumbled on to the road, falling to the ground then scrambling to his feet, running towards the fire. As he hit

221

the back of the crowd, he shoved through the immobile bodies. He ignored the muffled shouts of indignation, the wild, angry looks, as he pushed past. The hoses were deafening. Scrambling over the front wall of Tŷ Gwyn, he burst into the blackened house, flinging his arm to his mouth as the smoke hit his lungs. The house had been transformed by the fire, internal walls burned to the ground, furnishings scorched. The heat was incredible. As he tried to get his bearings, work out how to get to the basement, a pair of hands fell heavily on his shoulders, a deep murmuring in his ears. He pushed himself forward but he was being dragged back by a stronger man, arms flailing as the backs of his shoes scraped the ground. He was dropped on to the front wall, his backside hitting the cold stone. His legs spasmed.

He looked up at the rough face of a fire fighter.

"My sister is in there!" Noah shouted.

The man held him down harder. "No one is in there now," he said.

Noah looked up. "Did they get her out? Where is she?"

The officer stared down at him, eyebrows crumpled, face dripping with sweat beneath his helmet.

* * *

It might have been many minutes or only a few seconds later when Noah tried to stand again. The fireman re-established his grip on his shoulders, holding him down.

"I'm not going to go in again," Noah shouted, smacking his tongue against the roof of his dry mouth. "I need to find my wife. Please!"

The man hesitated then let him go, watching as Noah swung his shaking legs over the wall and stumbled back through the crowd. He went towards the school, the playground quiet and empty beside the nearby chaos of the lane. There was a ringing in his ears as he wandered through the open gates. The noise flattened, turning to a dull hum. He moved towards the railing and held on to the cold metal, lowering himself to the ground.

He hadn't heard her footsteps but Megan was there now, moving close as he crouched against the hard metallic rail. His head seemed to be swishing around, full of liquid. He closed his eyes, noting before he did that Megan's mouth was moving. He couldn't hear anything she was saying, though it was quiet in the yard.

He opened his eyes again, looking up at Megan. His hearing returned in a rush of sound.

"Noah!" she was saying, shouting in his face as though he'd gone deaf. "They're saying someone was in the cottage. I don't understand! Why would there be? Who was it?"

Vomit surged up from within him, pushing him violently forward to spatter the ground between his knees.

"Oh God! Noah? Are you okay? What is happening?"

He edged away from the vomit, crouching against the rail, clinging to the metal.

"It's Imogen," he said.

She moved round, bending down to face him. "What did you say?"

He closed his eyes again. "I said, it's Imogen!"

CHAPTER SEVENTEEN

Megan

She led him back to her car, his body a dead weight, his movements stumbling and uncoordinated. He stopped now and then, saying he wanted to lie down where he was on the cold concrete ground.

"No," she said. "We're going to the car."

She couldn't think straight with the commotion around them. Besides, it was cold, barely sunrise on an early November morning. Last night's rain had given way to a fierce overnight wind, circling them now, gusts of cold air whipping up the leaves and twigs at the foot of the school yard. She had only a coat on over her nightie, her sockless feet shoved inside wellies, and felt the wind moving around her bare legs, long T-shirt flapping.

This — fourth of November, the day before Bonfire Night — would be remembered, when the rushing events had gained clarity and order, as the day Imogen died. For now, Megan could not believe it. Though a police officer had told her that a dead woman had been recovered from the basement of Tŷ Gwyn, taken in the ambulance to the mortuary, and while Noah seemed certain this was Imogen, the story refused to settle. Why was she down there? How had she got in? Only Megan had a key to Tŷ Gwyn. And if Noah had known she was there, why hadn't he told anyone, including her?

She settled Noah in the car, slumping him against the passenger seat, and went round to the other side, climbing in behind the steering wheel. She pulled the door closed, shutting out the blowing cold, encasing them in stillness. The wind groaned outside, lifting scattered leaves fallen from the late autumn trees. Fewer than a hundred yards down the lane, the cottage still burned on one side, smoke rushing across the face of the moon. Distantly, she could hear the thud of hose water.

She was cold, her feet stiff inside her wellies. She started the engine and turned on the heating, warm air building slowly in the vents. She looked at Noah. There was enough light from the strong moon and the flames ahead to see that his face was stricken, his eyes disturbed within the familiar frame of his face. Beyond him, a low field gate revealed rolling farmland, sheep huddled in shadow. A tentative early light emerged in the sky beyond, pushing against the authority of the moon. In his lap, Noah's hands trembled gently, the only movement from the limp frame of his body.

"Is she definitely dead?" he said.

His voice was high and strange. Megan looked steadily at him.

"A police officer told me they recovered a body. A woman. Dead. I haven't seen her, though, so I don't think we can be sure it's her?"

"It's her," said Noah.

"How do you know?"

He didn't say anything.

"Noah — I need you to tell me what's going on."

He brought his fingertips to his forehead, closing his eyes.

"She was in the basement," he said.

"Why?"

"I took her there."

225

She stared at him. "What do you mean?"

"Megan," he said, "I can't do this now."

"But the police are going to ask me why she was there. I was in charge of the cottages — I had the keys. What am I going to say?"

"I don't know," he said. "Oh my God, Megan. This can't be happening."

Within the quietness of the car, their reactions were suspended and slow. Phantom feelings hovered around them. Megan didn't know what to think. She didn't yet understand what had happened, or why. Suddenly, violently, Noah smacked the dashboard, making her flinch. He collapsed against her, clutching at her coat, his mouth yawning soundlessly. He gasped, letting out a wail of despair. As he cried — loudly, his body shaking — she thought someone was bound to hear. But between themselves and the silent figures crowding the fire there was nothing but darkness.

* * *

When they got back to the farm, a police car stood in the murky light of the drive. Megan slowed the Land Rover, looking over at the officer standing at the front door. From inside the shed, Mai barked frantically, desperate to sniff out the stranger on her turf. Down the track, trees were silhouetted against the early light. Birds were singing, manic and shrill, as though telling each other the story of the morning's fire.

As she got out of the car and walked to the house, she saw that it was Chris Roberts, the officer who came on the day of the slaughter. She knew Chris a little, as most people did. He turned to her, saying nothing. They looked back at the Land Rover, where Noah sat motionless in the passenger seat.

"How is he?" said Chris.

"He just needs a minute. Let's go in."

She went past Chris and unlocked the door, which she remembered locking a couple of hours earlier, as though it had happened in a dream. She removed her wellies and looked for something warm to put on her feet. Her slippers weren't there. She found a pair of Noah's, putting those on instead. Chris followed her through the house, the tread of his boots hard and heavy behind the light patter of her moccasins. His martial uniform looked silly in the light of the kitchen, and vaguely threatening. She thought she should offer him tea or coffee but she couldn't summon the energy. She sat down in the armchair, closing her eyes. When she opened them again, she felt overwhelmingly tired. She wondered if she should go and check on Noah. But all she could manage was to sit here against the cold leather, waiting for Chris to speak. Through all of this, she worried about the baby, and she finally knew — if she ever hadn't — that she was keeping it.

She heard the front door open.

Noah appeared, the whites of his eyes bloodshot, his unshaven skin streaked pink. Chris shifted his weight, averting his eyes as though there was something untoward about Noah's grief.

"I'm very sorry about Imogen," said Chris, looking across at Noah. "We're all in shock, I think."

Noah stayed near the door, gazing at the floor, his hands clasped in front of him. He reminded Megan of a boy outside the headteacher's office, waiting for his punishment. She had a sudden feeling that he was not in a fit state to speak to the police, that she should protect him somehow.

Chris held a notebook in his hand. He glanced at Megan. "You're the owners of Tŷ Gwyn?"

"Actually, no," said Megan. "I'm in charge of running the cottages but Noah's father owns them."

Chris nodded. "That's Ray Robinson?"

"Yes." She looked at Noah suddenly. "Has anyone told him? About Imogen?"

Noah shrugged, shook his head. Chris watched them with the air of someone intruding.

"And what about Aled, come to think of it?" said Megan.

"We've spoken to Aled," said Chris.

"Oh my God," said Megan. She put her face in her hands, thinking about Aled and Hari. She couldn't imagine what this meant for them, couldn't get her head round it. It was nearly seven o'clock. The light was sparse, the fields grainy through the window.

Chris cleared his throat. "Imogen went missing on Thursday?"

Megan looked at Noah. He was quiet, still staring at the tiles.

"Yes," she said. "Although we didn't know until yesterday."

"Why was that?"

"That's when Aled told us."

"And he didn't report her missing until then, either?"

Megan could see the suspicion in Chris's question, that the police were assuming certain things about Aled and the fire.

"Only because he wanted to find her himself. He didn't want to make a fuss until he had to. And he didn't want it to be true, I don't think. That she was gone again, that she might have to go back to the hospital? She had only just come home."

Chris considered Megan. If he understood her explanation, he gave no sign of it. He looked at Noah.

"And you don't know why she was at the cottage?" he said, directing the question specifically at him.

The room was quiet. Noah glanced at Chris. "I have no idea."

* * *

As Chris left, the sun was rising. Megan felt the budding despair of sleep deprivation. She was reminded of lambing, awake at all hours of the night, swapping shifts as the sun came up, moving past one another in the hall like zombies. She put Noah to bed, removing his clothes, lifting the duvet over him. She sat on the edge of the bed, watching him. She knew he needed to sleep — so did she — but she couldn't wait any longer.

"Tell me why you took her there," she said.

He opened his eyes, looking wearily at her.

"Please," she said.

He looked more exhausted than she'd ever seen him. But he summoned some deep store of energy, understanding that he owed it to her, and in the hazy light of the new morning he told her the story. She could picture the whole scene — Imogen's iron will, even when her mind was ridden with darkness and delusion; her susceptibility to Noah, in spite of it; his caution and pragmatism. She could see all of it and yet she couldn't absorb it as fact. She left him and went to the spare room, drawing the long curtains, climbing into the cool bed. Closing her eyes, she felt squeamish and raw, that she had been somehow violated. She tossed and turned, changed position, bringing the duvet tightly around her, trying to banish the feeling. She felt there was nothing holding her, that everything was slippery and insubstantial, that even the baby inside her was unsafe.

* * *

Eventually she slept, waking after ten. Last night churned up from the depths, a nightmare fusing with reality. She went to the bedroom. Noah was asleep, breathing heavily into his pillow. She went downstairs, wandering the quiet house. She remembered that Mai was still locked in the shed and went to let her out. The dog was whiny and upset, urgent for the toilet. She ran to the track, squatting in the tufting grass, her hot urine absorbed in the cold earth. The ground was hard with cold, a light frost sheening the grass, and mist capped the mountains. Mai raced back, pushing her wet snout against Megan's palm. Megan stroked the dog's hard head uncertainly, as sceptical about her as she felt towards her husband.

She went into the house and found her keys, changing out of Noah's slippers and into her winter boots. Getting in the Land Rover, she couldn't quite believe how wintry it was, the autumnal wetness and mild wind sliding overnight into bleak frost. The car interior was icy cold. She adjusted the heating. Starting the car, she realised she was thirsty, not having had a drink since she went to bed the night before. She had the morning nausea she now knew to be pregnancy sickness, merging with the deliriousness of missed sleep.

She drove down the bypass, ordinarily busy on a Saturday morning, and past the industrial estate, waiting for a slow tanker to manoeuvre itself before she could go past. Eventually she pulled into Gethin's street, sitting in the car, staring at that red door as she had the evening before. She wasn't sure she could go ahead with it but if she was keeping this baby, she had some sense Gethin should know. Her only hesitation was whether she should talk to Noah first. But Noah was in no state to talk about anything.

As she climbed the steps to the terrace, she saw that the door was open, which she had not noticed from the street. She reached for the bell then changed her mind. Instead, she pushed open the door and walked inside.

There were no lights on. The hallway was quiet. She went to the living room, putting her head round the door. The curtains were closed to the street. Gethin's books were on the shelves as usual, stacked in their neat piles on the coffee table and floor. She went back to the hall, looking down the corridor at the unlit kitchen, counters shadowed, the floor lit by the dull light through the back windows. In the hush of the house, she knew she should make her presence known. But something prevented her calling out.

She went to the stairs and looked up at the shadowed landing, a square of light from the bathroom window planted against the blue-painted wall. Slowly, she walked upstairs. Cold wind fluttered in from an open window. She heard a movement in Gethin's bedroom, the creaking of floorboards.

The door was ajar. She went towards it, the tread of her boots absorbed in the carpet, and pushed it open.

His room was in disarray, drawers open, things thrown around. Gethin was there, topless and barefoot in navy joggers, facing away from her as he sifted through a sprawl of clothes on the bed. He shoved a fistful of T-shirts into a sports bag. The window was open, his half-naked body apparently immune to the cold air filling the room.

"What's going on?" said Megan.

He jumped, turning to her. "Fuck!" he said. He looked shockingly pale, his light hair oddly dark against his drained face. "How did you get in?"

"The front door's open," she said.

He looked at her as though he didn't quite believe her. "Did you close it?"

"Yes. What's going on?"

"You need to leave," he said, shaking his head.

"Where are you going?" she said.

He didn't answer and went back to his hurried packing, crouching to pull his phone charger from the socket beside his bed, throwing it in the bag.

"Imogen is dead," said Megan.

His body turned still. Megan saw the muscles in his back tensing.

"I know," he said, not looking at her. "I'm sorry."

He went on packing.

"She was like a sister, really," Megan said, folding her arms, leaning against the door frame. Gethin was too wildly distracted to listen but that was how it had been, she thought — complicated, difficult, exasperating, protective. Rooted in love. Like a sister, but without the rivalry. Megan had never been jealous of Imogen, even when her crises had dominated Noah's attention for days, weeks. Imogen had been too vulnerable to be threatening.

"Can you tell me what's going on?" said Megan.

He was pulling on a long-sleeved top. He turned towards her and she was struck again by the paleness of his face. "I really need you to leave."

He looked past her, as though remembering something, then hurried into the bathroom, pushing open the frosted window, checking the street below. He came back to the bedroom, brushing past her, and began frantically closing drawers, putting things away. Pleadingly, he turned to her once more. "For once can you do what someone asks? I shouldn't have got involved with you."

"That's nice."

"It's the truth."

"If you want to leave, just leave. You don't have to be a bastard about it."

"I need you to go. And you won't unless I upset you. That's what you're like."

"You'll have to try harder, then, won't you?"

He walked up to her, placing his hands on her shoulders. She felt the urgency in his grip and saw a dreadful fear in his eyes.

"You will regret it, if they come now."

"If who come?"

"The police," he said. "I'm in trouble, Megan. You don't want to be here. Trust me."

She stared at him. "What kind of trouble?"

"You'll know soon enough. But you have to go now. Do you understand what I'm saying?"

"Not really, no."

He couldn't be talking about the lambs or anything like it. He was acting as though he'd killed someone.

"Oh my God," she said. She put her hands over her mouth. No. It couldn't be that. She was not thinking clearly.

Gethin turned back to the bed, mounting the sports bag on his back like a rucksack. His shoulders tensed, the fabric of his top straining under the straps. He came back to her, pressing his cheek against hers.

"Please tell me it's not what I think," she said.

He sucked in a mouthful of air, his warm breath exhaling against her ear.

"I want you to know that I never — ever — would have done it if I'd known she was in there."

He lingered for a second, his body pressed against her. Then he fled downstairs and was gone.

* * *

She heard his car roar out of the street and left the house, closing the front door behind her. The quiet of this street had always pulsed with the secrecy of their affair. Now it felt clandestine in a far more disturbing way. She got into her car, shaken, and stared through the windscreen, tracking the last two months like a film that had passed by without her attention. She'd been distracted, missed something important. The books in his house. The man in the pub. The confrontation about the cottages the day they met. His emotional distance, which now felt calculated. The way he had refused to let her in last night, the evening before someone set fire to Tŷ Gwyn. Had he been preparing? Did he do it himself? Or was he part of something bigger? She couldn't get her head round it. She felt she must have misunderstood. At the same time, she was barely surprised.

When she got back to the farm, Noah was slumped at the kitchen table, bleary-eyed and unshaven in his dressing gown. Through the kitchen window, the sun was low and blinding. Undrunk tea sat inside a mug in Noah's hands like the festering mess of their lives. Megan sat across from him, tired in the deepest way imaginable, as though a lifetime of sleep wouldn't cure it.

"I'm pregnant."

Noah stared at her, blinking.

"It's the worst time to tell you, I know. But I can't begin to think about how to handle anything else without telling you this first." She watched him, waiting for any hint of a reaction. His expression was withdrawn, waiting. "I had an affair. It's over now. I can't be completely sure who the father is but . . . I'm going to keep the baby. I know how wrong that is. Selfish, especially now. I was going to get rid of it. But I couldn't do it. I can't do it. I'll never forgive myself if I do. I don't expect you to understand. Or maybe you will, one day. I don't know."

She felt monstrous in her pragmatism, her betrayal, putting the baby before Noah. She couldn't justify what she was doing, at least not within the terms of her marriage. But this was how it was. She couldn't do anything else. She knew it would be better if she cried in regret, begged for forgiveness. But she was wrung out.

"I knew about the affair," Noah said evenly.

She was surprised for a moment. Then she thought — of course. That was how he'd been behaving.

"When did you find out?"

"A few weeks ago. I was following Gethin. I thought he was behind the lambs, as you know. The police weren't taking it seriously. I got a bit obsessed for a while. Anyway, I saw you."

He was looking at her so resignedly, speaking so matter-of-factly, she was suddenly overwhelmed, like a barrier lifting within her. She felt the buried shame rising up. Tears came, after all.

"I'm so sorry, Noah," she said. "I don't know how to explain it. I really don't. I just felt so alone."

"I know why you did it," he said.

She looked at him. "Do you?"

"I turned my back on you. After we stopped IVF. I don't know why. I was ashamed, I think. For letting you down."

"You didn't let me down, Noah! We tried everything. You did everything you could. It wasn't your fault."

He smiled derisively. "Clearly it was."

She shook her head emphatically. "We still don't know for sure why we couldn't conceive. It might have been an incompatibility thing, I've heard about that. And this baby — it could be yours. It's not impossible. And even if it was you — that's still not your fault, is it?"

"Is that how you would feel?" he said. "If you found out you were the reason we couldn't have kids?"

"I did think I was the reason — for years. I hated myself for it."

"Exactly."

She brushed her hands across her wet cheeks. "What about the baby?"

He considered her. "Have you told him?"

"No. And I'm not going to."

"Why?"

She looked at him. "He was involved."

"Involved in what?"

"The fire."

Noah looked at her. "What makes you say that?"

"I went to see him this morning. I thought I should tell him about the baby, one way or another. But he was leaving. Running from the police. And he told me. He said . . ." She took a breath. "He said he never would have done it if he knew she was in there."

Noah stared at her for a long time.

"One of the times I followed him," he said. "He left his car and rode a motorbike to this field just outside Llanberis. He had a meeting there, in this abandoned farmhouse."

"Did you see who he was meeting?"

Noah shook his head. "I left quite quickly. I didn't like the feel of it."

She looked at him. "Should we tell the police all this?"

"I don't want to draw attention to myself."

"Isn't that the effect of not telling them?"

"I don't know. Maybe."

"I think we need to act as we would if you hadn't known she was there."

"What if someone saw me?"

"The police would know by now if they had."

"Maybe they do know — maybe they're collecting evidence against me. And what about the fireman?"

"What fireman?"

"When he pulled me from the house, I said to him, 'My sister's in there.' Won't he have told the police?"

She looked at him. "But Noah — it's not a crime, is it? What you did. I mean, didn't you say she agreed to stay there?"

He nodded.

"And did you lock the door?"

"No. I was going to. I changed my mind."

"So what is the crime, exactly?"

He shrugged. "I don't know. But she wouldn't have been down there if it wasn't for me."

"But that would be true of a hundred situations. There could have been holiday guests in there — and I would have arranged that. That wouldn't make me to blame, would it? That's why you don't go around setting fire to buildings!"

"It's not the same, though, is it? I didn't tell anyone she was there. Maybe if someone had known, it wouldn't have happened. They wouldn't have done it if there were guests."

"Why not? I mean, how do you know that?"

He looked at her. "Do you remember when those holiday homes round here were firebombed?"

Megan shook her head. "No?"

"It was a militant campaign in the eighties. We bought the farm a couple of years after it stopped. People were still talking about it. The police were still investigating. They burned down over two hundred holiday homes."

"Jesus. Did anyone get hurt?"

"No," he said. "That's my point. Not a single person died. And I'm sure Imogen wouldn't have, if they'd known she was in there. She's dead because of me."

CHAPTER EIGHTEEN

Noah

December came with a morning frost that evaporated under the low sun. As the days darkened, Noah watched over his pregnant ewes. He was grazing them on winter crops, which kept his feed costs lower but required careful management. The distraction was helpful. It had been seven weeks since the fire and there was hardly a minute he wasn't thinking about that night. Obsession had crept over him in the early, shock-blazed days when he answered condolence texts and phone calls, planned the funeral, and eventually lowered her coffin into the ground. All the while, flashes of the fire burst in his mind, fragments so real they were like he had lived it. Except that his mind was concocting snapshots, springing them on him when he least expected.

As the weeks passed and the fuss died away, the chaos of his mind turned to a rumination in which he sorted through known details to find a clear sequence of events. He created a timeline, starting when Imogen came to the farm, and went over it through the day, his mind working constantly, finding a strange comfort in this morbid ritual.

The police had told him it was smoke inhalation that killed her. The flames had never reached the basement, moving upwards through the house before being extinguished. Noah was thankful for that, at least. He didn't know what she had been doing in the hours between leaving her (just before ten) and the explosion, four or so hours later. Had she slept in the den? She might have found the floor uncomfortable, in the end, and moved to the bed. It was possible she had slept through the explosion, which was created by a basic homemade letter bomb and wouldn't have been loud (none of the neighbours had heard it). But something had woken her, whether it was the bomb itself or the smoke, because she was found on the floor near the bottom of the staircase. The door to the garden had been locked but the door at the top of the stairs wasn't. Had she known this? Noah wasn't sure he had ever made clear to her that she wasn't locked in.

For a while, the firebombing was on the news. There were photographers at the cottages, taking pictures of the decimated house. A handful hung around the entrance to the farm. One morning, Noah had come out and found a man on the drive. He must have walked down the track from the main road, as his car was nowhere to be seen. Short and weedy looking, he asked Noah if he could interview him for one of the tabloids about what the firebombers had done to his family, trying to express sympathy as he intruded on his land. Noah looked at the man, who seemed almost deranged by his wish to speak with him, and told him if he found him here again he would call the police.

There had been no suggestion that Noah had anything to do with Imogen being there. As the police questioned family and neighbours, Noah had waited for someone to come forward and say they had seen him taking her there, or coming and going in the days that followed. Nothing. Apparently, everyone believed Imogen had left the farm alone that evening, taking Megan's keys, and walked, through the darkening lanes, back to the village, letting herself into Tŷ Gwyn.

Meanwhile, Gethin, having taken a ferry to Ireland and back, had handed himself in at a police station in Caernarfon a week after the fire. He was charged with arson and manslaughter. At his hearing he pleaded guilty to everything.

* * *

At night, Noah tossed and turned in dreamless fits, falling into sleep close to sunrise. This was when Imogen came to him. He saw her vividly, knocking on the farm door, urgently ringing the bell. She was running from something. She needed his help. She didn't speak in the dream. She was a ghost, vivid and silent, her wide eyes despairing at her brother's cautious reluctance. Within the stark world of the dream, Noah felt there was a powerful, overwhelming force preventing him from doing whatever it was Imogen was asking and he became as despairing as her, before waking in the gathering light, muttering her name.

* * *

On Christmas Day night, the dream altered itself. Instead of staring at him with her helpless expression, Imogen looked him in the face.

"What are you waiting for?" she said.

He awoke, startled to hear her speak, her voice so life-like in his sleeping mind. He lifted himself on to his elbows, looking around the dark bedroom. Megan was asleep beside him, almost four months pregnant. Quietly, he whispered the words aloud to himself.

"What are you waiting for?"

As he lay back on his pillow, he felt as though his entire life came down to that question.

The next day, he drove to the police station in Caernarfon. Parking his truck on the street, he walked through the front door to the reception. He knew the officer behind the clear screen, whose name was Elis. Elis's father was a farmer and

Noah had known them since Elis was a little boy. He didn't know Elis worked here, though, when he thought about it, Elis's father did perhaps mention once that Elis was training to become a police officer.

"Hi, Noah," said Elis. "How are you?"

Elis lacked that shifty, awkward air that Noah had become accustomed to since Imogen's death. It made him wonder if Elis knew. But he must have done; everyone knew. They made small talk about Christmas. Elis had worked the day before, upsetting his mother and girlfriend. Now he was working Boxing Day, too.

When there was a lull, Noah said, "I don't suppose Mandy's around?"

"Richards? She's in. Let me check if she's free."

As Elis picked up the phone, Noah moved away from the desk. Elis spoke quietly in Welsh.

"She'll be out soon," he said, putting down the phone.

"Thanks," said Noah.

He sat on the hard bench. No one else was there except him and Elis. It was not yet ten. The reception was draughty and cold, with dull, blue-painted walls. A coffee machine stood in the corner, tall and black. Noah was considering whether he had the energy to use it when the doors to his right swung open and Mandy appeared. Noah stood. It took him a moment to realise what was different. It was her clothes. Not the smart suit he'd seen her in before but blue jeans and a soft turtleneck jumper. Her hair was changed, too, not pinned back but full and loose around her shoulders.

"Do you want a coffee?" she said, walking over to the machine. "I'm getting one for myself."

"Americano, please."

She nodded. She made the black coffee first, handing him the hot cup. As he struggled to secure the lid, he noticed how sweaty his hands were, wiping them on his trousers.

"Come with me," she said, holding her own coffee in front of her. She led him to a different set of doors. Over her shoulder, she said something to Elis. Noah understood that she was telling him which room they would be using.

Noah followed her down a cold corridor.

"No uniform today?" he said.

She turned her head. "I'm not meant to be here at all."

"Sorry," said Noah.

She stopped at a teal-painted door, turning the handle, and led him into a small room. There was a white table and black plastic chairs, a leather armchair in the corner. There was no recording equipment in sight, thankfully. It was even colder in here. Mandy walked over to the radiator, crouching to adjust the knob.

"I had a feeling I wasn't finished with you," she said, standing up. She didn't say it unkindly, but Noah became even more sick with dread. Perhaps he was making a terrible mistake. She gestured for him to sit at the table and sat down opposite, removing the lid from her coffee as she placed it on the table.

"Looks like you were right about your lambs."

He looked at her. For a second, he had no idea what she meant. The slaughter of the lambs felt like another life, one that barely mattered. Then he thought back on his fanatical belief that the crime was not the work of the gang, that it had been Gethin. Given this was only three months ago, he tried to show some interest now.

"Oh?"

She nodded. "Those men — they admitted to all the live-stock thefts in the area. But not butchering your lambs. They just wouldn't say it was them. Eventually we didn't think it could have been."

He nodded. "What about Gethin?"

"It wasn't him, either. We asked him about it again after he handed himself in for the firebombing. I don't see why he would deny it if he'd done it, given he was admitting to far more serious things."

Noah nodded. "I suppose I was wrong about that, then."

"You were right to suspect him of something. Just not that. What can I do for you?"

Noah stared at his coffee, too anxious to drink it. He licked his lips. Mandy watched him, calm and receptive.

"I want to report something," he said.

"Okay."

"You know my sister died in the firebombing?"

"Oh, Noah," she said, putting her hand to her mouth. "I should have said something. I was so sorry to hear about it. I really was. I knew Imogen a bit."

"Did you?"

"Not very well. She was in my yoga class. She was lovely."

He nodded. He wasn't sure he had known Imogen did yoga. Not for the first time, he wondered about the aspects of her life in which he had taken no interest. Mandy watched him. He moved his dry tongue over his teeth and cheeks, trying to stimulate some saliva.

"I don't know if there's anything you can do about this," he said. "Maybe it's crazy to even bring it up. But I owe it to her."

Mandy's eyes were locked with his.

"Two days before she died, she asked me to bring her here. She said she'd been abused. As a child."

Mandy's expression turned solemn. "Okay. Did she say who by?"

Noah paused, swallowing. "She said it was my father."

Mandy nodded. "When did she say this happened?"

"When she was nine. We lived in the Midlands. She said he came into her room at night. I didn't bring her in. In fact, I talked her out of coming down here."

"Why?"

He sighed. "Maybe I was wrong. I really don't know anymore. But she was not well at the time. You know my sister was schizophrenic?"

"I knew there was something," she said.

"Well, she'd come off her medication. She was delusional, saying all kinds of things that certainly weren't true. I didn't want her getting herself into something she couldn't pull back from.. My sister was very . . . vulnerable. I don't think she would have been able to cope with a police investigation, let alone a trial. And she was susceptible to . . . believing things that aren't true. Even when she wasn't psychotic, I mean."

"So you weren't sure you believed her?"

"Well, yes. But more than that. If it had turned out to be false, it would have been worse for her, wouldn't it?"

"How do you mean?"

"The lawyers would have proved it wasn't true. Found all the inconsistencies. They would have made her look like a liar. They would have destroyed her. I didn't feel she could withstand that."

Mandy nodded. "I can understand that."

"The thing is, it does make sense of a lot of things. The abuse allegation, I mean. My mother brought us here at exactly that time. My father stayed in the Midlands. There was a lot of anger between them. And there are letters, where she had accused him of something."

"Do you have the letters?"

"I have his letters to her. She kept them. Her letters might be at my father's house."

Mandy nodded. "So your mother knew."

"I think so. I think that's why we came here. And I think—" He paused. "I think maybe I knew, too. I don't know. I pushed it down, I suppose."

"You were a child yourself."

"But I've been remembering things, since she died. The arguments between my parents. How everything happened so quickly. I remembered that, while we were waiting for the purchase to go through, my mother slept in Imogen's bedroom."

Mandy pursed her lips. Noah sighed.

"Anyway," he said. "I think my father thought she would forgive him, eventually. My mother, I mean."

"Some mothers do."

"Well, she didn't. He wasn't allowed to set foot at the farm. I don't remember him coming, even once. Not until

243

after she died. I didn't think about it at the time. I was just relieved to be away from him."

Mandy nodded. "Listen. I'm going to take a statement. Everything Imogen told you — I want you to tell me, exactly as you remember. Everything you can remember from that time, too. But I have to tell you — it might not be easy to bring charges. Historic sex abuse is difficult to prosecute without witnesses. Or evidence. In this case, we don't even have the victim, only your account of what she told you. The CPS may feel there isn't enough. Not because they don't believe Imogen, but just if it doesn't have a chance of conviction. Does that make sense?"

Noah nodded. "I understand."

* * *

The next morning, Noah's phone rang, his father's number flashing on the screen. He was alarmed. He and his father had not spoken since the family meeting. Even at Imogen's funeral, they had said nothing to each other. Staring at his phone, he didn't know what to do. He wondered if the police had questioned him already, and whether they'd told Ray it was Noah who brought the complaint, in spite of him asking Mandy not to.

"I'm here and I need to talk to you," said his father when he answered.

"What do you mean 'here'? And what about?"

"Let's meet at the place by the water. Today."

"You mean Y Foryd?"

"Whatever you want to call it."

"What do you want to talk about?"

"We still have business, don't we?"

"You mean the farm?"

"I'm not doing this over the phone."

"Fine," said Noah. "I can be there by twelve."

* * *

244

Y Foryd was the local name for a stretch of hinterland over-looking the strait separating the peninsula from Anglesey. Scrubbed land, wild yellow flowers, water lapping dirtily against thin pebbled beach. To the east, the castle loomed over the water. Westward, the deep strait opened into the wide sea. On a clear day, you could see the distant rise of Ireland.

It was a stark white day. Seagulls circled the strait and cried out in the cold air. The water stretched, rippling and colourless, as Noah drove his truck along the empty lane. Noah had not asked his father what he planned to do about the farm and cottages, now that Imogen was dead. As far as their lawyers were concerned, Noah's legal challenge was going ahead. His father's solicitors had — before the fire — sent their letter of response, declining to resolve out of court. A trial date had been set. As for Tŷ Gwyn, the house was being rebuilt by his father. Megan had urged Noah to ask Ray what was going to happen, desperate to know whether, in the first months of their new baby's life, they would be fighting a court battle against its grandfather. She didn't like the idea of this. Neither did Noah. But he was sure nothing had changed. In which case, why give his father the opportunity to knock him down again?

When he got there, the Range Rover was parked silently on the dry ground. His father stood at the water's edge, back turned, his figure small against the expanse of sky. At his feet the ground dropped abruptly to tangled seaweed and cold grey pebbles.

Noah parked his car next to his father's and walked to the water, standing beside him. Ray didn't acknowledge his son's presence, staring ahead. In the distance, sunlight glowed through thin clouds.

"Megan's pregnant, then?"

Noah looked at his father, surprised for a second. But of course he was bound to still be in touch with Aled.

"Due in June."

His father nodded glumly. "Congratulations."

"What did you want to talk about?" said Noah.

His father was silent for a moment. Then he said, "I've always tried to do right by you kids. By your mother, too. I bought her the farm, didn't I?"

"In the end."

Ray turned his head. "What do you mean 'in the end'?"

"You know what I mean," said Noah. "She begged you for years."

Ray looked back at the water, shook his head.

"What is it you wanted to talk about?" Noah said again.

"I want to sort out this business with the farm and cottages. I can't manage a trial, Noah. I'm not well."

"The precancer?"

"No. It's my heart. It was always my heart. I didn't want to say anything before."

Noah looked at him. "The thing is, Dad — I really wouldn't put it past you to say that just so I agree to do things your way."

His father put his hand in his pockets. "Is that really what you think?"

Noah shrugged, looking away. "I'm not going to give in," he said. "I don't care how sick you are. I'm not giving you the farm."

"Not me — Aled."

"And how can Aled manage the farm now? Who's going to look after Hari?"

"His mother will help."

"She'll be there every morning at five thirty?"

"It's not your concern."

Noah shook his head. "My case is stronger all the time. Whereas you just look more and more unreasonable. Not wanting to resolve out of court. Not having a good reason for taking the farm to begin with. Now Imogen is dead and it looks worse — how will you explain taking a hundred acres from your son, who has worked it for thirty years, and giving it to someone who isn't even related to you? You will come out looking vindictive. And you'll lose. Meanwhile, everyone will suffer."

Ray shrugged, hands still in his pockets. "It's your choice."

Noah laughed. "No. You're doing this. Not me." He paused. "So you're still going ahead with it?"

"I'm not going back on my agreement. It wasn't only Imogen who wanted the farm. It was Aled, too."

"Imogen never wanted the farm!"

His father turned to him. "She wanted it very much. She might not have said it to you — she was afraid of upsetting you. But she wanted Hari to grow up there, like she did. She told me as much."

"You didn't understand her at all, did you? She had all kinds of fantasies, Dad. They were fleeting. They weren't . . . grounded in anything. You had to learn the difference between what was real and what wasn't."

"You're an expert in that, I suppose?"

"I understood her better than you did. I spent a hell of a lot more time with her, for one thing. Think about it. The things she wanted, she did them. Swimming in the sea alone, even when the doctors said it could be dangerous for someone like her. Having Hari when everyone told her she was taking a huge risk. If she'd wanted the farm, she would have lived there with me. She didn't want it."

His father shrugged. "Believe what you like."

"Well, she's dead now. And you reckon you're giving my farm to a man you hardly know."

His father eyed him. "It's for Hari, too."

"Nothing you do makes sense."

"How is it you always find something to complain about? The cottages that I'm giving you on a plate — if you run them properly, you won't have to work another day in your life. What exactly are you whining about?"

"I like work," said Noah. "Even you can't be so blind not to have noticed that." His father's jaw tightened. Noah went on. "Don't pretend any of this is about making me happy. We both know it's the opposite."

"It's not about making you happy, Noah. It's about doing what's best. A distinction you've never understood because your mother spoiled you half to death and now you don't know the difference."

"How can it be 'best' for me to open holiday cottages that people round here resent so much they'll burn them to the ground? How do you expect me to raise a child in those conditions?"

"Don't give me that. I'm not letting an arsonist who killed your sister dictate what I do and don't do. We're going to do exactly what we were going to do before."

"What if no one wants to stay in them now?"

His father waved a hand in the air. "That won't happen."

Noah was quiet. "What if they do it again?"

"He's in prison, isn't he? The lad who did it?"

"He didn't do it on his own. The police think there were seven or eight of them involved — and that they're planning more."

"We won't hear from them again. Not after what happened to your sister. The lad was ashamed — I saw it on his face when he went into court."

Something occurred to Noah for the first time.

"Aled wouldn't agree to run the cottages as holiday homes, would he? That's why you wanted to do it this way round. Okay. But I want it even less, now. After what happened to Imogen, I don't want anything to do with them."

"What do you expect me to do, Noah?"

"Sell them," he said. "Give the cash to Aled and Hari, if you want. Let me keep the farm. Why is that so much to ask?"

His father shook his head. "You never reach the right conclusions. The information is there but you put it together wrong. You've always been the same. When those lads came and butchered the lambs, you could have realised it was time to move on, that you've had one crisis after another. But you hold on with both hands. You're like a toddler with a broken toy."

"It's not true," he said. He swallowed, hot tears springing to his eyes. "I've made a lot of progress. It's been slow. But it's been getting better all the time. You can't see it because you don't know how bad things were. And because you only see what you want to."

They were quiet. Noah thought of something. "What do you mean 'those lads'?"

"What?" said his father.

"You said when 'those lads' butchered the lambs. As though you knew them or something?"

"Calling them 'lads' doesn't mean I knew them. Did you think they were girls?"

"Well, that's how it sounded."

"You're talking nonsense, as usual."

Noah looked at his father. "Do you know who did it?"

"How would I know who cut up your lambs?"

"I don't understand," said Noah. "If you know who did it, why haven't you told me?"

"All I know is that I heard it was a few lads from Trefor. That's it."

"How do you know? And why haven't you said anything until now?"

"It was just something I heard."

"From who?"

"Don't start getting worked up, Noah. I don't want a row about this."

"I'm not getting worked up. I'm asking you a simple question."

"Okay," said his father, licking his lips. "But I don't want a fight. Do you understand me?"

Noah nodded.

"I arranged it."

Noah stared at him. "What do you mean? You arranged what?"

"Killing the lambs."

Noah blinked dumbly at his father. Bleak sunlight pressing against the clouds, the white sky seemed to become blindingly bright. He closed his eyes, opened them again. He took a step back from the rocky edge.

"Sorry," he said. "I'm sorry — what? Why would you do that?"

Casually, as though explaining why he left open a gate, his father said, "I just wanted to make the transition easier, help you see it was time to move on from the farm. It wasn't supposed to turn into such a drama. I didn't think the police would care about a few lambs."

Noah looked at the water, his father's words settling inside him. Ray's voice contained no remorse or regret. Only reproval, as though Noah had failed another test.

"How did you arrange it?"

"A friend of mine just asked some lads he knew. It wasn't a big thing."

Noah looked at him. "You hired criminals to come to my farm in the middle of the night and kill my lambs? And you think it wasn't a big thing?"

"They weren't criminals, Noah."

"You hired them to commit a crime. That makes them criminals."

"I own the land, don't I?"

"The sheep are mine," said Noah. "So that's a crime. I can report you for this."

"You won't."

"It would help settle our fight over the farm, wouldn't it?"

"No one could prove I had a thing to do with it, Noah."

Noah looked at his father. "Do you know what I went through after the attack? How it affected me?"

"That's exactly what I'm talking about. You're not made for all this, Noah. I tried your whole life to toughen you up, but you're weak. Always have been."

Noah thought back over those early years of his childhood. He understood now that he had been unable to recall what his father did to Imogen partly because he had never wanted to think about the emotional abuse the man had inflicted on him. It had to stop now — but he was too tired to fight. When he thought of a long trial to determine ownership of the farm, possibly alongside a criminal trial over the abuse of his dead sister, he felt utterly exhausted. He couldn't bear to go through any of it. But nor could he just give in.

He looked at his father. "The police are investigating you."

His father looked at him. "What?"

"Imogen told me what you did. Before we moved to the farm. I told the police. I wasn't going to, but that's what she deserves. She was planning to tell them herself when she died. There'll be an investigation. You'll be ruined, even if you're not convicted. You'll be destroyed either way. And I can't see any judge siding with you over the farm in such circumstances."

Ray stared at him, anger glinting in his eyes. "Jesus, Noah. Don't you know any better? Malicious allegations by two sick women? What is the fucking matter with you?"

Noah shrugged. "There's nothing the matter with me."

"Why the hell would you go to the police without talking to me first? Don't you know there's two sides to every story?"

"You can tell your side in court."

Ray shook his head, eyes shining with rage. "You sneaky bastard. You've always been so useless. Always running to your mother."

"Why do you think I did that?"

"Because you're a mummy's boy, you always were. Why couldn't you have been on my side, just once?"

They went quiet, looking at each other. His father's expression changed.

"You do realise there's absolutely no case, don't you? It's nonsense and the police will laugh in your face."

"I've been to the police," said Noah. "They certainly didn't laugh. They have Imogen's word. And your letters."

"I've no idea what letters you're talking about but I can guarantee you I've never written a single word that incriminates me of anything. Let alone the kind of thing you're talking about. And they don't have Imogen's word, do they? They've just yours. Imogen and your mother said nothing like this to nobody — certainly not the police — not in all these years. Yet now, weeks after she dies, here you are, saying this despicable thing happened thirty years ago, when she's not here to ask about it. And neither is your mother. And this just happens to come out while you're trying to keep hold of my farm, that I'm trying to give to my murdered daughter's grieving husband — and my grandson? Are you off your head, Noah? You went to the police and said that — and you think I'm the one going to be destroyed?"

Noah's body had gone very still. He felt the ground was slipping from beneath him. Meanwhile, his father's face was contorted in contempt as he went on, badgering, mocking.

"A spoiled, bitter baby, jealous of your sister, jealous of your nephew. Making up lies in a desperate attempt to keep your hands on the farm. You really are useless, Noah. There is nothing you can do properly. Your pregnant wife will get the fat end of all this chaos you're going to bring down on everyone. And your new baby. Is that what you want?"

Ray's lips had become pale, his face draining of colour. Noah himself felt unwell, his vision starting to blur at the edges.

"Well?" Ray croaked at him.

"What?"

"Is that what you want? Or are you starting to understand that you're out of your depth here?" As he talked, his breathing was becoming ragged. And he was still pale as the winter morning. "These ridiculous lies and your nonsense legal letters. You can't stand up to me, Noah! You should know that by now. Now, I'm willing to think about some kind of compromise. But you'll have to compromise, too."

"You're not taking my farm," said Noah. "I'm not compromising about that."

His father coughed, wheezing a little. "Maybe we could talk about *when*. Make a transition plan. We could discuss a managed handover between you and Aled, over a period of time."

He coughed again.

"Aled can help on the farm if he wants," said Noah. "He can work on the farm. But there'll be no handover."

"Oh grow up, Noah. Aled's not going to want to . . ." He broke off, gasping now.

"What's wrong?" said Noah. "Are you having a panic attack?"

"Course I'm not having a fucking panic attack!" But he was rasping horribly, sucking air between words, the flesh at his neck folding in like he was choking.

"What's happening?" said Noah. "What's going on?"

Ray tugged at his shirt collar as though he wanted to rip it open. He closed his eyes, opening them again with a frown of confusion. Noah thought he was going to collapse but instead he staggered towards the water. Noah grabbed his arm, pulling him away from the edge. Ray stumbled backwards against Noah. He began beating his chest dumbly, repetitively, like he'd gone mad.

"Fuck," said Noah, scrambling for his phone.

Ray shook his head. In a whisper he said, "Unbutton it."

Holding his father's weight against him, Noah reached round from behind to unbutton his shirt, fiddling painstakingly with each button. Aware that they were still dangerously close to the water's edge, he lowered him gently to the ground, laying him on his side in the dirt, crouching beside him. His father's chest was hot pink, the skin inflamed behind tufts of white hair. As Noah began to punch 999, his father reached up and batted the phone from his hand, knocking it to the ground.

"No."

Noah looked at his father.

His voice still a whisper, Ray said, "Listen to me for once. Leave me be."

"Dad?" said Noah.

Ray held his gaze. Then his eyes rolled back, whites flaring. His head rolled to the side. His body went still. Noah sat beside his father, staring at his unmoving body. He placed two fingers against the side of his neck, then checked his wrist, too. He looked up at the sky, the sun pressing against the sheet of clouds, and felt very alone. Then the clouds opened and sunshine spilled over the water, lighting the dirt ground around him.

* * *

Spring came with blue skies and damp mornings, daffodils blooming in cluster. Noah was in the thick of lambing, knee deep among his flock. One of his ewes was having an aversion to nursing, her udders swollen and red, butting her little ones away when they came near, even though letting them feed was the one thing that would relieve the pain. Meanwhile, her twin lambs bleated, hungry. He would have to give them a bottle if she didn't give in soon.

Megan was eight months pregnant and quarantined in the house against the risk of foetal infection that came with birthing ewes. She didn't come out to the farm at all, now lambing had started. Noah didn't go in the house during the day, either, and when he came back at night or in the early morning, he stripped to his underwear in the cold, stuffing his clothes and coveralls in a bin bag. Then he went to the downstairs shower, running the water as hot as he could tolerate, soaping himself thickly. It was all becoming quite tedious, but there was only a month to go.

Megan was happier than he'd ever known her. She had created a nursery next door to their bedroom, dragging in furnishings collected from strangers on the internet or the emporium by the beach, her belly was taut and enormous as she rushed around in a flurry of prenatal anticipation. Noah maintained a basic scepticism. He hadn't said so to Megan but given their history it had seemed overly hopeful to assume she would carry this baby to term. He wouldn't relax until he saw the baby, mewling and kicking in the flesh. It was like retrieving a lamb. He was only satisfied when he heard the fresh bleat, felt the pounding of its tiny heart.

So when he heard her shouting for him at thirty-seven weeks, the first thing he thought was: it's happened. The late-term miscarriage, an imminent stillbirth. It was finally here. He ran from the shed, finding her on the drive, denim maternity dungarees wet around the crotch, holding her swollen belly.

"I think my waters broke."

"You think?"

"I'm pretty sure."

"Is it too early?"

"It's fine. But we need to go."

Her hospital bag was at her feet, he realised. Momentarily, he was stunned. This was not meant to happen now. He looked down at his clothing, shining with the fluids he had been keeping away from his pregnant wife.

"Yeah, you need to change," she said. "And shower. Quick!"

He rushed, heart pounding as he pulled off his clothes. Stepping out of the shower, he ran a towel roughly over his dripping body and glanced in the mirror, taking in his wet hair and damp face. Unexpectedly, he thought of Gethin. He pictured him in his cell, reading a book, keeping to himself. Then he heard Megan calling and ran upstairs to find clothes.

* * *

The night was long and almost endless, Noah helpless in the face of Megan's ordeal. Confronted with his wife's guttural screams, it occurred to him that thirty years of sheep farming had given him a false impression of birth. Then she was there, a baby girl, unspeakably tiny and light as air (though six and a half pounds, really) with shocking dark hair.

"Am I imagining it?" he said to Megan when the midwives had left.

"I don't think so," said Megan. "But it's hard to know. She doesn't really look human yet."

Megan leaned back, closing her eyes. Under the glow of the hospital lights, she looked like she'd been through a violent ordeal, fresh red blood smeared on her belly and thighs, darkly soaking the sheets beneath her. Her hair was wet, skin glistening with the sweat of labour. Her complexion was almost bleached, all over her face tiny specks of red that the midwife told him were the blood vessels that had burst with the strain of pushing.

She had an air of contentment that might have been simple relief that it was over. She opened her eyes, leaning across the bed to hand him the swaddled bundle. He took the baby with great care, bringing her slowly to his chest. Megan lifted the blanket from her legs, shifting her weight to the edge of the mattress until she was able to lower her legs over the side. Every movement seemed to cause her pain. Pushing herself up to standing, she winced, sucking air through her teeth.

"Are you okay?" he said, looking across at her.

"I don't know how I'm going to do this."

"Look after a baby?"

She looked back at him. "Use the toilet."

He looked down at the baby. Surely he was imagining the resemblance. But her hair was very dark, like his mother's and Imogen's, and his own. Her eyes were almost black. They were calling her Rhian.

* * *

The next day, Aled and Hari came to the farm to see the new baby. Hari carried a white floppy-eared rabbit, rushing to the living room and stopping in the doorway to stare at Megan and baby Rhian, who were settled in the nursing chair. Slowly, he approached, lifting his head. The chair was reclined,

Megan's eyes closed, baby Rhian tiny and limp against her chest. Megan had not separated from the baby since they returned from the hospital. Even in the milk-white haze of these early hours, Noah wondered if she would become one of those mothers, so long denied a child, who could not then bear to leave it.

Noah watched from the doorway as Hari crept closer, placing his hand on the edge of the chair, craning his neck and stretching up on his tiptoes. Megan opened her eyes, forcing a weak smile. She looked so tired. She lowered Rhian, letting Hari touch her feathery head. Standing next to Noah in the doorway, Aled muttered something to Hari, telling him to be careful. Hari stroked Rhian's forehead, glancing up at Megan for reassurance. After a moment, he withdrew his hand and gently placed the stuffed rabbit against the baby.

"Do you want to hold her?" said Megan.

Hari nodded. Noah lifted him on to the couch, gently taking Rhian from Megan. She was light as air as he lowered her into Hari's outstretched arms, positioning pillows around them. Aled stood behind, reminding Hari to support Rhian's head. "Do you want a *panad*?" said Noah, looking at Aled.

"A quick one, please," said Aled. "We can't stay long."

Noah nodded. As he left the room, he heard Rhian stirring, that high, cat-like cry. Aled looked a lot better, Noah thought, as though he might have emerged from that early, gripping grief. He had showered and was wearing clean clothes.

"I have someone viewing Tŷ Gwyn later," Aled said, following Noah into the kitchen.

"Oh yeah?"

After his father's death, Noah had inherited everything. The farm, the cottages, the house in the Midlands, a flat in Sicily. Noah was in the process of selling his father's house and the Italian property. He planned to use a fair chunk of that cash to pay off debt and invest in the farm. He would put some aside for Hari, and for himself and Megan and Rhian, and set up a charity in Imogen's name. The cottages he had given to Aled, who had put two of them on the market while the builders finished rebuilding the burned-down cottage. The first two houses had sold already, both to local families. The work on Tŷ Gwyn had recently been completed. Noah had worried that Aled would struggle to sell and end up lumbered with it. But he seemed confident about the viewing.

"Young couple," he was saying. "They have a boy starting at the school next year. I know the mother from years back. Fingers crossed."

* * *

When Aled and Hari left, Noah went out to the drive to wave them off, wandering up the track. The Hughes boys were supervising the lambing and he raised his hand to them as they leaned at the opening to the shed, smoking, and drinking from cans of pop. They were no more than sixteen — twins — but they'd probably been lambing since they were six. At the hospital Noah had rung Anne Hughes, an old friend of his mother's who owned the fields surrounding the village, to ask her advice about leaving the ewes while Megan was in labour. Anne was in the thick of lambing herself but immediately sent her grandsons over.

He stopped at the top of the track and looked down at the fields. Several new lambs had been turned out, tottering after their mothers on wobbly legs, dipping their heads to find a milk-giving teat. He knew he should go and send the twins home. But he was finding it hard to contemplate throwing himself back in with the ewes. It felt wrong, somehow, with the new baby only just home. Everything felt different now, that was the truth.

* * *

Back in the house, he went over to the nursing chair and took the baby from Megan.

"Why don't you have a bath?" he said. "I can have her."

She looked up at him uncertainly. There was fear in her face, like she wasn't sure Rhian would be okay without her. Then she nodded, a little tearful as she pushed herself from the chair. With the water running upstairs, Noah walked to the window, baby Rhian in his arms. He looked out at the fields, noticing, not for the first time, that he had a heightened view of his environment since Imogen's death. Somehow, the land and sky were more intensely coloured, the world enhanced to technicolor, as though, now she was gone, her elevated experience had become his own. She used to say the sky was talking to her, that when the clouds moved quickly she knew someone was angry. Looking at the land, bathed in brilliant sunshine, he was overcome with grief and a dizzying wave of regret. His mind no longer worked over the events of that day — somehow, sometime, that had stopped. All he was left with now was the unbearable loss of her passing, tainted by the shame of what he had done. He didn't believe this would ever leave him, nor did he think it should. It was part of him now, like the sun in the sky and the wind passing through the trees.

Scrunching up her face, Rhian opened her mouth and let out a shrill cry. Noah lifted her to his shoulder, taking in her consoling newborn smell, repeating the words his mother used to whisper to Imogen when they first came here and she woke crying in the night.

"*Ti'n saff yn fama.*"

You're safe here.

THE END

ACKNOWLEDGEMENTS

My sincere and grateful thanks to everyone at Joffe Books, in particular Kate Lyall Grant for her encouraging, enthusiastic and insightful early feedback and edits. I would also like to thank Kate Ballard, Jasper Joffe, Jon Appleton, Hanna Myers, Sasha Alsberg, Gemma Carr, Tia Davis, Imogen Buchanan and Elizabeth Hinks. Huge thanks also to my agent, Cara Lee Simpson at Susanna Lea, for her ongoing and invaluable guidance and support.

When deciding to write about schizophrenia, I did not want to sensationalise, patronise nor misunderstand the condition. Imogen became very real to me over the course of writing this book; I came to care for her deeply and I truly hope nothing about my depiction was offensive to anyone who lives with this complex illness. In getting to grips with what it might be like to be her, I deeply thank and highly recommended the following accounts: *The Collected Schizophrenias* (2019) by Esmé Weijun Wang and *The Centre Cannot Hold: A Memoir of Schizophrenia* (2008) by Elyn R. Saks. *An Unquiet Mind: A Memoir of Moods and Madness* (2014) by Kay Redfield Jamison — about manic depression rather than schizophrenia — was just as enlightening and vital to me.

I took on a similarly sensitive topic with Welsh militancy and the issue of second homes in the Welsh-speaking heartlands. Thank you to these excellent books: *To Dream of Freedom: The Story of Mac and the Free Wales Army* (2020) by Roy Clews, *Hands off Wales: Nationhood and Militancy* (2022) by Dr Wyn Thomas and *The Story of Wales* (2013) by Jon Gower. Books are never enough, though, and I count myself lucky to live in one of those heartlands. To the people of the Llŷn Peninsula, and particularly the community around Ysgol Llandwrog, I would like to say thank you. These communities are a daily example in how a culture can be welcoming and compassionate to the people who come here from elsewhere while fiercely protecting their unique, and sadly threatened, language. This balance is a fine art and an inspiration to me.

When I started this book, I knew shockingly little about sheep farming, a complex practice variable according to climate, terrain, resources and tradition. Yet I was keen to make Noah as authentic, within his specific circumstances, as possible. I could not have done this without Ellen Pierce Jones, Julie Webb and Iwan Williams. A *panad* and chat with experts, followed by the endless back and forth via WhatsApp and email, was infinitely more valuable than any article or documentary. *Diolch o galon am eich gwybodaeth, amynedd a'ch haelioni.*

Diolch o galon hefyd i Siôn Fôn, so generous with his time and expertise, and indispensable in drawing my attention to "promissory estoppel" and helping me to understand the legal rights and processes around land disputes and family promises. As for rural crime and police procedure, retired police officer Mark Watkins was a superb asset: informative, knowledgeable and always to-the-point. I would also like to thank the communications department at North Wales Police, in particular Sergeant Peter Evans of the Rural Crime Team.

Ni fyddai wedi bod yn bosib i mi gyhoeddi'r llyfr hwn heb lygad craff a dawn ieithyddol a thraws-gyfryngol fy ffrind Angharad Blythe; *un sy'n gallu ystyried sensitifrwydd y Gymraeg, arcau cymeriad, hanes cenedlaetholgar a themâu emosiynol ar yr un gwynt. Diolch o galon.*

I don't know how I'll ever thank or repay Amy Ludlow, my beloved friend and first reader. Even more importantly than her shrewd literary insight, Amy gives me encouragement and self-belief when I need it most. Likewise, Siôn has remained the solid root from which I can grow and thrive, not only providing rigorous feedback on everything I write but the emotional support and domestic partnership I rely on to write books. Thank you also to my Auntie Diane and my parents, in particular my mother, for helping lighten the overwhelming domestic load. And thank you to Gwilym, Menna and Celyn, who do nothing to help me write books but everything to remind me there are more important things in life.

THE JOFFE BOOKS STORY

We began in 2014 when Jasper agreed to publish his mum's much-rejected romance novel and it became a bestseller.

Since then we've grown into the largest independent publisher in the UK. We're extremely proud to publish some of the very best writers in the world, including Joy Ellis, Faith Martin, Caro Ramsay, Helen Forrester, Simon Brett and Robert Goddard. Everyone at Joffe Books loves reading and we never forget that it all begins with the magic of an author telling a story.

We are proud to publish talented first-time authors, as well as established writers whose books we love introducing to a new generation of readers.

We won Trade Publisher of the Year at the Independent Publishing Awards in 2023 and Best Publisher Award in 2024 at the People's Book Prize. We have been shortlisted for Independent Publisher of the Year at the British Book Awards for the last five years, and were shortlisted for the Diversity and Inclusivity Award at the 2022 Independent Publishing Awards. In 2023 we were shortlisted for Publisher of the Year at the RNA Industry Awards, and in 2024 we were shortlisted at the CWA Daggers for the Best Crime and Mystery Publisher.

We built this company with your help, and we love to hear from you, so please email us about absolutely anything bookish at feedback@joffebooks.com.

If you want to receive free books every Friday and hear about all our new releases, join our mailing list here: www.joffebooks.com/freebooks.

And when you tell your friends about us, just remember: it's pronounced Joffe as in coffee or toffee!